# POWER PLAY

## DUSK BAY DEMONS
### BOOK 3

## MAGGIE ALABASTER

Cover design by The Book Brander Boutique

Paperback interiors by Dexpress.

Edited by Lily Luchesi

Proofread by Nora Hogan

# TRIGGER WARNINGS

Hey lovely reader. Your mental health matters, so read with care. This book contains violence, consensual non consent and a consensual, sexual relationship between stepsiblings.

*To all the girls who tried to say 'highland cow' with a mouth full of cock.*

# CHAPTER 1

## WREN

I glared at Bray. "I don't make pendants shaped like cocks."

He leaned his hip against our parents' kitchen island. A smug smile graced his lips.

Yeah, what the fuck was new? My stepbrother was the bane of my existence. From the moment our parents got married, he'd made it his life's work to be a shithead to me.

Braylon fucking Ellis, right-winger for the Dusk Bay Demons ice hockey team. First line, if you please. As if he'd let anyone forget it.

For some reason, he blamed me for our parents getting together. Why, I have no idea. I was ten years old at the time. He was twelve. He'd harboured some belief his mother would get back together with his father. That was never on the cards. My father and Jenny were heads over heels for each other since the day they met. Fifteen years later, they were still adorably besotted.

Bray crossed his arms over his ridiculously burly chest and leaned back. "You keep saying that, but I don't believe you." His dark eyes lingered on me, gaze full of mocking amusement.

He tipped his head to the side to flick his dark brown hair off his face. His favourite look was 'freshly fucked,' messy hair and all.

Add the three days worth of growth on his chin, and he was too stinking hot for his own good.

If he wasn't an asshole, I'd set him up with one of my single friends. Because he was, I wouldn't even give him their names, much less their details.

"This might come as a shock to you, but what you believe doesn't matter to me," I said. "Why do you even care?"

He shrugged. "I don't. I love seeing how angry you get whenever I mention it." One side of his mouth tugged upward.

Did I mention my stepbrother is a massive prick?

"I think you do care," I told him. "I think you're scared that if I made penis shaped pendants, they'd put your tiny little dick to shame."

I glanced down at his groin. What the front of his jeans covered was far from tiny. Not that you'd ever hear me admit it. No way.

He chuckled. "For someone who hates my guts, you seem very interested in my cock. You want some of it?"

He dropped his hands to the button of his jeans as though he might undo them and push them down his muscular thighs.

I waved my hands in front of me. "Ugh, don't. Yours is the last cock in the world I ever want to see."

"That's a lie and we both know it." He lowered his hands from his button, and swivelled around to pick up his cup of tea. He never drank coffee.

"You don't want to see Nicholas Fiorelli's. Or any of those guys that abducted you last year." He watched me over the rim of his cup before taking a sip.

"That's a low blow," I said softly.

My friend Sinclair and I were abducted from her house and held in a filthy motel room for about three days. Our abductors didn't touch us, but it was an ordeal, regardless.

Bray lowered his cup. "Yeah, sorry. I guess it was a dick thing to say."

"You guessed right," I snapped.

I sighed and took a moment to compose myself and shrug. "It's nothing less than what I'd expect from you anyway. Every time I see you, I think, 'Wren, what dumbass thing will Bray have to say today?' Do you lie awake at night running through plays, and planning how to give me the shits?"

If I didn't hate him so much, his grin would have me ruining my panties.

"As a matter of fact, I do," he said. "I think, 'Bray, you gorgeous stud muffin, what could you say that would make her get on her knees and suck your cock?'"

I made a face. "I don't even know where to begin with what's wrong with that. Let's go with *everything*. For a start, you have a face that would make a potato jealous."

He laughed. "At least it wouldn't make a potato cry."

"Nah, I'm pretty sure it would do that too." I nodded. "If anyone could make a potato cry, it would be you."

He was so fucking hot, he could make a potato ruin her panties. The problem was, he knew it. Of course he did. How could he *not* know, when he was told on a regular basis by all the gorgeous puck bunnies?

As far as I was concerned, they could have him. I didn't envy them for a moment. If I did, it wouldn't be because of him. It would be because most of them were beautiful and seemed to have their shit together.

Me, on the other hand? I was short, my bright red hair untameable. I carried an extra layer of fluff.

Oh, and I actually *did* make pendants in the shape of cocks and pussies, that my father, who was also my boss, wasn't supposed to know about. If he did, he'd be livid. He'd think I was putting his jewellery business into disrepute or some such.

What I was actually doing, was making a butt ton of money on the side from the designs. Enough that, someday soon, I may need to stop working for him and focus on Danglies, my own company.

One day, when I was rich, I'd sponsor the stadium where Bray and his team were based. Danglies Arena had a ring to it. The fact it would piss him off would be a delightful bonus.

"Talking to you is such an experience," he said dryly. "I feel like I'm back in year three."

"I'd suggest that's a couple of years' step up from your normal conversations, but that would be an insult to your entire team," I said. Most of whom I actually liked.

Tiberius 'Tiger' Pennington, in particular. He never admitted it, but he killed a man for me last year. The man who orchestrated my abduction. A few people had remarked shortly after the incident, that he was furious anyone dared to take me. He'd insisted on accompanying Coast Riggs, the team's centre, when they went to find Sinclair and me. It was Tiger whose arms were around me first when they found us.

He'd barely said a word to me since.

"I'm sure they've heard worse," Bray said. "From you and from people better than you."

"How could they have heard from people better than me?" I scoffed jokingly. "Who could possibly be better than me?"

I fluffed the back of my hair and found half of it had fallen out of my messy bun. Ignoring his smirk, I wound it all back up and clipped it into place.

"I don't know how to answer that," he said thoughtfully. He snapped his fingers like he had some kind of revelation. "Actually, that brings us back to the potato we were talking about earlier."

"If you're implying that a potato is better than me, I'm okay with that," I said. "Potatoes are awesome. Everyone loves them. They're better than all of us put together."

He shook his head. "Only you would favourably compare yourself to a potato. Year three must have been a compliment. Talking to you is like being back in preschool."

"Ahhh, preschool," I said slowly. "The year you peaked. Wait a minute, two years. You had to repeat preschool, didn't you?"

He tipped his head back and laughed. "I think you might be confusing me with yourself."

I felt my face heat. I walked straight into that one.

I didn't repeat preschool, but I wasn't very good at school. I was better at making things with my hands than I was at academic stuff. I left high school and went to work with my father before I failed and they kicked me out, or made me do it all over again.

"The education system isn't tailor-made for individual needs," I said finally. "You know that as well as I do."

He hadn't done brilliantly either, but his skill at hockey more than made up for it. If it hadn't, his looks would have gotten him through life. He was the kind of guy who was always going to succeed, regardless.

"You took the first shot," he said. "I wouldn't have

said anything if you hadn't."

"Yes, you would," I said. "You would have found some other way to insult me. If that was a competitive sport, you would have…" I closed my mouth so quickly my teeth clicked together.

"Would have what?" he asked darkly.

I blew out a breath through pursed lips. "I was going to say you would have won the cup, but even I know a low blow when I think one up."

The guys made it so far, only to lose the finals in overtime. To fall, painfully close to your goals, was the ultimate suck. I didn't hate Bray enough to poke him in that open wound.

"We're going to take it this year," he said, his teeth gritted. "Last season was a practice run."

He was determined to win, even if he had to do it all by himself. If there was anything he hated more than me, it was losing.

I won't lie, I was as competitive as he was. Lucky for me, if I lost, it wasn't in front of an arena full of fans.

"I believe in the team," I said. "You've come up from the very bottom and almost got to the very top. That's one hell of an achievement."

"If I didn't know better, I'd think you're proud of me." His smug expression was back.

"Like I said, I believe in the team," I said. "Don't get a big head."

As if it wasn't far too late for that. His ego was so healthy, it was a miracle he fit into the arena at all. Or into a hockey helmet, for that matter. Not that he had a monopoly on having a big ego. It seemed to come with the territory of being a professional hockey player.

He grabbed his groin. "I can't help it when I was born with it. You sure you don't want to find out? I'm told my cock is very tasty."

I bet it was. Cocks usually were.

"I bet you fifty dollars you've tried to find out for yourself." I mimed bending over and trying to suck my own imaginary dick.

"I won't take that bet, because there's not a guy in the world who hasn't." He was grinning when I straightened back up. "You're very flexible there, step-sister dear."

"I'm incredibly flexible, and you'll never get to find out just how much, stepbrother *dear*," I said.

No matter how much my body wanted his, I would never, ever go there. In real life. In my fantasies, when I was alone in my bed…

"You say that now—" he started to say. "Oh, hi Mum." He hugged Jenny as she stepped into the kitchen. "I thought I heard the doorbell."

"Nothing wrong with your hearing." Dad carried a pile of pizza boxes and placed them on the island. "Are you two hungry?"

"Ravenous," Bray agreed. He glanced over at me when he said it, like he wasn't talking about food.

I rolled my eyes.

*Dream on, dickhead.* I was not on his menu.

# CHAPTER 2

## WREN

"He's insufferable." I picked up a chip from my plate and bit into it like it was part of Bray.

Hazards made the best chips and burgers in the entire country. That and the atmosphere, made it one of the more popular pubs in Dusk Bay, especially amongst the sporting crowd.

"Which one?" Sinclair asked half teasingly. "Tiger or Bray?" She nodded to where they stood around a table, talking to other guys from the team.

"Yes," I replied. I ignored the laughter from her and Elenna and continued talking. "They're both frustrating and I want to slap them both silly." I mimed doing just that, my hand bouncing back and forth between two invisible cheeks.

That made my friends laugh harder.

"I'm sorry." Sinclair wiped tears from her eyes. "I relate to that so much. Guys can be infuriating."

"They really can," Elenna said, her tone steadier, like always. "Have you tried communicating with either of them?"

"Bray's idea of communication is flinging insults at me," I said. "Tiger's is to talk in grunts and filthy looks. Not aimed at me."

He glared at anyone who came close to where I sat, even if it was a server picking up empty glasses from the table. He didn't want anyone near me, but he didn't seem to want to be near me either. Talk about mixed messages.

"Anyway, I don't need to communicate with Bray." I broke a chip in half and put one half in my mouth. "He's only my stepbrother and a pain in my ass. If it wasn't for Jenny, I wouldn't even bother to speak to him."

"Right," Sinclair drawled. She gave me a meaningful look that suggested she didn't believe it either.

It wasn't fair, both of them knew me too well.

"Can you stop?" I grimaced. "There's nothing between us and there never will be. I guess at this point there's not going to be anything between Tiger and I either."

Certainly not both of them. My friends were the model for polyamorous relationships. They had three boyfriends each.

Me? I couldn't even get one.

"You know what you need," Elenna said. "You need to meet someone new."

"She's right," Sinclair said. "It worked for me, and there's tons of single guys here tonight."

Preseason training started in a couple of days. Tonight was a chance for the team to go out and enjoy themselves while they could. Burgers and beer would be off the menu for most of them for the next few months.

"If you put yourself out there, you might meet the man of your dreams," Elenna sighed and looked over to where her three stood at a different table, talking to each other and pretending they weren't watching everything she did.

Sinclair's three guys were doing the same thing, but Javey hadn't taken his eyes off her the whole time. He never did. The only time he looked away from her was when he was on the ice.

"I'm open to trying." I popped the other half of the chip in my mouth. "Any suggestions?" They both worked at the arena, so they knew the guys better than I did. They'd know the ones to avoid like the proverbial plague.

"Actually," Elenna said slowly. "I've noticed Lex, the team's strength and conditioning coach, looking at you more than once. He seems nice. Quiet and not with an ego bigger than Australia."

I searched the crowds for the attractive, dark-haired coach.

In his mid-thirties, he'd have his shit together better than me. In theory, anyway. Like a lot of coaches, he was a former player, but he never made it to the profes-sional level. I wasn't sure if that was due to his skill, or because the sport wasn't well enough developed in Australia yet. Lots of players went to America or Canada to play, but many chose not to.

"It wouldn't hurt to go up and talk to him, I suppose," I said. "What's the worst that can happen?"

Yeah, I should know better than to ask questions like that. Considering some of the things we'd been through in the last few months, the worst could be very bad.

"The worst might be that you find him boring," Sinclair said. "But then, maybe you'll make a friend. And maybe it'll be more than that. You know what they say about the quiet ones."

That had me looking at Lex more speculatively. "They do say that, don't they?"

Would he be adventurous and wild in bed? Was I getting ahead of myself? Absolutely. Did I regret it? Nope. Life was too short not to embrace dirty thoughts.

There was nothing wrong with having a healthy sexual appetite. And this little birdie hadn't been laid in far too long.

"Well?" Sinclair looked down at my now empty plate. "We don't mind if you go and talk to him. Do we, Elenna?"

"Of course we don't," she said. "We want you to be happy. If there is a chance he might do that, even if it's only for an hour or two, then you should take it."

"And you know what to do if you need to get out of the situation in a hurry," Sinclair said.

We had a code known only to the three of us, that would let the others know if we were in trouble or just needed to bail on a conversation. We'd only used it a handful of times since we met, but it got our asses out of some uncomfortable situations.

"Yes I do." I pushed my phone into my back pocket and got to my feet. I brushed hamburger bun crumbs off the front of my emerald green, knitted jumper and my black jeans, and squared my shoulders. "Here goes nothing."

Trying not to look too deliberate, I wound my way through the tables and crowds, wine glass in hand as though I'd just come from the bar. I stepped up to Lex and smiled.

"Hey." Okay, that wasn't the best, most articulate start, but it was a start.

"Hey." His gaze dipped down to where my cleavage was on display above the V-neck of my jumper. He quickly looked back up. "Wren, right?"

"That's right." I offered my hand for a shake. "Like the bird."

He smiled. His expression was warm and immediately put me at ease. "Lex. Like the bad guy in *Superman*."

I laughed. "I was going to say it rhymes with sex, but Superman is good too."

Fuck, did I just say that? Good job, Wren, he now

thinks you're a complete idiot. Maybe Bray had a point about my conversation skills.

Lex smiled more broadly. "You like Superman too?"

"Who doesn't?" I said. Okay, maybe he didn't think I was a nitwit. Yet. Give it a few minutes more.

"Not too many of the girls I've met," he said. "Their eyes usually glaze over when I mention it."

"They don't know what they're missing," I said. "So, are you a supervillain or just the regular kind?" What can I say, I'm secretly a massive nerd. Or maybe not so secretly.

He laughed. "I'm definitely not up to supervillain status. For one thing, I don't have a white cat. And I don't think I have the evil laugh down pat yet."

I grinned. Talking to him was refreshing. No insults. No grunts. Not even a death threat against me or someone else.

"I feel like having a cat is passé for a supervillain," I said. "You'd need something more badass than that."

He cocked his head and looked at me like I was the only other person in the whole pub. Maybe in the whole world.

I won't lie, his expression was compelling. There was something about an attentive guy that got my pulse racing.

"What would you suggest?"

"I was thinking you need a cockatiel." I nodded and held back a laugh.

He also nodded, as though seriously considering the

suggestion. "A cockatiel, you say? They are quite fierce. If I had one of those on my shoulder, I'd look like the model supervillain." He stroked his chin, adding to the whole vibe.

"How's that plan for world domination going?" I teased.

"Better now I know what's missing," he said. "It seems if I'm going to succeed in life, I need a little bird." The look he gave me was so intense my panties almost burst into flame.

"Everyone needs a little bird in their corner," I agreed. "We make everything more interesting."

"I have absolutely no doubt about that," he said. "How are you at playing pool?"

"It's not on the top of my list of best ball and stick skills," I said. "But I enjoy the game as much as the next person."

I wasn't bad, but I was nowhere near as good as Elenna. There wasn't a person in Hazards she hadn't taken on and beaten. If anyone was going to achieve world domination, it was her, if only at pool.

"Care for a game?" He waved toward the table.

"I'd love to." I grabbed up a cue and started to chalk the tip. I felt Tiger's and Bray's gazes boring into me.

I didn't turn to look at them. If they had a problem with me playing with Lex, in any capacity or context, that was their problem. Tiger in particular. He had plenty of chances to show me he was interested and he hadn't taken any of them. I wasn't going to sit around for the rest of my life and wait for him to decide to pursue me.

It was long past time for me to get on with it and forget about him. I'd noticed several women eyeing him off since my friends and I arrived. He could have his pick of them. He didn't need me.

I pushed him out of my mind and deliberately leaned over the pool table to line up the shot.

The angle gave Lex an eyeful of cleavage, and Tiger, a perfect view of my ass. In no way was I now thinking about him bending me over the table and fucking me. No way.

Okay, maybe a little. Like I said, this little birdie hadn't been laid in far too long.

I slid the cue between my fingers and drove the tip into the white ball. It hit hard, slamming it into the triangle of balls. They broke, scattering across the table and rolling into the sides. None obliged to me by dropping into a hole.

"Nice work," Lex said. He waited until I stepped aside and lined up his own shot. The white ball hit the six and sent it rolling, but it hit the side a centimetre or two from the hole. "I should have said I suck at this." He straightened up and smiled.

"Believe it or not, I like a guy who isn't good at everything," I said. "I'm surrounded by more than enough overachievers."

"That's another thing we have in common," he said dryly.

"You must have it so much worse than I do," I said, part sympathetic, part teasing. I'd seen him interacting with the team often enough to know he enjoyed his job.

"Definitely." He grinned and moved aside to let me take my turn. "We should start a support group. Hockey player victims anonymous."

Of course he said that just as I was about to drive my cue into the white ball again. His words made me laugh so hard I missed it completely.

"You really are a supervillain," I told him. "You totally did that on purpose." I shook my head at his smile.

If the start was any indication, I was definitely going to enjoy the rest of my evening.

# CHAPTER 3

## WREN

I let Lex beat me a couple of times, then he let me beat him a couple of times.

He tried to let on that I won fair and square, but I saw him miss a couple of easy shots at crucial moments.

I was so used to fiercely competitive men, this was a nice change. We took turns buying each other drinks and telling corny jokes. I couldn't remember the last time I laughed so hard.

I also couldn't remember the last time Tiger glared so hard. He didn't say anything or approach us, but whenever I glanced in his direction, he was watching us both.

For some reason, Bray looked equally annoyed.

Ignoring them both was one of the highlights of my night. If they had a problem with me hanging out with Lex, that was their fucking problem, not mine. I wasn't going to buy into their bullshit. Not anymore.

"I'm surprised my head hasn't caught on fire," Lex remarked. "The way those two are looking at me, I suspect they wish it would." He lined up the cue and took a shot.

"Is that going to cause a problem for you?" I asked. "You have to work with them."

He straightened up. "If there's anything I know about those two, it's that they aren't backwards in coming forward. If they have a problem with me, or anyone else, they'll speak out."

"I hope so, because I'd hate for you to get a puck in the head at the next training session." I placed the end of my cue on the ground and leaned against it.

"It wouldn't be the first time," he said easily. "But they know better than to do it on purpose. They might not like me talking to you, but they respect their coaches. They're a good bunch of guys, even when they do an impression of some kind of obsessive, possessive boyfriend." He frowned. "You're not dating either of them?"

"No," I said quickly. Too quickly perhaps.

"But you want to?" He raised an eyebrow at me in question.

I sighed. "It's complicated. I thought Tiger cared about me, but now I have no idea. As for Bray, he hates my guts, but sometimes he likes to act like an obsessive twatwaffle. I don't know what his deal is. In case you're wondering, I'm not using you to make them jealous. I genuinely like you and I'm done waiting for Tiger to figure things out."

"Have you tried talking to him?" Lex asked.

"You sound like Elenna." I made a face. "Which isn't a bad thing, but…"

I ran a hand over my hair. It was tangled, as usual. I patted it down as best I could.

"If he wanted to talk to me, he could have. Can we go back to having fun now?" I smiled hopefully. The pub was starting to empty out and there were only a handful of people left. Elenna and Sinclair had said good night and gone with their guys about an hour ago.

"Of course we can." Lex looked behind me.

I tried to resist the urge to turn around and look too, but I couldn't stop myself. I locked eyes with Tiger. His expression actually softened slightly. As soft as a stone wall could be.

Beside him, Bray was as hard as ever. He shot Lex what I could only interpret as a warning look, before they left the pub, leaving us to play in peace.

"We should finish up," I said. "They probably want to close soon."

"No hurry," Lex said lightly. "My brother owns the place. We can stay here as long as we want after closing." He stepped around behind me and said in my ear, "There's more than one way to enjoy a pool table."

His words sent a shiver right through me.

I turned to follow him with my eyes. "Is there now?"

I asked lightly. "Like what? Sacrificing virgins? If that's the case, I should tell you I'm not one."

"That's good to know," he said smoothly. "Neither am I."

"Why do I get the feeling you're not even a virgin to making use of a pool table in an unconventional manner?" I said.

He wouldn't be the first person to fuck on one. Probably not even *this* one.

He grinned. "If I'm not careful, my reputation for being innocent will be out the window."

I snorted. "Innocent, my ass. You're about as innocent as I am."

"So, extremely innocent?" he joked.

"If you keep saying things like that, you're going to have to pick me up off the floor, because I'm going to die laughing." I looked at him while I leaned forward over the table and lined up another shot. I made sure to give him a good view of as much cleavage as possible.

"If you're on the floor, I'll be right there with you." He gave me a heated look just in time for me to miss my shot.

"You're naughtier than I gave you credit for," I said.

"Is that a bad thing?" He waved for me to take another shot.

"Not at all," I said. "In fact, it's a refreshing change from tall, dark and brooding."

"You prefer tall, dark and naughty?" He was definitely not letting up on the distractions.

I preferred both, but I just gave him a wink and focused on getting the red ball into the corner pocket. It rolled all the way there. I thought it would stop half a centimetre short, but it dropped right in.

"That's what I'm talking about," I grinned and did a celebratory dance with my shoulders and hands, waving the cue around near my head.

"I've decided Tiger is an idiot," Lex said. "If you were interested in me, I'd never let you go." He stepped around the table, stopping behind me to lightly touch the front of his body to the back of mine. "Maybe I won't."

Another shiver passed all the way through me. I leaned back against him. "Really? Tell me, what would you do with me?"

He spoke right against my ear. "Everything." He moved away before I could swoon.

Several staff moved around the pub, picking up glasses and wiping tables. Once the tables were dry, they stacked stools upside down on top of them so the floors could be cleaned.

While I got ready to take another shot, Lex leaned his cue against the wall and went over to speak to them quickly and quietly. They nodded and turned the lights off inside the bar before slipping out the back door of the pub.

"Isn't this interesting?" I said. "We seem to be alone."

"There's no 'seem to be' about it," he said. "We're definitely alone."

"Excellent, there's no one here to see me kick your ass at this game." I grinned.

"You really want to keep playing pool?" he asked.

"Are you scared of losing?" I countered.

He chuckled. "No, but there are other things we could do." He stepped over to take the cue from my hand and place it back in the rack. He did the same with his, then stood in front of me, my back pressed against the side of the table. He put a hand on either side of me and looked me right in the eyes.

"I have a confession to make," he whispered.

"You really are a supervillain?" I teased.

He smiled. "I might be." His smile faded. "I've been trying to get up the nerve to talk to you for ages. I've seen you in here with your friends and I didn't want to interrupt. Sisters before misters and all that." He glanced down, then back up again. "I've also seen the way Tiger looks at you."

"Bros before hos?" I suggested.

He snorted softly. "You're no ho, but yeah, something like that. It's not cool to try to muscle in on a woman another guy is interested in."

My heart sank a little. "Is this where you tell me you want to be friends and you'll stay away from me for the sake of Tiger?"

Lex leaned in closer. "No. This is where I say he had his chance and didn't take it. I won't make the same mistake." He brushed his lips over mine.

I kissed him back. He tasted like beer with a hint of

salt and something purely masculine. It was instantly addictive. I swiped my tongue against his lips, wanting more.

He opened his mouth to let me slip my tongue inside. He gripped my hips with his hands and lifted me up onto the side of the pool table.

My arms went around his neck for balance and to bring him closer. As soon as he was close enough, I wound my legs around his waist and pressed my pussy against his erection.

We were separated by layers of fabric that felt like far too much. I wanted to see him naked, but I couldn't untangle myself from him. I ground my clit against him, driving myself closer and closer to coming.

"I don't want you to come like this." He unwound my arms from him and pressed me down on the felt. He managed to unhook my feet from behind him and undid my jeans to pull them down my hips. I lifted them to help him, then kicked them off my feet onto the floor.

He raised an eyebrow at my emerald green G-string.

"What? I like green," I said.

"I like red." He admired my curls, visible through the sheer fabric.

My skin was on fire. I sat up and tugged my jumper off over my head. I dropped it down beside me on the pool table, then started on my shirt—a blue and red Demons jersey. Of course, what else would I wear to the game?

Lex eyed it speculatively.

"It doesn't have anyone's number on the back," I said. That would send the wrong message to everyone. This was a generic jersey, to show my support.

"Take it off and let me see." Lex held out his hand.

I slipped it off over my head and held it out to him. He took it, turned it around and inspected the back.

"Did you think I'd lie?" I placed my hands on my hips.

"Of course not." He tossed the jersey down over the top of my jumper and admired me in only my panties and matching bra. "Green suits you."

He gripped my hips and pulled me to the edge of the table. Slowly, reverently, he ran the pad of his thumb up and down the front of my panties. Just lightly, but enough to make me quiver.

"Your pussy is beautiful." He leaned in to place a kiss on the fabric, right over my clit. He glanced at me with dark eyes, then hooked his fingers around the waistband of my panties and tugged them down. He parted my legs with big, gentle hands and knelt down in front of the table. He draped my legs over his shoulders, so his face was between my thighs.

He started a long, slow exploration of my pussy with his tongue. Every movement was deliberate and careful. Designed to drive me crazy without making me come too soon.

I pressed my palms against the felt and closed my eyes.

On some level, I was aware we faced the window leading out to the street. Anyone walking or driving past could glance in and see him eating me out. I didn't care. Let them look. They could be jealous they weren't the ones so expertly being driven to the very edge.

I wanted to tell him he had a talented tongue, but I had no coherent words right now. I'd be lucky if I could remember my name, much less put together a sentence. If this was how he feasted, he must be one hell of a fuck.

My whole body trembled. I moaned when he pushed a finger inside me, then another. He hooked his hand around to massage my G-spot at the same time as his tongue teased my clit.

Every touch felt so fucking incredible. Exactly what I needed, to feel desirable and wanted. Not kept at arm's length, or in the dark.

I pressed my lips together and groaned a couple of times, the only indication I could give that I was about to come. That and grinding myself against his mouth harder and faster.

I arched my back and came, long and hard, tangled up in a warm web of bliss with no beginning and, if I was lucky, no end. The only thing that existed was pleasure and his touch, along with the firm surface beneath my body.

My orgasm waned all too soon, bringing me down to earth with a gentle bump.

"Holy shit, that was—" I blew out from between pursed lips, still trying to catch my breath.

"Delicious." He slid his fingers out of me and stood. "You taste incredible. I love the way you sound when you come. We should do this again."

"Hell yeah, I'm in." I liked a guy who was generous with his orgasms.

# CHAPTER 4

## LEX

"Go!" I shouted.

Tiger and Bray gave me twin glares, but gripped the tethers attached to their waists, leaned forward and started to sprint across the ice on their skates. They pulled sleds with additional weight along the rink behind them.

Of course, the strength exercise had to be a competition between these guys, to see who could pull the sled across the ice the fastest.

It was my job to make sure it didn't get out of hand. Friendly competition was one thing, injuring themselves to prove a point was another.

At this level, they knew what was at stake. They weren't young and stupid, aspiring to turn professional. They *were* professionals whose livelihoods depended on their bodies. On and off the ice.

An injury could stop them from fulfilling sponsorship requirements and put them out of the game. When you were talking about thousands of dollars, it wasn't something the guys fucked with. Some of them might make the move to North America. If they did that, they'd be talking about millions.

Yeah, there was competitive, then there was smart.

That included these two, no matter how pissed off they might be at me. Just *how* pissed off that was, I wasn't exactly sure.

They both gave me long, dark looks, but neither said anything more or less than was required of them. Would they keep their mouths shut if they knew I ate Wren out on the pool table?

Lucky for me, I was a big boy and could stick up for myself. What she and I did was our business, not theirs. And what fucking good business it was. The taste of her pussy lingered on my tongue. The cries she made when I lapped at her as she lay on her back on the pool table, echoed in my ears. My cock twitched at the memory.

I blinked a couple of times to return my focus to the morning's training.

Tiger and Bray skidded to a stop at the end of the rink and turned carefully to come back.

Tiger's sled slammed into the boards, but he tugged it around and gave chase as Bray was getting away from him.

"Come on, Tige!" Coast Riggs shouted. "You're letting Bray beat you." He skated backwards, right in front of them.

"Fuck off, Coast," Tiger shouted back. "We all just saw Javey kick your ass."

"In your dreams." Coast grinned. "You must be thinking about Phoenix."

Phoenix was working with the goaltender coach, practising saves. "Leave me the fuck out of it," he shouted. "Besides, there's no chance Javey would be faster than me."

Javey was visibly unamused at being the source of ridicule. He was slightly smaller than Coast, but faster. That put them on an equal footing when it came to exercises like this.

"If you're not careful, you're going to make Javey cry." Tiger reached the end of the rink and grinned at Javey.

Javey glared at him before lunging at the defence-man, aiming a fist at his face.

Tiger ducked to the side and raised his own fist to strike back.

"That's enough," Aidan snapped from the other side of the rink. "Don't make me bench you both for the rest of the season."

Tiger glared at Javey but lowered his fist and sprinted away, the sled still behind him.

I made my way over to Aidan, skating casually. "They're on edge today."

I stopped and lightly rested my hand on the boards. I didn't need it for balance. I learned to skate not long after I learned to walk. It was second nature to me.

"When are they not on edge?" Aidan narrowed his eyes at Javey. "They're desperate to get the season underway and make up for the last one. Getting as close as we did and then missing out... It's fucking with all of us."

"It's ironic how much less pressure there was when we were losing all the time," I remarked. "The better you do, the better you want to keep doing."

"Exactly," Aidan agreed. "Now everyone knows what we can do, we have to keep doing it. Doing better. The moment we don't, everyone will be watching."

"They can do it this year," I said. "They're a lot more focused. Most of the Fiorellis are gone and all but one of the Mancinis. We might be able to focus on hockey for a while."

I glanced in the direction of Tank and BJ. I wasn't sure about Aidan's decision to let them and their girlfriend, Kaya Mancini, walk away from the attack on Sawyer's house. It wasn't my call to make. As far as I could tell, all three of them were firmly in line. If that changed, Aidan would be all over them before they could blink.

"That would be a fucking miracle," Aidan remarked, drawing my attention to him. "While Nicholas is still out there, I won't hold my breath for miracles."

After a moment, he added, "You're right though, they are a lot more focused. We need to keep them that way."

"You've noticed, huh?" I turned back to the ice.

"I wasn't born yesterday," he said. "I saw you with Wren. I'm seeing the death glares you're getting today. Playing with fire, are you?"

I grinned. "Nothing I can't handle. I like Wren. She deserves someone who actually spends time with her. Women like that don't wait around forever."

Tiger's loss was my gain. And Bray's. If he thought he was fooling anyone when it came to his interest in his stepsister, he'd have to think again. He was as subtle as a puck to the eyeball.

"No they don't," Aidan agreed. "Sometimes a man just has to take what's his."

That was very clearly his approach to Elenna. He'd set his sights on her the moment he saw her and laid claim within a matter of weeks. I didn't think she'd resisted, but he wouldn't have allowed her to. Once he'd decided she was his, that was that.

I was close to making that same decision myself, where Wren was concerned. My only hesitation was the potential of friction with Tiger and Bray. I didn't care about it, but she obviously did.

The solution was simple. I'd have to get under her skin so far she wouldn't be able to push me out even if she wanted to. I'd make her forget all about all other guys.

In the back of my mind, I acknowledged the possibility she might prefer the same kind of arrangement as Elenna and Sinclair had. Three boyfriends each. Was that something I could do?

Specifically, was that something I could do with Tiger and Bray?

I wouldn't have thought Coast, Phoenix and Javey would get along well enough to make it work with Sinclair. Aidan, Finlay and Orion were a different story. Aidan and Finlay had been friends for years. Finlay and Orion had something going on between them as well.

Tiger and Bray continued to sprint across the rink with sleds behind them. No one could deny they were good-looking, well-built guys.

I'd never considered either of them as anything more than hockey players I coached. Now I did, I came to no particular conclusions. I might be jumping to a few here though. Wren may have absolutely no interest in a polyamorous relationship. Once I got her to fall for me, she may only want me. I had no problem with that.

"That's exactly what I intend to do," I said. "Take what's mine, I mean. I have no reason to believe Wren will object."

"Are you going to be concerned if she does?" Aidan asked lightly.

"Would you have been?" I asked. "If Elenna objected."

He smirked. "Of course not, but that was never in the cards. Elenna and I were meant to be together. I knew it and she knew it. There was no reason for her to object."

"But if she had?" I pressed.

"Then I would have kept working on her," he said.

"However long it took. Sometimes we have to help people to see what's right in front of them."

I nodded. "Yes, we do. I'm going to make sure Wren sees very clearly. She's a smart girl, it shouldn't take too much work."

"If she's that smart, and you're the one for her, she'll see it," Aidan agreed. "But if you're not, she'll see right through you. And if she doesn't, she has Sinclair to help her out."

He rolled his eyes. For some reason, he seemed to have taken a dislike to Sinclair. I had no idea why; she seemed nice enough to me. Anyone who was a good friend to Wren must be a decent person. If she tried to get between us, like Aidan seemed to imply, I'd put a stop to it. As long as she supported us, then I was fine with her spending time with Wren.

"Coast, Phoenix and Javey can keep Sinclair busy," I said. "She won't be a problem."

"Famous last words," Aidan said with a snort.

I glanced over to him. "Why exactly do you dislike her?"

He shrugged. "She's mouthy. I don't like that in a woman."

"Elenna isn't mouthy?" I asked.

"Elenna knows when to keep hers shut," Aidan said. "She speaks her mind, but not the way Sinclair does."

I shrugged. We couldn't like everyone, I supposed.

I'd take a different approach to her than Aidan did.

I'd be so nice to her, she'd happily support Wren and me. I could be charming when I wanted to be.

I waved to Tiger and Bray to switch out with two of the other players. They could practice trying to get goals past Phoenix for a while.

They both gave me looks while they removed the tethers from their waists. At some point, we were going to need to have a conversation, but not today.

I had work to do first.

# CHAPTER 5

## WREN

I put down the ring I was working on, set my loupe aside and rubbed my aching back.

I'd been bent over my desk for at least an hour, trying to get the design just right. Making pendants shaped like dicks and pussies was easier than a custom engagement ring.

The customer was paying a fortune for it to be perfect, so that was what it had to be. Right down to the exact placement of the massive princess cut diamond. Not to mention the six smaller ones.

The bell tinkled as the door opened and closed. Dad coming back from his meeting with Caleb, I presumed. Some of our best diamonds came from the second oldest of the Brantley brothers. I didn't think too much about how Caleb got his hands on them. We bought them cheaper than we would anywhere else and sold them for only slightly less than other jewellers.

Ask no questions, make a bunch of money. That might be Dad's motto.

"It's about time you got back," I called out teasingly over my shoulder.

Sudden pain lanced through my head.

I was pulled backward by my hair, until my chin was raised towards the ceiling.

Tiger loomed over me, a fistful of my hair wound around his fingers.

"What are you playing at?" he growled. His dark blue eyes blazed with fury. His grip on my hair tightened.

I met his gaze evenly. He'd startled me, but I wasn't scared of him. Maybe I should be, but I knew he wouldn't hurt me. Not in a way I wouldn't enjoy.

"What are you talking about?" As if I didn't know. He'd been avoiding me for so long, let him work for whatever answers he thought he needed to hear.

He jerked my head back harder. "I'm talking about Lex Stone. You two were fucking cosy the other night. Did you think I wouldn't notice?"

"I know you noticed," I said. "You couldn't stop staring at me. But that's all you were doing. Staring. This might surprise you, but there's more to relationships than just looking at each other."

"No shit." He cupped my cheek with his other hand. "You know you belong to me."

"Do I?" I raised my eyebrows at him. "You gave me the impression you didn't give a shit. What was I supposed to do with that? Wait around for the rest of my life, guessing? You weren't exactly fighting Lex off me."

"Neither were you." He stroked his knuckles down my skin.

"Of course I wasn't, I enjoyed his company," I said. "He doesn't mind admitting he's interested in me."

"He's more than interested." Tiger's fingers moved slowly down to my neck. He wrapped his hand around my throat. "He wants you to belong to him. I've seen the way he looks at you. Not only the other night. Before then too. He's been waiting a long time to claim you."

"I know," I whispered. The pulse in my clit was throbbing like crazy. My panties were ruined and probably the chair I was sitting on.

He leaned in and spoke softly in my ear. "So have I. I've waited long enough." He squeezed my throat a little tighter.

"Why did you wait?" I asked.

His grip loosened. I immediately regretted asking, but I needed to know the answer.

"I've been waiting for Nicholas Fiorelli to resurface," he said. "I've focussed a lot of energy and resources on finding him. It's been a distraction, but a necessity. When he abducted you, you were collateral damage. He wanted Sinclair to get Coast's attention. The moment he knows I'm looking for him, he'll look for targets. If I was seen with you, that would make you one. If that prick comes anywhere near you, he's going to end up the same way Sawyer did. With a bullet in his brain, courtesy of me."

"You've been staying away to keep me safe?" I said.

"Exactly, but I can't do it anymore," he said. "Seeing you with Lex... Imagining him touching you, tasting your pussy..." He shook his head. A brief frown crossed his brow.

"Did you fuck him?"

I averted my gaze from his.

He jerked my chin sideways, forcing me to look back at him. "Did. You. Fuck. Him?"

"Yes." The word passed my lips before I could stop myself. I swallowed hard. Had I signed Lex's death warrant? Tiger was volatile at the best of times. I could totally imagine him killing Lex for touching me.

Tiger stared at me for the longest time, conflict flashing through his eyes. Finally, he let go of my hair and throat and stepped back. He turned away from me and ran a hand over the back of his head.

"Fuck."

I slumped in my chair and tried to catch my breath. Tiger was like an ice storm, fierce and unpredictable. Deadly.

"I had no idea—" I started.

He turned around. "No. Of course you didn't. How could you? I suck at stuff like this. I should have told you. I was so hellbent on revenge because of what he did to you. So focused on that, I neglected to tell you. I should have."

I shook my head and pushed myself up out of the chair. "I can't blame you for trying to keep me safe." I glanced down at the floor for a few moments, trying to compose my thoughts.

"I could have come to you and asked you what was going on, but instead I hooked up with him in front of you." In front of Bray too. I had a feeling that would bite me in the ass at some point.

"The truth is, I like him too. I'd appreciate it if you didn't kill him."

He opened his mouth as though he was about to deny even thinking that, but closed it again.

Yeah, that was what I thought.

"If he was a lot of other guys, I'd have no choice," he said slowly. "But Lex is… Better than most." A brief, rare flash of vulnerability crossed Tiger's face. "Are you choosing him?"

Was I? I was attracted to Lex, but what I felt for Tiger was like a magnet. As compelling as gravity. I couldn't escape it if I wanted to.

"Can I choose you both?" I asked tentatively. That was a big deal to ask anyone.

We were surrounded by groups that made it work, but that didn't mean he wanted to be a part of that.

It was his turn to glance down at the floor. When he looked up again, he was fully in control of himself.

"You belong to me," he stated. That was a stone cold fact and he wasn't budging a hair on it.

I won't lie, it was hot as fuck. Knowing he wanted

me as much as I wanted him, that he felt the same magnetic draw. We were as inevitable as the sun rising in the morning.

"But if the only way to have you is to share you, then that's how it has to be," he said. "I have the balls to do that."

My whole body relaxed and I smiled. "I have no doubt you do. We can make this work if we want it hard enough." I glanced down at the front of his jeans. Hard was the right word for it. The fact I did that for him was hotter still.

"You're not going to want seven boyfriends are you?" He winced. "My brother is one of seven."

I rubbed my cheek as though I was actually contemplating exactly that. "I mean, if that's what happens, then…"

I needed seven boyfriends like I needed seven holes in my head. I didn't know how his brother's girlfriend managed. She must be one hell of a woman. Or absolutely out of her mind. Possibly both.

Tiger sighed out his nose. "Whatever it takes, I'm here for it."

"I know you will be," I said. I wasn't sure if Lex was, but that was a conversation for later. There were other things we needed to discuss before that.

"Have you found Nicholas?" Tiger was right, he would come for me if he knew Tiger was sniffing around. He'd come for both of us and anyone we cared about.

Personally, I thought if he knew what was good for him, he'd stay right out of everyone's way for the rest of his life.

Like the rest of his family, he was ambitious, and it only took one to rebuild. He still had a lot of contacts and a shit load of influence.

"I have some leads," Tiger said. "Nothing concrete. It seems like he's getting desperate. He wants to make a big play, to return to the way his family was under his father."

"So he may come after Reuben or Caleb?" I guessed. "Or Samuel Bell and his daughters." The best way to make an impact would be to take out the biggest players. Once they were on ice, he could step right into their shoes.

"Or he might start with the Brantleys' biggest supporters," Tiger said. "People like Aidan, Phoenix's brother Ric, Coast because he's Aidan's right-hand man at times. Me because I'm up to my eyeballs with all of them."

"Potentially all of us," I concluded.

Tiger stepped closer to me and placed a hand on my hip. "I will personally not let anything happen to you, even if that means I have to stay away from you in public for a while longer. If Nicholas tries anything, I'll pluck out each one of his pubic hairs, one by one. Then I'll staple his balls to his leg. Then a bunch of other shit I haven't thought about yet." He pulled me to him. "Nothing will happen to you."

"That's a shame, I wouldn't mind *something* happening to me," I said with a flutter of my eyelids and a smile.

He gave me a long look before he crushed his lips against mine. His tongue demanded entry to my mouth.

I opened to let him inside.

He swiped across my lips and tasted my tongue and the inside of my mouth.

He pushed me back against my desk and pulled up my thick, woollen skirt. He hooked his fingers into the top of my panties and tore them in two. He tossed the scraps aside and slid his fingers down my seam to my pussy.

"You're so fucking wet for me." His voice was rough, gravelly.

"Of course I am," I said. He drove me wild.

He wrapped his large hands around my hips and lifted me up onto the edge of my desk. He parted my legs and leaned back to look at my pussy like it was his prize.

"So fucking gorgeous," he whispered. "So fucking mine."

He leaned forward to run his tongue from my rear hole to my clit. "So delicious." He licked around my pussy, tasting my arousal and driving me even crazier.

I pressed my palms flat to the desk on either side of me, careful not to lean on my tools or the ring I was making. After all the hours of work, I didn't want to ruin it. The only thing I wanted ruined was my pussy.

He slipped a finger inside me, then another. "Who does this belong to?"

"You," I said breathlessly.

"That's right. Who's going to tell you when you can come?" He drove his fingers in and out of me hard and fast, his tongue flicking against my clit every few moments.

I groaned. "I'm going to—"

His hand stilled and he pulled his face back. "Who's going to tell you when you can come?" he asked again.

"You are," I ground out.

"That's right. No coming until I say so." He lowered his face back down to me and worked me even more thoroughly than before, keeping me right on the edge without letting me tumble over.

"Tige—"

"Not yet," he insisted, barely taking his mouth off me to speak.

I was so close. I wanted to launch myself over the edge of the waterfall, right into the deepest water. Only his determined words kept me from flinging myself into the abyss.

Instead, I opened my eyes and looked up at the ceiling. It could use a coat of paint.

"Look at me." He lifted his face, his blue eyes intense, commanding. "Look at me while I eat your pussy."

I swallowed and focused my gaze on him, watching his head between my legs, glancing at me every few moments.

"I need to come," I whispered.

He didn't answer and for the longest time I didn't think he was going to. He just went on licking and grazing his teeth over my clit, his fingers working inside of me.

Finally, he nodded. "Come for me." He nipped my clit and sent me right over into a whirlpool of bliss that spun me around and dragged me under. If this was how I died, drowning in pure pleasure from his touch, then it was a hell of a way to go.

I arched my back, but managed to keep my eyes locked on his while I came, rocking my body on the desktop.

I flopped back, panting and trying to catch my breath.

"You're fucking hot when you come," he said. He kissed his way down my thigh before he stood and adjusted his pants.

I sat up. "Do you want me to—"

He waved me off. "Yeah, but not here. We have plenty of time. Enjoy walking straight while you can."

# CHAPTER 6
## WREN

"When does it stop being complicated?" I asked.

The first game of the preseason was about to start. Elenna, Sinclair and I had seats in the team's box, giving us a good vantage point of the ice and each play.

In this case, the warmup. Sinclair was half-listening to me while watching Phoenix doing groin stretches.

"Who says it ever stops being complicated?" She tore her eyes off her goalie boyfriend and his pseudo ice humping, long enough to look over at me and grin.

I groaned. "Why did I know you were going to say that?" I hadn't even talked to Lex yet and already my stomach was in knots.

He may decide he didn't want to see me anymore if I was involved with Tiger. Or worse, he may insist I choose between them.

That would be difficult, to say the least. I could easily fall for him *and* Tiger. I knew Tiger wasn't going to walk away, but knowing I still had one guy wasn't a consolation if it meant hurting another. Tiger wasn't a consolation prize, or a fall back. Neither was Lex. I didn't care if it was greedy, I wanted both of them.

I peered down toward the ice.

I couldn't see Lex from here, but Tiger and Bray were talking about something while they did a warm up skate. Whatever it was, it seemed intense. Every so often, one of them would look up in my direction.

Why the fuck was my stepbrother talking about me?

Yeah okay, it didn't take a genius. No doubt he was warning Tiger about me. Reminding him I was with Lex the other night. Potentially telling him my deepest, darkest childhood secrets, like the time I failed a maths test even after copying from the kid beside me.

If you're going to copy, make sure the other person has the right answers.

He might be telling Tiger about when I learned to shoot. I used to visualise Bray standing in front of me at the gun range. I learned quickly. Especially head shots and how to place a few handy bullets in the right shoulder. Why there? Ruin his shoulder and he'd never play hockey again.

Of course, he was always good at hitting heads and hands. To say we were competitive was an understatement. We'd done whatever we could to get praise from my father. And didn't we hate it when it went to each other instead?

There was always the possibility I was being paranoid. Tiger and Bray should be talking about the plan for the coming game. The Koalas were a tough team, in spite of their name. They'd give the Demons no mercy. If the guys weren't focused, they'd get their asses handed to them.

There Bray went, glancing at me again. The prick actually smiled.

Yeah, they were definitely talking about me. Why did he have to be so hot though? As a kid, he was as gangly as fuck. Then he hit puberty. He filled out into a smug wall of muscle, with a hockey ass made for grabbing.

I was tempted to flip him off, but it would be just my luck if someone had a camera aimed my way as I did it. That would not look good for the team. Instead, I leaned forward and gave him an enthusiastic wave, like I gave a shit.

His grin widened and he blew me a kiss.

Smartass.

"To the casual observer, you two might look like a couple," Sinclair remarked.

I stuck out my tongue in disgust. "Only if the casual observer doesn't know any better. He's good at fooling people. Believe it or not, there are people who think he's actually nice."

Sinclair put a hand over her heart and pretended to look shocked. "They do? How is that possible?"

"He seems nice to me," Elenna said. She had the night off from assisting Finley, the equipment manager.

She'd worked all day to help get everything ready for the game. Usually, she was down in the locker room with him anyway, but tonight she opted to sit with us and watch the game.

"That's because you're nice," I told her. "You want to think other people are nice. Trust me, Braylon Ellis is a dick. He only thinks with his dick. Half the reason he started playing hockey was for the puck bunnies."

"You seem to think about his dick as much as he does," Sinclair teased.

I swatted her with my fingertips. "His is the last cock want to think about."

That brought me right back to the conversation with him in the kitchen the other day. My good mood melted away like ice in the middle of summer.

The memory of being abducted, pushed into the back of the van and held at gunpoint for days, flooded back. My whole body tensed.

"Are you okay?" Sinclair looked concerned at the abrupt change in my expression.

She and Elenna were frowning at me like they expected an answer.

I sighed and explained why Tiger stayed away from me.

Neither of them looked surprised. Elenna in particular, nodded in understanding. Whatever Tiger knew, Aidan knew. And whatever he knew, he told her. Most of it anyway, from what I could gather.

"Of all the words I'd thought I'd use to describe

Tiger Pennington, sweet isn't one of them," Sinclair admitted. "Protecting you like that, even when you're both going crazy, is kind of adorable."

Yeah, sweet wasn't a word I'd use either, but I understood where she was coming from. Everything he was doing, he was doing for me, including trying to find Nicholas. I'd never had a man trying to get revenge on my behalf before. I wasn't sure how I felt about it. It was hot, but it could get Tiger killed. That was the last thing I wanted.

"I have no idea what he'd think if he knew you described him that way," I said with a forced laugh. "Sweet and adorable. I don't think that's what he's going for."

She laughed. "Fine. Brooding, grumpy and vengeful. Is that better?"

"Much more accurate," I agreed. "Those are three of my favourite things."

Elenna smiled. "Funny, mine too."

I'd guessed that about her. Aidan was a broody asshole. Orion was just broody. Finley probably fit the vengeful criteria the best. He'd smile while putting a bullet in someone's head.

"Bray is all of those things too." Sinclair gave me a sly smile.

I snorted. "What does he have to be vengeful about? Oh, right. My father had the audacity to marry his mother. He better not decide to act on it. I'd stab him in the eyeball with one of my cock pendants."

"If he's upset about that, it's only because he thinks you're off-limits," Sinclair said. "Some people frown on stepbrother-stepsister relationships."

That was true.

"We virtually grew up together," I said. "I've seen him naked more times than I care to count."

"That explains why you can't get him out of your head," Sinclair teased. "Is his cock that big?"

I stuck out my tongue. "Please. Yes it is, but I don't want to think about it." If I did, I'd imagine how it felt to run my hand up and down his length. How he'd feel sliding into my pussy. Pounding into me. Our sweaty skin sliding together. The sound of his moans when he came...

I shook my head to clear the thought away before I ruined my panties. I admit I was curious about what it would be like to fuck him, but he was still an asshole. There was no way I was going there.

Not again.

"Did your pupils just dilate?" Sinclair asked. "Elenna, did you see that?"

"I did," Elenna agreed. "Are you really attracted to your stepbrother?" She'd leaned forward in her chair and kept her voice down.

"I was thinking about Tiger and Lex," I said quickly. Now I was. An image of them touching each other popped into my head.

My panties were officially ruined.

Neither of my friends looked like they believed me,

but they both nodded and sat back to watch the start of the game.

Right from puck drop, Coast had control of the puck, driving it toward the Koalas' goal. Orion and Bray stayed close, Orion taking possession when the Koala's defense closed in on Coast, trying to smash it away from him.

Orion slid the puck over to Bray, who lost possession when one of the opposition's defensemen slammed him against the boards and skated away.

Someone shouted, "Fuck off," but the defenseman skated away like nothing happened.

Elenna winced, confirming what I suspected. It was Aidan who shouted. Of course, who else would it have been?

The Koalas' right-winger tried to sneak the puck past Phoenix, but he stopped the goal with his stick and smashed it back to Javey.

Javey drove the puck behind the goal and around before sending it spinning back to Coast right before a change of shift.

"They're playing better than they were at the beginning of last season," Sinclair said. "They all have their heads in the game."

"They definitely didn't last year," Elenna said. "The coaches have done a lot of work with them to give them the right mindset. It seems like half the battle sometimes."

"It really does," I agreed. If I wasn't in the right

mood to work, I didn't get as much done as when I was. Now my Danglies were making me money, I was in the mood a lot more often. Also, I enjoyed making cocks, especially ones with piercings on them.

Bray was back on the ice for a shift. He now had the puck in front of him. He was keeping careful control with his stick. What he was doing was harder than it looked, but he made it look so easy.

I could skate and hit the puck, but the one time I asked him to teach me how to control it like that, I failed miserably. Of course, he'd laughed hysterically. For days.

Ever since then, I left the ice hockey to the experts.

He feinted to the left before flipping the puck and sending it to the right, straight into the goal. The arena erupted in cheers.

I clapped and cheered as loud as anyone. Even if I hated his guts, I appreciated his ability. And when it came down to it, I wanted the Demons to win.

After Bray scored the first goal, the Koalas were fiercer, angrier than before. They fought back, right up until the end of the first period, blocking every goal and keeping us from hanging onto possession for long. By the time the horn sounded, the score remained at one to nothing.

The players filed off the ice for a few minutes of rest and water, and a chance to regroup.

"If this is any indication of the way this season is going to go, it's going to be exciting as fuck," Elenna said. "I'm going to have no nails left by the end of it." She held up her perfectly manicured, dark red nails. Totally unchewed, as far as I could tell.

I laughed. "Me too." My bright pink nails were also unchewed, but they may not stay that way for long.

"Orion is going to be in a mood after the game." Elenna's smile faded. "He always thinks the team didn't win by enough goals. Aidan is just as bad. Winning isn't sufficient."

"Nothing less than total annihilation." I nodded. I had a feeling Lex would agree. I chewed my lip at the idea of talking to him, but it was something I had to do.

Tonight.

# CHAPTER 7

## WREN

"That was a great game," Sinclair said. "Edge of our seats stuff."

"Yeah, it was," I agreed.

Half of my mind was on the game, the other half on *after* the game. I felt as if I was going to drop a nuclear bomb right in the middle of my whole life and hope like hell I wasn't the one annihilated.

We stayed in the box for a while as the crowds dwindled. The guys would have to shower and meet with the press before they could leave to celebrate the win. Some would do a quick work out if they didn't have enough time on the ice.

Finally, on some unseen signal, we rose from our seats and headed out the box and down the elevators to the main part of the arena. In North America, we'd have a private elevator and corridor, but here we had to mingle with the public. The budget for purpose built arenas was limited at best. Some day…

"I'm always nervous after a game," Elenna admitted. "After that attack last year, I keep wondering if they'll come after us here again. It's silly, I know. The arena has much better security now than it did even then. Everyone is on alert, and unless Aidan is mistaken, Nicholas doesn't have the resources. But still."

I hooked my elbow through hers, while Sinclair did the same on the other side.

"After what happened, it's perfectly normal and logical to be anxious," I said. "It was a traumatic experience for everyone. Especially you."

"What she said," Sinclair agreed. "I couldn't move out of my house fast enough after Wren and I were abducted from there." She didn't bother to contain a shudder. "Not that the guys would have let me stay there alone after that anyway. If I had, the guys would have quit and become my bodyguards, so they could stay home and make sure nothing happened to me."

"They would have driven you crazy in… How quickly?" I teased.

"By the end of the first day," she said with a smile. "They're all too active to sit around in a tiny house like that, hour after hour. They would have taken turns to run around the block and burn off excess energy."

"Yeah, that's how they would have burnt off energy," Elenna said knowingly.

Sinclair grinned. "That too. But a girl needs to sleep once in a while. And so do they."

We stepped out of the elevator, into increasingly thinning crowds that were filing out the glass front doors.

We made our way to the press area. Elenna flashed her badge and we stepped past security.

The guys were still talking about the game, Coast with enthusiasm. Aidan with approval, but as always the suggestion there was room for improvement.

"The team played well. We're looking forward to the season ahead," he concluded. He nodded to the press, rose and stepped away.

The journalists looked ready to ask more, but the press was ushered out. They left reluctantly, filing past us and glancing but not saying anything.

Sinclair and I faced our share of questions after the abduction, but that died down and if I had my way, it wouldn't flare back up again.

"Hey." A hand clasped the back of my neck. Tiger's hair was damp from the shower, slicked back off his face. Like that, the resemblance to his brother was easier, more obvious. I might be biased, but Tiger was the better looking of the two.

"Hey, yourself," I said back. "Good game."

"It wasn't bad," he said. "We could have handled the puck a bit better."

I exchanged looks with Elenna and Sinclair and we all grinned. Of course he couldn't just be happy to win.

"Did I say something funny?" He gave me a look like he wasn't sure if he should be amused or irritated.

"No, it's nothing," I said quickly. "Just girl talk."

"I don't think I'll ask," he concluded. "Unless you were discussing my pucking skills."

"Not the ones you're actually referring to," I said. I didn't kiss and tell.

"Good, I wouldn't want to show anyone up." He squeezed the back of my neck.

"In your dreams, Pennington." Coast draped his arm over Sinclair's shoulders and kissed her mouth.

"Fuck off, Riggs." Tiger looked at him with half lidded eyes. He turned us slightly, putting himself between me and the Demon's centre.

"Always so nice to have a conversation with you." Coast hadn't missed the manoeuvre. He glanced at me, clearly wondering what I saw in Tiger.

I wasn't going to let that worry me. I liked Coast, but I didn't need his blessing to have a relationship. Although, it would be easier for us girls if the guys got along with each other.

"Of course it is," Tiger said. "I'm articulate and charming. I might also reconsider my stance on not showing anyone up. I might embrace my awesomeness instead."

"Are you talking about me?" Phoenix appeared on the other side of Sinclair. "You must have been, I heard the word awesome."

"No, we were not talking about you," Tiger told him. "If we were, that's not a word we'd use."

"Funny, I was going to say the same about you," Phoenix said. He glanced toward Coast. "Let me guess, you were telling Wren she can do better?"

Tiger dropped his hand from the back of my neck and took a step towards Phoenix.

I grabbed his arm before he could take a swing.

"Can we *not* punch the shit out of each other?" I asked.

"He fucking deserves it," Tiger growled. "It's about time someone rearranged his face for him."

"Maybe, but that doesn't have to be you." I shot Phoenix an apologetic look. I had nothing against the goalie. If anything, I liked him because he made Sinclair happy. Anyone who did that for one of my friends was all right in my book.

"My face is perfect the way it is," Phoenix said. He gave me a shrug like he agreed with Coast's suggestion Tiger wasn't good enough for me.

"Who said it wasn't?" Javey stepped up behind Sinclair and leaned around to kiss her cheek.

"Tiger." Phoenix nodded at him.

Javey frowned at Tiger, then at me. Evidently all three of them were in agreement.

"What about Tiger?" Finley, the team's equipment manager, snaked an arm around Elenna and pulled her to him.

"They're doing some team bonding exercise by being assholes to me," Tiger said.

"While I applaud team bonding, that's not what it looks like to me," Finley said. He whispered something in Elenna's ear. She nodded and whispered something back.

"What about sausages?" Coast grinned as if he could hear from further away than I was.

"Wouldn't you like to know?" Finley grabbed Elenna's hand and pulled her towards the exit, where Orion and Aidan were waiting. "We'll see you later. Don't forget to get lots of sleep."

"Don't do anything we wouldn't do," Coast told him.

Finley winked and whisked Elenna away.

"Could you be more cringey?" Tiger asked Coast.

"Yes, I could," Coast replied. "I could have been you."

It was a good thing I was still holding Tiger's arm, or he might have taken a swing at Coast.

"We should get out of here," I said. I took a step away, but turned back to Sinclair's guys. "If… When… Nicholas Fiorelli comes at us, we need to be united. As a team, you need to be united. Being shitheads to each other isn't going to help anyone."

"That's my girl," Tiger said as we stepped away. He placed his hand back on my neck, fingers tangled in my hair.

"Your girl?"

I hadn't seen Lex come into the room, but he was

there now, a clipboard in his hands. He looked from me to Tiger and back again.

"We need to talk," I said softly.

"So I see," he said. "Let me put this down and we can do that."

He stepped out of the room, leaving us alone with only a handful of others who were talking in small groups while inching towards the door.

Bray was deep in conversation with one of the Demon Girls, the team's cheerleading squad. She was a cute blonde who hung off every one of his words. She was exactly his type, breathing and with a pussy. He was nothing if not predictable.

"Do you want me to leave?" Tiger asked. "The conversation could get messy."

"Please don't," I replied immediately. "If we're even going to *think* about doing this, we need to be all in. Right from the start."

He was right though, this could get very messy and complicated. What was I saying? It already was. Not helped by Tiger's own teammates' animosity towards him.

"I'm all in," he said. "Don't listen to the bullshit from guys like Coast. They wouldn't know what their own asses looked like if they walked up and bit them on the face."

"That's very specific," I said with a grin.

Tiger chuckled. "It's true though. He thinks he knows everything. He's a dumbass."

"Maybe he is, but I meant what I said about you guys getting along," I said. "For all our sakes, you need to try."

Tiger looked pained. "I'll make an effort if he does. No promises."

Lex stepped back into the room. He nodded towards Tiger and me. "So, we're doing this?"

That wasn't what I expected him to say. I quickly realised his putting the clipboard away wasn't from necessity. It gave him a chance to compose his thoughts and decide how he felt about what he saw.

It seemed he wasn't going to back down or step away.

"That depends what you think 'this' is," Tiger said.

"You, me and her," Lex said bluntly. "Sharing. Both of us dating Wren." He cocked his head at Tiger. "Did I get it right?"

Tiger grunted. "More or less. Yeah, that's what this is. I'm not giving her up. You want her, you're in like this. Or you're out." His tone gave no room for alternatives or arguments.

Lex leaned in towards us both, the smile fading from his lips. "I'm not stepping away. If this is how it'll be, then that's how it'll be." He leaned back, his expression relaxing.

"It's a good thing you and I get on better than you do with most of the team."

"If I hated your guts, I'd still refuse to walk away," Tiger said. "I'd have to kill you instead."

Lex smiled. "Not if I killed you first."

"Well, this is a lovely conversation," I said wryly. "I'm starting to wonder if I should—"

"No," they both said at the same time.

"You don't get to walk away from us now," Tiger growled.

"Not a chance," Lex agreed. "You're ours now."

I hadn't seen the possessive look on his face before, but it was there now. Their expressions matched.

They were all in with me, jumping in with both feet and to hell with the consequences.

"Great," I said lightly. "I know this won't be easy, but if we take it a day at a time, neither of you will need to kill the other." I'd like to think they were joking, but I knew better.

Maybe they wouldn't have literally killed each other, but if they hadn't agreed, things would have gotten bloody. That shouldn't have been a thought that ruined my panties, but here we were.

"Will there be any more than us?" Lex asked carefully. "I know your friends have three each..." He exchanged glances with Tiger, who gave a curt nod.

"Whatever happens, happens," Tiger said. "I don't give a shit as long as it doesn't get between us."

"We'll make sure that doesn't happen," I assured them both. And myself. My head spun. I needed to get used to the idea of having two boyfriends before I thought too hard about a third.

I won't lie, it was nice to know where they stood if that happened though.

"Deal, but we have plans," Tiger said. "Lex got to play pool with you. I have plans for the rest of the night." He took my hand and led me from the room before Lex could object.

# CHAPTER 8

## TIGER

Not gonna lie, I wasn't sure if I was relieved or not. I tolerated Lex and I wanted Wren to get what made her happy, but if he'd decided to walk away, I would have gotten over it.

There were worse fates than having her to myself for the rest of my life. Lex was going to make things interesting, but the rest of the night, this was for her and me.

I opened the door of my black Maserati and helped her inside before stepping around to the driver's side. I slipped in and started the engine. Of course, the car purred like a kitten. Or a tiger cub.

"Where are we going?" Wren asked.

"You'll see when we get there," I told her. "It's a surprise. For the record, we're not going to a Wolf Venom concert."

I'd lost count of how many times women asked me to take them to see my brother's band. So fucking many,

I started to wonder if they were interested in me, or good tickets.

When I told them no, I didn't see them again. Didn't want to.

I wasn't my brother. I spent enough time in his shadow, I wasn't going to do it now. If they just wanted to fuck me, I was there for that. That was about me. Okay, that was about me being a hockey player, but it still wasn't about my brother.

Wren never showed any interest in the band, not before and not now.

"I didn't think we were," she said. "I got the impression this was a you and I thing. Not a group thing." She peered out the front windscreen. "Are we going to the beach?"

"No." I preferred the beach in autumn, when there weren't so many people around, but that wasn't tonight's plan either.

"Some little hole in the wall restaurant?" she asked.

"No," I said again. I preferred those to the fancier places, although I didn't mind Hazards. The atmosphere was casual. No expectations.

She hummed for a moment. "Not the beach, not a restaurant..."

"If you don't stop asking questions, I'm going to have to shut you up," I growled.

She grinned over at me. "Are you now? In that case... Are we going to the movies?"

I grunted in annoyance and pulled the car over to

the side of the road. I stopped in the shadows between two trees and killed the engine.

Rougher that I should, I shoved my door open and stomped around to the passenger side. I yanked the door open before grabbing her hand and pulling her out. I undid my jeans with one hand and pushed her down onto her knees with the other.

I shoved down my jeans and boxers until my cock popped free. My fingers tangled in her hair, I pressed her face until her mouth was right in front of my tip.

"If you're going to keep asking questions when I tell you not to, you're going to take my cock down the back of your throat. Open up."

She looked up at me, smiled and opened her mouth.

I slipped my cock between her soft, luscious lips. She swirled her tongue over my tips before sucking me eagerly.

Fuck, she felt good. Better than good. Warm, wet and eager. Three of my favourite things.

She gripped my balls with her hand and massaged them while I thrust in and out slowly, fucking her mouth.

"Bloody hell, woman, your mouth is something else." I gripped her hair, holding her while I slid myself slowly in and out of her.

Just like when I ate her out on her desk, I locked my eyes on her, watching the way her lips wrapped around my length like she was made to suck me off.

A couple of cars drove past, but I ignored them. If

they saw anything in the shadows, who cared? Let them know my woman was sucking my cock on this cool autumn evening. They could be as jealous of me as they wanted. That was their problem.

Mine was not coming too quickly. The way Wren's tongue swirled over my tip drove me absolutely fucking wild.

I thrust in deeper, my balls getting harder at the way she gagged each time I hit the back of her throat.

"That's the way, gag for me," I said. "Take everything." I gave her everything. As far in as I could go, as much as she could take. I wanted to push her to her very limits and then beyond. I wanted to know how far she'd let me go.

"Have you learned not to ask so many questions?" I asked.

I smiled at the way her eyes shone with mischief in response to the question. That was what I figured. She'd push me if she got to suck my cock as punishment. I knew she was my kind of girl. I didn't know which was better, playing hockey or having her on her knees beside my car, her lips decorating my cock.

Probably this.

My balls tightened, my pulse raced. I gripped her hair tighter.

"I'm going to come down your throat and you're going to swallow what I give you," I instructed.

I didn't wait for her to respond, I came with a roar,

squirting a mouthful of cum between her lips. I went on thrusting until every drop was gone from my balls.

Finally, I slid off her, tugged her head back so her chin raised before she swallowed.

She smiled. "Now will you tell me where we're going?"

I snorted a laugh and pulled her to her feet by her hair. "Stop asking so many questions or I'm going to spank your ass. Get into the car, woman, let's get going." I shoved her towards her door and into her seat.

"If you keep threatening me with a good time, I'm going to keep the questions coming." She shot me a cheeky grin before closing the door behind her.

Brat.

I slipped into the driver's seat. "If you do that, I'm going to steal some of Phoenix's kneepads. You're going to need them." I shut the door behind me and restarted the engine.

She laughed. "You say that like it would be a bad thing."

"You like sucking my cock that much, hmmm?" I glanced away from the road to look at her before looking back. My body was still buzzing. I didn't need to go too fast with her. We had the rest of our lives to enjoy each other, but I could go for a round two soon enough.

Instead of answering my question she asked another one of her own. "What do I get to do to you if you're a brat?"

I snorted softly. "You get to punish me by letting me fuck your mouth."

"So, win-win." She sat back against the seat.

I shook my head. She really was something fucking else.

# CHAPTER 9

## WREN

"You're full of surprises," I said.

"I've been told I'm full of lots of things, but not surprises," Tiger remarked. "Usually shit." He slipped out of the driver's seat of his car and walked around to help me out of mine.

I smiled my thanks and let him take my hand and lead me into the planetarium.

Built on the tallest of the hills to the west of Dusk Bay, I hadn't been here since I was a kid. It wasn't the kind of place I pictured Tiger Pennington going to, much less enjoying.

He shrugged. "Tigers have layers."

I laughed softly. "I'm beginning to see that."

We pushed in through the glass front doors with a nod from the security guard, who was clearly expecting us.

"I'm surprised there aren't more people here," As far

as I could tell, the planetarium was empty apart from us.

"I'm not," Tiger said simply.

He led me through the main reception area, into a vast viewing space, long and wide, topped with a glass dome. Stars glittered, visible through the ceiling. Other rooms housed telescopes, but this was just looking straight up at the sky with the naked eye.

On the floor, lay a thick, square rug. On top of that were several cushions and a large basket.

"You arranged this," I said. "You bought out the whole place, so you could bring me here for a picnic."

In my wildest dreams, I wouldn't have thought he was a romantic. "No one has ever done anything like this for me before." I brushed away a tear before it fell into my cheek. I wasn't usually so emotional, but he'd taken the time to do something special for me. For us. The gesture got me right in the feels.

He helped me down onto one of the cushions and sat on the one beside me. "They should have. You deserve to be treated like a princess."

He opened the basket and pulled out a bottle of wine and two glasses. He filled them both and handed one to me.

"Would that make you a prince?" I took a sip. The full, rich flavour was delicious on my tongue, warm and sweet all the way down my throat. Almost as delicious as his cum.

The way he 'punished' me by getting me to suck

him off... The thought made me hot all over again. If that was his idea of punishment, I was definitely going to be bad more often.

"Prince Tiger," he mused. "That has a ring to it. Not as good as Princess Wren." He set his wine aside and pulled out plates of food. "It's all within my dietary plan. You don't have to go off and tell Lex I'm eating shit I shouldn't."

"Are you suggesting I'd snitch?" I teased.

"No, but he'd ask." Tiger handed me a plate of lean chicken and vegetables which looked and smelled delicious. He pulled out a couple of rolls and added them to our plates. "It's his job to be a bossy prick. I brought cake for you to have after."

I snagged up a fork and stabbed it into a piece of chicken. "A picnic under the stars and cake. What more could a girl ask for?"

"You're my dessert," he added.

"This date just went up ten notches." I pushed the chicken into my mouth.

"Good. I intend to spoil you for all other guys. By the time I'm done, you might not want Lex after all." He gave me the slightest hint of an eyebrow wiggle before starting on his own food.

"Or you might inspire him to go one better," I said.

"Then I'll go one better than that." Tiger looked unruffled. "I don't mind working hard for what I want. If I have to work hard to impress you, that's what I'll fucking do." After a moment he added,

"Asshole better not take you to a Wolf Venom concert."

"I'm guessing that's a sore spot for you," I said, gentle but direct. "You don't get along with your brother?"

"Beauregard Pennington is a massive prick," Tiger said. "Everything was always a competition with him. As far as he and everyone else was concerned, he always won. Both of us chose professions our parents hate, but they hate mine more than they hate his." He paused for breath. "If I was the musician and he was the hockey player, that would be flipped. Didn't fucking matter what I did."

I reached out a hand and placed it on his arm. "That sounds rough. Competing with a brother can be a pain in the ass. It's no fun when you're not related to them by blood either. I *think* my father prefers me, but Bray's mother always preferred him. I guess that's fair enough, but I always felt like I missed out on having a mother."

"Yours not around?" Tiger asked.

I put my plate aside and leaned back to look up at the stars. "She was around. At first. She got married again, had more babies. She got busy. Eventually she stopped coming, and I stopped going to stay with her. We talk to each other on the phone sometimes, but I don't really know her anymore, y'know? If I saw her face to face, I wouldn't know what to say to her."

"I'd tell mine to fuck off, so yeah, I get it," he said bitterly.

I looked over at him. "I'm sure they're proud of you. Sometimes people don't know how to express things like that."

"Not gonna lie, it's been a long time since I gave a shit whether they were proud or not. I don't see them. Or my brother, for that matter. He's probably forgotten I exist. I'd forget him but his band is on the fucking radio all the time. I don't know how many times I've done a warm up to the sound of their bloody music."

"They are a little bit popular," I said. They were one of the biggest bands in the world. It was understandable he wouldn't be able to get away from them. They were everywhere.

I never gave much thought to how often I heard their songs, but now I did, I realised it was a lot. I sang along to most of them when they came on. Their songs were so catchy.

We looked up at the stars in silence for a while, admiring the way they twinkled. Each one a tiny diamond in the night sky.

"Did you organise the cloudless weather too?" I asked.

He snorted. "Yeah, I'm that fucking influential the weather behaves for me."

He glanced over and smiled. "Naw, just looked at the forecast and picked a night that looked like it would behave itself."

"What would you have done if it hadn't?" I asked. "Choked it?"

His smile broadened to a grin. "For you, I'd choke the shit out of the clouds."

I laughed. "If anyone could do it, it would be you."

"I'd rather choke you," he said. The darkening of his eyes, and the heat behind his words made my pulse race and my clit throb.

"If you choke me right, I'll see stars," I said. Ones in other universes.

"Princess, I would never choke you wrong," he said. He rolled over and pressed his mouth to mine.

"Of course you wouldn't," I replied.

He pulled back and looked at me with a serious expression on his face. "There's something I want to talk to you about before this goes any further."

"Should I be concerned?" I frowned.

Things were going well, weren't they? Shit, now I was worried he was going to tell me something bad. Like this was a test and somehow I failed. That wouldn't be fair, I didn't even have time to study.

Yeah, the very *thought* of exams filled me with anxiety. They always would. Thank fuck I didn't have to worry about them again. Not school ones anyway.

"That depends on you," he said. "I want to tell you something about myself and I don't know how you'll take it. People in the past have had a big problem with it. They can get fucked, but you're different. I need you to hear this and if you want to run away, I won't stop you."

Whatever it was, it must be a big deal for him to say

something like that. He'd made it clear he wasn't letting me go without a fight. What could he say that would make any difference to that?

"Okay," I said slowly. "I'm listening. I can't imagine you saying anything too scary. I know you've killed people. I know you'll do it again if you catch up to Nicholas."

"*When* I catch up to Nicholas," Tiger corrected.

"When," I repeated.

I glanced around, half expecting to see the last of the Fiorellis jump out at us and kill us both. He didn't appear, no one did. Tiger and I were still alone.

"Do you like anchovies? Or something even nastier, like chicken hearts, or unborn pigeons?" I was babbling, but he had me nervous. I was ready to be all in, but now he was telling me there was something that might change my mind? I was trying not to freak out, to be honest.

"Fuck no, fuck no, and never tried it," he said. "Is that even a thing? If it is, I'm pretty sure it's also a fuck no."

He took a deep breath and plunged on. "I'm bi."

I blinked.

Waited for more.

"That's it?" I asked. I quickly added, "I mean, of course that's a big deal, but it doesn't change how I feel about you. Should it?"

"I don't think so," he said, his voice low with contemplation. "Like I said, it has in the past. I've had friends who freaked out when they found out. Thought I'd try to date them or some shit. As if I was into their ugly mugs."

"Your parents didn't approve?" I guessed.

He glanced down at the rug. "You could say that. It was the icing of disapproval on their judgey-as-fuck cake."

He shook his head. His eyes glazed as he thought back. "I've never seen that look on my mother's face. Like she didn't even know me. It was bad enough when I told her I wanted to play hockey. They wanted me to be a doctor or something that would have made me miserable. No idea why they thought I'd be any good at it. I'd probably tell my patients to shut the fuck up and get better. As if that would work."

I smiled. "I think you would have been a better doctor than you think, but you're certainly an amazing hockey player. A happier one too."

"A-fucking-men to that," he agreed. "If I even got into med school, I would have done what my brother did and drop out."

"Your brother went to med school?" I asked.

Tiger snorted. "Fuck no. He went to the Sydney Conservatory of Music." He spoke in a fancy tone, but rolled his eyes. "Decided not to be a classical pianist. He dropped out and joined a rock band."

I couldn't help smiling. "I can't say I blame him. It looks to me like rock stars have a lot more fun."

"Not as much fun as hockey players," Tiger said

with a hint of a smile. "Except that we work a lot harder."

I suspected they both worked as hard as each other, but decided it was better not to voice that opinion. Whatever problem Tiger had with his brother, that was something they needed to work out.

I snuggled up to him. "I don't care that you're bi. It doesn't change how I feel about you. If you feel the need to explore that side of yourself, you have my full support. As long as it's not behind my back."

"I would never cheat on you," he said. "I expect you to be there, taking part. Or…watching."

*Yes please.*

"Then that's what I'll do," I said. Now my head was full of thoughts of him and Lex together. Yeah, that image was hot enough to melt my panties off.

"If you're not careful, I could fall for you," Tiger whispered.

"I could say the same to you," I said.

I was already falling, hard and fast. With absolutely no safety net beneath my feet.

# CHAPTER 10

## WREN

The minute I stepped foot inside my townhouse, I knew something was wrong.

Nothing looked out of place, not that I could immediately tell. Nothing seemed broken. The place wasn't on fire. None of the windows were open.

I placed my bag down beside the door and moved through slowly. The hairs on the back of my neck rose. Goosebumps broke out on my skin.

If this was a horror movie, I'd call out, asking who was there. Since the characters who did that tended to end up dead first, I kept my mouth shut.

In the junk drawer in my kitchen—yes, I also have one—I keep a gun. If I could get to it before whoever was here got to me...

Movement flashed in the corner of my eye. I started to whip around.

I was grabbed from behind and shoved face first against the wall. I squeaked in surprise and fear.

"What the hell are you doing?" Bray growled.

I was almost relieved it was him. Almost. I was still pinned. To. The. Fucking. Wall.

"What the hell are you doing?" I growled back. I shoved, trying to push him off me. "How did you get in here?"

"I swiped Dad's key." The asshole was like an immovable wall himself." Answer the question. What are you doing with Lex and Tiger?"

"That's what you're on about?" I scoffed. "It turns out, it's none of your business."

"My stepsister is my business," he said. His hot breath swiped past my ear.

I snorted. "Since when?"

"Since you started messing around with my team-mate and my coach." His grip on my right arm was almost bruising. "I can't turn around without falling over you."

"Not my fault if you're clumsy." That wasn't what he meant. I didn't care. He was being an even bigger asshole than usual. Part of me was scared, but the other, less rational part, was turned on. Stupid pussy that didn't know not to be aroused by Bray. Sometimes I wondered who was in charge here. Her or me.

Still, I hadn't ruled out going for my gun. Not completely. If he gave me a reason, I'd use it. Even if it meant breaking Dad and Jenny's hearts. For their sakes, I hoped he didn't force me into that.

"Has anyone told you, you have a smart fucking mouth?" His lips lightly touched my ear. Either that was a gun in his pants or something else was poking into my hip.

"As a matter of fact, they have." My mind skipped back to kneeling on the gravel by the side of the road, Tiger's cock down my throat.

Provoking him was fun and his response was more than worth it. If I wanted Tiger to stop, he would have stopped immediately. Letting him take control like that was liberating. I'd never been dominated like that before. I liked it.

"That figures. You're a pain in the ass. Why would you only be a pain in mine?"

"I wouldn't want you to feel special," I told him. "You might start to think I care."

"I'm not that stupid," he snapped.

"Says you," I retorted. "Get the fuck off me." I pushed back again.

"What? You're not enjoying our little conversation?" He pressed his body against me.

That was definitely his cock. Pinning me to the wall like this was making him hard.

Unfortunately, it was doing things to me too. *Almost* making him want to touch me. To taste his mouth on mine.

I must be getting low on oxygen or something.

"Is that what you call it?" I replied. "A little conversation. I think I can feel something little, but it's so small I can't tell."

He chuckled, deep in the back of his throat, sending a surge of heat coursing through me.

"There's nothing little about any part of me, stepsister dear." He ground himself against my hip.

My traitorous pussy pulsed like crazy in response.

"You would say that, wouldn't you?" I taunted. "You probably think a toothpick is big. Then again, compared to your cock, they probably are."

He stepped back, spun me around and pressed me against the wall again, this time facing him.

His dark brown eyes blazed with anger and something else. Pure, carnal need.

He slammed his mouth down onto mine. At the same time, he gripped the front of my blouse and tore it apart so the buttons popped off and went flying.

Without thinking, I was kissing him back and grabbing his shirt to haul it over his head. The harder our lips and tongues ground on each other, the more I needed him to fuck me. Right. Now.

He barely took the time to unhook my bra before yanking it down my arms and dumping it on the floor. His jeans and my skirt were next. Followed by him tearing my panties in two.

My breath was ragged, crazy, desperate. If he wasn't inside me soon, I was going to explode. Or implode. Or whatever. The need was too much to ignore or express coherently. This was about blind, animal lust. The need to touch and be touched. To fuck and be fucked. All rational thought went right out the door. If rational thought and I were ever acquainted when it came to him.

He cupped my ass and picked me up. Pressing my back against the wall, he wrapped my legs around his waist. He positioned my pussy carefully, looked me right in the eyes and pulled me straight onto his cock.

I cried out in surprise and pleasure as he drove himself all the way to his balls with one thrust.

He grunted and went still, his eyes closed. "Fuck, Wren..." Holding me in place, he drove into me, over and over, completely merciless, violent. Perfect.

I gripped his shoulders to keep my balance. With every thrust, he grazed my back against the wall. It was uncomfortable, painful, but it added to the whole experience, driving me even wilder. Nothing about this was soft and gentle or slow and sweet and I was loving every minute of it. I could have stayed like that for hours, letting him drive himself into me. Holding him fast with my feet hooked around each other, my heels pressed against his ass.

I didn't want it to be over too soon, but his relentless pounding forced me to come. I couldn't have stopped it any more than if I was standing in front of a runaway train. I shattered right there against the wall, coming apart completely in a rush of hot, messy pleasure that lasted and lasted.

I dropped my head back and screamed out his name. I came so hard I'd probably feel it in the next lifetime or two.

He grunted and drove in harder and harder until he let out a shout and came inside my body. He pumped and ground, groaned and panted until letting out a long breath and sagging forward.

"Fuck," he whispered. "That was…" He panted for a while longer. "Told you my cock was bigger than a toothpick."

I couldn't help myself, I started to laugh. "Yes, I suppose it is."

My stepbrother's cock was still buried deep inside my pussy. Braylon fucking Ellis, the asshole I'd hated for a long time. The guy who just made me come so hard I could have touched another universe.

"Just a little bit," I added. Wouldn't want him getting a big head. He might start to think I liked him or something.

Bray drew his head back and narrowed his eyes at me. "I'll give you 'just a little bit.'" He thrust a couple of times before pulling out of me.

"Does this mean you don't hate me?" I asked as he lowered me to the floor. He was gentle this time, as though worried that if he dropped me I might break.

"I still hate you," he said. He pressed his hard, muscular body against mine, pinning me to the wall again. "But I've realised something. I'm not going to stop fucking you. Your tight little pussy is made for my cock."

He pressed a hand to my stomach and slid his thumb back and forth across the top of my seam. Slowly, as though memorising every centimetre of me. As though trying to leave some sort of permanent mark.

I tilted my head and raised my eyebrows. "Is that so?"

My pussy had enjoyed his cock, but reality was coming back into focus.

He was my stepbrother and I was involved with two other guys. What the hell was I thinking, letting him fuck me?

Oh, right. I wasn't thinking. I wanted him. If I was honest with myself, I'd wanted him for a long time. Between me being his stepsister, and our animosity toward each other, we'd held back. But now? Everything was different.

When I looked at him it was like I hadn't really seen him before. He was still as smug and hot, but fucking changed our relationship. It blurred every line we'd drawn in the sand. Shattered a butt load of inhibitions too. But then, it also created a bunch of complications.

He hooked a hand around the back of my neck. "Yeah, that's so." He was already growing hard again, and my pussy was still throbbing and eager.

"Lex and Tiger—" I started to say.

I was going to have to tell them about this. I wasn't going to go behind either of their backs. I had their blessing, but I needed to tell them Bray and I fucked. I needed to know they meant it when they said they were willing to share. I had to be certain that extended to Bray.

Bray interrupted. "I don't care if you fuck with them too. Now I've had another taste of your pussy, I need more." He pinched one of my nipples with his other hand. "I've been wanting to do this for too long. Now we have, there's no going back. You want this as much as I do, I see it in your eyes."

His eyes were dark, his tone firm, his mind made up.

I knew what he was like. Once he'd decided on something, there was no budging him. He was a stubborn prick. Of course, he had to be to play at the level he did. But this, this was something different.

I'd never seen him look at a puck bunny the way he was looking at me. The absolute need to possess me.

I hadn't realised it until now, but he'd been looking at me like that for a long time. I hadn't wanted to see it until now. Hadn't wanted to want him back.

"Even though we hate each other," I said. The way he was rubbing his thumb around and over my nipple was driving me wild.

"In spite of that. Maybe *because* of it. I don't know and I don't give a shit. I want you." He pinched my nipple again.

"I must be losing my mind, because I want you too,"

I said. The moment he tore up my blouse, I was done for.

That was going to go straight to his head, wasn't it? Both of them. To hell with it. If Lex and Tiger didn't mind one more, why shouldn't we go at it like we wanted to?

Later, I'd worry about what my father and step-mother would say.

# CHAPTER 11
## WREN

To my surprise, Bray was still in my townhouse in the morning. Still in my bed.

I lay awake watching him a while before his eyes opened. He blinked a couple of times, glanced around to orient himself, then looked at me and smirked.

I decided to get in before he did. "Figures you'd snore like a train."

He snorted like a smoke stack. "Good morning to you too, stepsister dear." He ran the pads of his fingers up and down my bare arm.

His words sent a shiver up and down my spine. "You make this sound dirtier than it is. We're not related."

"Not by blood," he agreed. "Some would say we're practically brother and sister."

"You love that don't you?" I asked. "You get off on the fact some people would find this taboo."

The skin around his eyes crinkled. "I've always been a shit stirrer. You know that about me."

"Yes, I do," I agreed. "Bad boy Braylon Charles Ellis. Puck boy and fuck boy. The biggest asshole on the first string Demons hockey team."

"Wren Elizabeth Valentine, Queen bitch and high school dropout." He traced tiny circles around the inside of my elbow.

I grinned. "That's me. Although, Princess is fine. I'll leave being the Queen to other people."

"You're not calling my mother a Queen bitch, are you?" he teased.

"I would never. Jenny is amazing." She was my mother too, as far as I was concerned. And here I was, lying naked next to her son. A guy I was definitely *not* related to by blood. Thank fuck. Otherwise all of this would be very weird.

"Of course she is. That's where I got it from." He looked pleased with himself.

"Your awesomeness is diluted," I said with a smile. "So diluted it's almost not there. But don't worry, you make up for it by being a prick."

He chuckled. "You wouldn't know awesome if it crept up and bit you in the ass."

"I know awesome all right," I retorted. "I see it every time I look in the mirror, or at Tiger and Lex. Remember them? The guys with bigger cocks than yours."

He rolled me over and straddled my body, my arms pinned above my head. "Really?" He pushed my legs apart with his knees. "You weren't complaining about that last night."

He nudged the head of his cock against the entrance to my pussy.

"That was last night." I bent my knees to give him access. "I lost my brain for a little while." I waited until he was fully inside me to say, "Is it in yet?"

He squeezed my wrists. "We can both feel it is. Even though your pussy is looser than one of Coast's lucky socks."

"We both know it's not loose, but I object to being compared to one of his stinky socks." I grimaced and hooked my legs around each other, holding him tight.

"Sorry not sorry, Socks," he teased. He eased out before shoving back in.

"No you're not, Bray-Bray," I said, using the nickname his mother called him when he was a kid.

He smiled. "No, I'm not. Insulting you is fun. Especially if it ends like this." He thrust in a couple more times. "Don't tell me you're hating this."

"Not as much as I hate you." When he thrust, he hit me inside and out, touching the right spot every time. I wasn't going to compliment his cock, or his skills, but I was enjoying the hell out of both of them.

He leaned in to nuzzle my neck. "You want to know what I think?"

"Not really," I replied. There was no way he was expecting me to respond in any other way.

He grinned. "You won't be surprised to learn I'm

going to tell you anyway. I think you don't hate me at all. I think you've been waiting all these years for me to fuck you. How many nights have you lain awake thinking about me? Do you get yourself off imagining what it would be like to have me touch you all over?" He thrust slowly in and out of me.

"Of course not," I retorted. "If I was going to lie awake in the middle of the night thinking of you, it would be ways to get you back for every time you were a dick to me."

He smirked. "We both know that's a lie. Admit it. Tell me how many times you got yourself off thinking about me." He stopped balls deep inside me and raised an eyebrow expectantly.

I looked back at him, unflinching. "I think you're projecting, Bray-Bray. How many times have you wrapped your fingers around your skinny little cock and jacked off thinking about me?"

He chuckled. "Tons of times, except for the skinny little cock part. Sometimes sleeping in the room next to you was a special kind of hell. Although, a lot of that was because you have shit taste in music."

I snorted a laugh. "You're so full of it. My taste in music is the best. I heard you sing along to it plenty of times."

"There's a difference between catchy and good," he said. "Just because a song lives rent-free in my head doesn't mean I want it there." He gave me a meaningful look.

"So I've been living rent-free in your head?" I teased.

"Only since I took your virginity," he said softly.

"That was—" I gaped. "Nearly a decade ago."

Dad and Jenny went away for the weekend and Bray and I got into a huge fight. Somehow we ended up in bed, fucking frantically and with a lot of mess. Afterward, we were both horrified and didn't talk about it.

Or maybe we weren't as horrified as I thought we were.

"Like I said, once I got a taste, I didn't want to stop." He thrust slowly a couple of times. "Since you regretted it, I figured it was better to stay away from you. Keep you at arm's length. Yesterday I was done. I couldn't do it anymore."

"Who says I regretted it?" I asked. I could have. It wasn't until afterwards that I asked Jenny to take me to the doctor to go on birth control. She hadn't asked why and I hadn't volunteered an explanation. She was just grateful I felt comfortable talking to her about things like that.

Thankfully, Bray hadn't got me pregnant at sixteen. Life could have ended up very different if he had.

"Your body language ever since." He rolled us over so I was straddling his hips. "No regrets now." It was a statement, not a question.

"None yet," I said. I placed my hands on his chest and rose and fell, riding him slowly while rubbing my clit against him each time. "Why? Do you want me to?"

He chuckled again. "Believe it or not, no. But then,

why would you? Haven't you always wanted to surrender to your inner puck bunny?"

I slapped a hand on his chest. "No, I have not. I don't give a shit if you or Tiger play hockey or clean toilets for a living. You know me better than to think that makes any difference to me."

He grinned, pleased with himself that he got a rise out of me. "And yet you frequent a pub that's always full of professional hockey players."

I sniffed. "I frequent a pub my friends like to go to. In fact, we were going there long before any of the Demons were. I have to conclude that you're following me, not the other way around."

"Whatever you want to think, stepsister dear." He gripped my hips with his large hands and guided me on and off his cock. "Either way, we've ended up here, together. Right where we belong. How are you going to explain the situation to your other boyfriends?"

"Firstly, referring to them as my other boyfriends suggests that you're my boyfriend," I said. "That's a bit presumptuous."

He grinned. "Of course it's presumptuous, I'm me. It's what I do."

I rolled my eyes and my hips.

"What's the second thing?" he asked.

"The second thing is your assumption that I'd tell them, not you," I said slowly. "But you're right, I want to be the one to do that. I'll explain everything to them as long as you can tell Dad and Jenny."

His eyes widened slightly. Clearly he hadn't thought that far ahead.

"No take backs," I added quickly.

He rolled us back over and pounded into me harder. "I'll worry about that bridge when we get to it. Right now, the only thing I want to worry about is fucking your pretty little body. I never should have stopped. Once I claimed you, I should have gone on claiming you. All night, every single night."

"Our parents would definitely have noticed," I pointed out. Especially Jenny when she realised I needed the birth-control so her son couldn't get me pregnant. That would have been an awkward conversation.

He shrugged, mid-thrust. "They forced us together, they'd have to deal with the consequences of that."

"Is that all this is?" I asked. "You were *forced* to be with me?"

He slowed down for a few moments. "No, I was forced to live with you, but I wanted to bury my cock inside you as soon as I was old enough to understand that was a thing. I started fights to push you away, but also because you set my blood on fire. The first time I slid myself inside you was like heaven. I've never forgotten it. Every woman since then, I've compared them to you. Not favourably. You're the one I wanted, needed." He thrust to punctuate his words.

"I never forgot either," I whispered. "It was just easy to go back to being nasty to each other."

"That's not going to stop," he said with a cheeky smile. "It's fun to get under your skin."

I smiled back. "It's even more fun to get under yours. Toothpick cock."

He snorted. "I'll give you toothpick cock." He thrust harder, slamming himself into me with all the strength of his muscular hips. "When I'm done with you, you won't be able to walk for a week."

"Promises, promises," I said.

"Have I ever lied to you?" He grabbed my legs and draped them over his shoulders. Each thrust hit deeper and deeper, all the way inside me.

I didn't answer with words. I didn't have any more. Nothing but moans of pleasure at the way he felt inside me.

He was wrong about me having regrets about our first time. I'd freaked out, and assumed he still hated me. But that wild, messy fuck was memorable. Neither of us knew what we were doing, but it didn't matter. We connected like I'd never connected to anyone before that.

I hadn't connected to anyone like that since, not until recently. Not until Tiger and Lex and now this. I hadn't realised what I was missing until now. Things all fell into place. Even as complicated as it all was. I wanted this, all three of them.

I groaned and looked at him cross eyed. "I'm going to come."

"Let me see you come, stepsister dear," he said.

"Come around my cock."

He really did like thinking all of this was taboo. That he was sliding his length in and out of his stepsister. Not just Wren, his long-time nemesis. He was thinking that I was being fucked by my stepbrother. That our parents and potentially the rest of the world would frown at our relationship.

Maybe he was imagining the headline when the press got hold of this.

*'Dusk Bay Demons winger has sexual relationship with his stepsister.'*

Something like that.

We should make sure Dad and Jenny found out first.

Wanting to goad him further, I moaned again.

"Yes, yes, I want to come around my stepbrother's cock."

His response was a guttural groan and frantic thrusting. He came at the same time I did, grinding our bodies together and crying out in unison while frantically clinging to each other.

"Fucking hell," he said breathlessly. "I…ahhh, fuck yeah. I love coming inside my stepsister's body. So fucking hot."

We sagged back down against the mattress, both puffing and sweating.

"So good," he breathed. "So mine."

"So yours," I agreed. I lay there for the longest time, my stepbrother's cock still buried deep inside my pussy.

# CHAPTER 12

## WREN

The day was unseasonably warm for autumn. Most of the trees near the beach were evergreens, so it could pass for summer, or maybe spring.

If the sand was swarming with people, it would complete the picture.

Fortunately, it was the middle of the day, in the middle of the week. Most of Dusk Bay was at work or school.

Technically, I should have been at work, but I took an early lunch at the same time the guys weren't training, meeting or doing interviews. I didn't know when we'd get another chance and this was something better done without an audience.

I set up a blanket on the sand, under the shade of a couple of trees. On one corner, I placed a bag of sandwiches and a cardboard tray with cups nestled inside.

Three held coffee. The fourth was tea for Bray, the tea bag string and label dangling from the side.

I sat down and tried not to let the anxiety get the better of me.

I didn't have to wait long. Tiger's Maserati was the first to turn into the car park. He was barely out and starting towards me when Lex pulled up beside him.

Absolutely no shock that Bray was last. He probably did that to piss me off.

"Took him long enough." Tiger sat down on one side of me. "He saw us make our move and decided it was finally time."

It took me a moment to realise he was talking about the relationship between Bray and me, not Bray's lateness. Was it that obvious?

"Lucky he's not that slow on the ice," Lex remarked as he sat in front of me, where he could see me and smirk at Bray at the same time. Evidently it was. That explained why Lex asked me about a third guy. They saw before either of us did. Certainly before I did.

"Fuck off." Bray flopped down on the blanket. "I always know when the time is right to act. When it is, I'm all over it, right Socks?" Apparently he was running with the nickname.

"If you say so, toothpick cock," I retorted.

Tiger and Lex both chuckled.

"They've seen my cock, they know it's bigger than a toothpick," Bray said with a shrug.

"Longer, maybe not thicker." Tiger eyed him like he wasn't sure if he was friendly or unfriendly competition. He hadn't decided if he was going to kill Bray yet or not.

A day or two ago, I might not have been concerned one way or another. Today, I preferred he not kill anyone currently sitting on the blanket.

"It's both," Bray said. "So, what the fuck are we all doing here?"

"Having a picnic," I said lightly. I handed him his cup of tea, but then added, "I brought your favourite. Vegemite sandwiches."

"I hate Vegemite." He peeled back the lid of his tea and looked inside as though maybe it held urine or seawater instead.

I smiled. "I know. I decided I couldn't go too easy on you too soon. Wouldn't want you to get comfortable."

He flipped me off, but took a sip of the tea. "Is it poisoned?"

"If she wanted you dead, you'd be dead," Tiger told him. "I would have killed you long before you went anywhere near her."

"Or I would." Lex opened the bag and pulled out the sandwiches. He tossed one to Tiger, handed one to me and kept another for himself.

Tiger nodded his thanks, opened his and started eating. "Cheese and salad."

Bray rolled his eyes at me, but leaned over to grab the last sandwich. "Are you clowns sure you want to get involved with her? You can see what she gets like when she's known someone for long enough."

"Only when they're an asshole," I told him.

"That's it, you're both fucked." Bray leaned back and rested his weight on one hand.

"I'm an asshole, but she wouldn't do that to me," Tiger said. "She must really hate you."

"I can't admit to being an asshole," Lex said. "Not openly. I think I'll leave that to you two guys."

"She might have a type," Bray suggested. "She might prefer assholes."

"She prefers people who don't talk about her like she's not here," I said. "Anyway, we aren't here to talk about where any of you fall on the asshole scale."

"Wren and I fucked," Bray said.

They both turned to look at him.

"We know exactly where he falls on the asshole scale," I muttered. "Right in the morally grey section."

"Your favourite colour is morally grey," Bray said.

"My favourite colour is shut your fucking mouth," I told him.

I didn't want to start the conversation like that.

"Like I said, it took him long enough," Tiger said.

"We figured that much when you asked to meet us all here," Lex said. "We already said we don't mind sharing and figured if there was another it would be him."

"You don't mind sharing with him too?" I asked tentatively.

"As long as you're not planning to choose him over me, then no," Tiger said.

"Yeah, that." Lex jerked his head towards Tiger.

"Definitely not," I said firmly. "His cock is too small to keep me satisfied by himself."

Bray tore off a piece of crust and flicked it at me. "You're such a bitch."

Tiger narrowed his eyes at Bray. "It's not too late for me to kill you."

"Don't kill him," I said. After a moment I added, "Unless I ask you to. You never know, things might change."

Bray flicked a piece of cheese at me.

"Stop wasting food," Lex said. "I know exactly how much of it you need to eat."

The winger groaned. "Oh shit, do I have two stepfathers now?"

Lex grinned. "Yeah, because you're lucky that way. Actually, this could be a beneficial arrangement for both of you. I can keep a very close eye on your diet and exercise—"

Tiger flicked a piece of lettuce at Lex. "Leave work at work." He spoke to him in a similar tone as he spoke to me. A little harder, a little more bro-to-bro, but not as harsh as he spoke to most other people.

I realised he spoke to Bray the same way too. Apparently my stepbrother was in before either of us admitted it to ourselves. That was reassuring. Tiger would probably not get pissed off at Bray and kill him. Maybe.

"I'm only looking out for your best interests," Lex argued, but his eyes shone with humour.

"It's in your best interest to separate work from not-work," Tiger said. "Lucky for you, I'm focused on trying to find Nicholas Fiorelli. You get a free pass for a while."

"Is there anything we can do?" Bray asked. "No one abducts my stepsister without my permission." He looked furious and, for once, it wasn't directed at me.

Lex mentioned he was angry, even scared, when I was missing, but I hadn't seen it myself until now. He'd played it cool and arrogant, like usual. This was an interesting side of him. I liked it. He might hate me less than he thought he did.

"Excuse me, but under what circumstances would you give anyone permission to abduct me?" I asked.

He grinned. "If I told you that, you'd be waiting for it to happen."

Tiger growled. "No one abducts her without my permission either."

"No one is going to abduct her without *her* permission." Lex said it firmly. He turned to me and raised an eyebrow.

My heart was racing. Was he suggesting what I thought he was suggesting?

"You'd kidnap me if I asked you to?"

"We'd do whatever you ask us to," Lex said. "But we should call it what it is. CNC. Consensual non-consent."

My face was suddenly warm. "I've read about it in romance novels, but I've never... That's a thing people do? Can we do it?"

"We have to discuss boundaries and safe words, but if that's something you want to do, I'd be down for it," Lex said.

"CNC," Tiger said slowly. "So, rough but with her permission? Anything goes unless she says it doesn't?"

"Exactly." Lex nodded. "We do what we want to her, but we stay within those boundaries and stop immediately if she says the safe word."

"I'm in," Bray drawled. "But we should talk about Nicholas Fiorelli first."

Of course it was him tipping the bucket of ice cold water onto all of us, but he was right. We shouldn't let our guard down until Nicholas was dealt with.

I'd feel a lot safer being abducted if I knew, without a shadow of a doubt, it wasn't by him.

"I really, really hate to say this, but Bray is right." I pointed a finger at him before he could speak. "This might be the first and last time, but you're right, right now."

He smirked. "Good enough for me. But I've been right before and I'll be right again." With a subtle tilt of his eyes, he reminded me that I screamed his name when he made me come.

I responded with the sides of my mouth pulling up slightly, reminding him that he screamed mine too. It was his cum that leaked out of me after we were done. Because he couldn't keep his hands or cock off me.

I turned to Tiger. "What can we do? I'd offer myself as bait, but we all agree it wasn't me he went after. I'm not offering any of my friends."

As far as I was concerned, the further from Nicholas Fiorelli any of them were, the better. For them and myself, I'd rest easy knowing he was dead and gone. With no one left to get revenge for him.

Technically, he wasn't the last Fiorelli, but his sister Amity was with Lucas Brantley and a couple of other guys, having babies. Last I heard, they were up to number four. She was no threat. I hoped.

"I wouldn't ask you to," Tiger said. "We all know there's no chance their guys would agree to it anyway. Since I don't feel like being murdered by Coast, Javey, Phoenix, Aidan, Orion or Finley, or any combination of those, let's rule that out."

"Nicholas would see that coming anyway," Lex said. "That's exactly the kind of thing he'd expect us to do." He looked frustrated.

A nice trap to catch a big mouse would certainly be an easier way to deal with the problem. Unfortunately this mouse wasn't going to take our cheese. Not after pulling the same thing on his stepbrother.

"So we should do it," Bray said. When we all turned to look at him, he continued. "Not literally, but we set something up that looks like bait. We know he won't take it, but it'll pique his interest. Use it as a distraction. Then we hit him where it hurts."

"His business interests," I said. "He still has a stake in lot of things here in Dusk Bay. And outside Dusk Bay, too."

"Especially in Sydney," Tiger said.

"Where we have a bunch of games this season," Bray said.

"I picture some sightseeing in our future," Lex said.

"I picture a dead Nicholas Fiorelli in our future," Tiger said. "We might even get a medal from Reuben or Caleb." He rolled his eyes as if that mattered or was something he cared about.

"There's only two prizes I want," Bray said. "The Goodall cup and Wren's pussy. I want to drink champagne out of both of them."

"You have to win first," I said.

He grinned. "I always do. Sometimes it takes a while, but I always win in the end."

# CHAPTER 13

## BRAY

I sat through that whole picnic, listening to them talk, while watching Wren.

I couldn't remember exactly when she got so fucking hot. Or when I stopped hating her.

I probably never had, not really. I was pissed off when my parents separated. Bitter as fuck when my mother remarried, but she could have done a lot worse than Martin. Hell, she could have married someone like me. Someone who holds a grudge for too long. Someone who has more ego than brain cells.

Yeah, I don't know if that's possible, but if it was, I fit the category. If I had any sense, I would have told Wren how I felt about her a long time ago. That I wanted to be more than stepsiblings that hated each other.

Instead of telling her, I buried myself in puck bunnies. Literally. I was never short of a willing pussy.

Every single time, they left me feeling cold, empty. The hookups were meaningless.

Hate-fucking Wren should have been just as meaningless. Two people working out their frustrations. The minute my cock was inside her, I was gone. I couldn't imagine fucking anyone else.

That was as terrifying as hell. What did I know about commitment? What did I care? Guys like me were supposed to screw anything with a pulse and move on after an hour or two. I couldn't do that with her. I didn't want to.

Also, being her, she'd never let me forget it anyway. If anyone knew how to make my life hell, it was her.

"Worst sandwiches ever." I tossed the empty wrapper into the bag, and the teacup with it. So I cared about her, that didn't mean I was going to go easy on her. That wasn't who we were. We lived to give each other shit.

"Vegemite for you next time," she said easily. "Or better yet, peanut butter."

"Ouch." Lex grinned.

Tiger looked at all of us like we were crazy. "The fuck you on about?"

"I'm allergic to peanuts," I said. "Anaphylactic. One little bite and I'm dead meat."

While I spoke to Tiger, I flipped Wren off. In the corner of my eye, I saw her return the gesture.

"Good to know," Tiger said, as if he planned to use that information against me.

"With friends like this, who needs enemies?" I said to myself.

"Who said we're friends?" Wren folded the empty sandwich wrapper before placing it into the bag.

Yeah, folded, not scrunched. I've often wondered if she wasn't slightly unhinged. She probably folds toilet paper too. She's also the kind of person who carefully, slowly, opens presents so she can reuse the paper.

I don't think I've actually seen her reuse wrapping paper, but she always claims that's why she does it. Truth is, it's probably to piss me off. I have absolutely no patience when it comes to opening gifts. I treat wrapping paper like I treated Wren's blouse. It's made to be ripped, to expose the goodies inside.

Don't get me wrong, she likes to give other people shit too, not just me. But mostly it's me.

"I didn't say anything about us being friends," I said. "Tiger and I drink together, that almost makes us friends."

"Almost," Tiger agreed.

"And Lex is cool," I added. "We don't dislike each other, right?"

Lex leaned over and slapped my shoulder. "No we don't. We could count each other as friends."

"One out of three ain't bad." I shrugged. At least things weren't going to be boring.

"Poor Bray-Bray," Wren teased. "I'm sure all those puck bunnies like you." There was something in her eyes, like she wanted me to deny what she said, or reassure her. For a gorgeous, smart, competent woman, sometimes she could be insecure. Fair enough, this thing between us was relatively new. Fragile.

I could have told her I had no interest in touching another woman, but that would be too easy.

"Like you?" I asked. "You're a puck bunny, aren't you?" She was sitting with two players and a coach. She'd denied it the other morning, but I couldn't help giving her another serve, just for fun.

"I don't want to be with any of you to score points," she said coolly. "I think that means I'm not a puck bunny. In fact, if you say that again I'll tell you to puck off."

I laughed. "I'll tell you to go puck yourself."

"You're such a puckwit," she retorted.

"Better than being a puckhead," I said.

"There's a difference?" she asked.

I grinned. "Definitely. I don't know what it is, but I'm sure there is one."

"You're a pucking idiot." She shook her head.

"That's not the first time you've told me that, and it won't be the last," I said.

"You two are out of your pucking minds," Tiger said. "I'm starting to think we shouldn't have let Bray into the club."

"There's a club?" Lex asked.

Tiger swallowed down the last of his coffee and tossed the cup into the bag. "Whatever you want to call it. Wren and us. Club. Group. Team." He was silent for a moment before quietly adding, "Family."

I always figured there was more to him than just a grumpy defenceman. I knew his brother was ridiculously famous and for some reason they didn't get along. I've seen Tiger become aggressive with someone because they wouldn't stop playing music from his brother's band. I mean, their music wasn't *that* bad.

"Family works," Wren said, her hand on Tiger's. "Even if some of us are dysfunctional." She shot me a sneaky glance.

"You can't have dysfunctional without fun," I said.

"You might be the stepdad," Lex told me. "You're here with all the dad jokes."

I tried not to bristle. "I learned them from Martin." My voice was tighter than I intended.

My biological dad and I were close, in spite of only spending every second Saturday together, from the age of ten until I turned sixteen and got too busy to bother.

We still talked on the phone every week, but only saw each other a couple of times a year.

For a long time, I lay awake at night trying to figure out ways of getting my parents back together so I could be with both of them. Even when my mother was happy with Martin, I struggled to see past my own needs.

Looking back, I saw how ridiculous it was. We were a happy family, and I would have sabotaged that for myself, to put back together two people who didn't work.

Like I said, I have more ego than brain cells.

"He learnt well, didn't you Bray?" Wren said. "If there's anything we can rely on him for, it's for bad jokes."

"You're not so bad at bad jokes yourself, Socks," I told her.

"Socks?" Lex looked amused.

I explained my comparison of Wren's pussy to Coast's lucky socks. "It seems appropriate." I grinned at her while she rolled her eyes.

"I suspect if you keep comparing her to lucky socks, you won't get lucky," Lex said.

Wren laughed at the expression on my face. "Lex is absolutely right. You definitely won't. Unless..."

"Unless I take a couple of puck bunnies home," I finished for her. "They might have tighter pussies than you."

"They might appreciate your toothpick cock better than I do," she retorted.

"You love my toothpick cock," I said.

"At least you admit your cock is as thick as a toothpick." She grinned.

"Whatever you say, Socks." I picked up the bag and pushed myself to my feet. "I don't know about anyone else, but I'm ready to figure out a plan to deal with Fiorelli. I'm guessing this is where you all say we should include Aidan."

"It's always safer to include Aidan. Otherwise you risk him being pissed off at you when you have to fill him in on the details later," Lex said.

That sounded accurate. The head coach was also in charge of plans for dealing with our enemies. Nothing much went on with the team that Aidan didn't know about. And if he didn't know, he found out pretty quickly. Lex was right, it was better to speak to him first.

"I'll be glad when all of this is over," Wren said. "It would be nice to spend a few days not having to worry about looking over my shoulder."

I sighed. "How long will it be before another threat pops up? The Bell family might decide to go after the Brantleys once and for all."

That would get very messy, given the relationship between Lila Bell and Hunter and Parker Brantley. Either they'd have to side against their own family or she'd side against them.

Maybe the DiMarco family would decide they were sick of sitting at the feet of the Brantleys, waiting for scraps. It was only a matter of time before something happened there. If not them, then someone else.

"As long as we keep our heads down, we should be fine," Wren said. "At least after Fiorelli is dealt with. Although, we might become more noticeable if we act against him. More of a threat to whoever might pop up next."

"That's why I was keeping my distance from you,"

Tiger said. "But we can deal with whatever comes after us. And whoever. And if we can't, we'll have Bray tell them his stupid dad jokes until they surrender." He gestured at me with his thumb.

"Let me at them," I said with a grin. "I have a million of them. Ready to release a barrage."

"They'll be begging for mercy just being in your company," Wren said to me. "Add in a joke or two and they're completely fucked."

I snapped my fingers and pointed in her direction. "That's a great idea. We could put them in your company and they'll go insane even quicker. They'll be begging us to let them out." I mimed clawing at an invisible door in front of me.

"You could show them your cock and they'll die laughing," she retorted. Her eyes sparkled with her special kind of mischief, the look she got when we flung insults back and forth at each other. She loved nothing more than to score a hit off me. We had that in common; I loved scoring points off her too.

I pressed a hand to my chest. "You know how to hit a guy where it hurts."

"Yeah, your chest, not your balls. Those are too small to feel pain." She laughed. She was on a roll today.

I grabbed her hand, pulled her to her feet and against my chest. I placed her hand over my groin. "Does that feel small to you?" I was immediately hard. The pressure of her palm made my cock want to split my seams.

"Tiny," she whispered.

"Liar," I growled.

"Your ego is too big for the truth," she said.

She lifted her chin and tried to stare me down. This was classic Wren. She never gave in, never backed down, especially with me. If she could get the last word, the last insult, she'd do it. She was more stubborn than a fucking mountain and I loved that about her. No one would walk all over my woman. Not even me.

"Tell me anyway," I insisted. I rubbed against her hand, getting harder still.

"Fine." She exhaled in mock annoyance. "Your cock and balls are huge. At least a match for the size of your arrogance."

I chuckled. "That's better." I didn't care if she came after my arrogance. That was something I'd admit to. It came with the territory.

"See, a bit of honesty didn't hurt you." I undid the front of my jeans and pressed her hand inside. She curled her fingers around my cock. The warmth of her palm was a jet of flame all the way through my body. How the hell did I go so long without her touching me? Without claiming her as mine, permanently?

I didn't care that we were in public; there was no one on the beach but us. No one to see me slide my jeans down my hips and thrust into her fingers.

# CHAPTER 14
## WREN

Bray was hot and hard in my hand. His cock thick and veined and ready. Seeing him like this washed away a bunch of old memories and sensations.

I couldn't think of him as my stepbrother. He was my boyfriend. My lover. A pain in my ass, yes, but so much more than that. I wanted to touch him, feel him. Hear him shout my name again.

"Does he know how well you suck?" Tiger asked. He brushed hair off my face and pushed me slowly, gently to my knees.

I looked up at him and Bray before teasing his tip with my tongue.

Bray hummed with pleasure. "I want more than that."

He got a teasing smile in response before I shuffled over on my knees and undid the button of Tiger's jeans.

"Brat," Bray muttered.

I laughed softly and slid down Tiger's zipper. I tugged down his jeans and black boxers, letting his erection spring free. I teased him with my tongue the same way I teased Bray: lightly, softly.

I gripped Bray's ass and pulled him closer before switching over to wrap my mouth around his cock. I sucked him hard for a minute or two before switching back to Tiger.

Lex sat down beside me and unbuttoned my pants. He pushed them down my hips just far enough to be able to slide his fingers over the gusset of my panties.

"Is she wet?" Tiger asked.

"A bit," Lex replied. "She could be wetter." He pushed my panties down and waited until I raised one knee, then the other to pull them all the way off.

I hadn't forgotten we were in a public place, but I didn't care. Even if a crowd of people turned up, I wouldn't.

As long as they weren't the press taking photos. That was the kind of publicity Sinclair wouldn't want to have to handle. Not as a friend and not as a member of the Demons' PR department.

I knelt with my thighs apart, giving Lex room to fit his hand between them. He slid his middle finger inside me, while his pointer finger rubbed over my clit. I groaned and switched back to Bray's cock.

They were both tastier than the sandwiches. I could happily have them for lunch every day.

"She's much wetter now," Lex reported. He pushed

two fingers inside me and let his thumb take over circling my clit.

Tiger looked down at me with dark eyes. "I need to see her naked."

Bray slipped his cock out of my mouth and leaned down to help pull my shirt off over my head. He tossed it aside and unhooked my bra before pushing the straps down my arms and onto the blanket.

"Perfect," Tiger said softly. He ran his knuckles down my cheek and over my hair. When Lex pulled his fingers out of me, Tiger guided me back onto the blanket. He climbed on top of me and parted my legs with his knees.

"I've waited so long to be inside you." He didn't wait any more. He positioned his cock outside my pussy and pushed straight inside me.

I gasped out loud, the sensation of his thick length sliding past sensitive muscle and nerves almost enough to make me come then and there.

Added to that, Lex kissing my breasts and sucking one nipple then the other.

Bray sat down beside me and turned my face so he could press his cock back into my mouth. "This is perfect. You can't be a smartass with your mouth full of my dick."

I gave him a look to suggest I could do just that, without saying a word.

He chuckled and thrust slowly between my lips.

Tiger slid his cock out of me and slammed back in,

all the way to his balls. He thrust over and over. There was nothing gentle in the way he fucked me. He'd held back for so long. He wasn't holding back anymore. He was giving me absolutely everything and then some.

I was loving every moment of it.

Lex slipped his hand over my belly and down to my pussy. He found my clit again and started to rub two fingers around my sensitive nerve endings.

Between all three of them, they touched me just the way I liked to be touched. Inside, outside, all the way down the back of my throat.

Every part of me was being spoiled rotten, to perfection.

"You feel fucking incredible," Tiger breathed.

"Her pussy is something else," Bray said.

Tiger glanced at him. If there was any envy over Bray having his cock inside my pussy first, he gave no sign. Maybe he didn't care, he was the one in there now.

Lex had the front of his jeans undone, his fist curled around his own erection.

Watching him pump himself a couple of times made me come completely undone.

My muscles clenched around Tiger's cock. I exploded in a shower of fireworks. My whole body was swamped with an intensity that pushed me further and harder than ever before. My vision went dark, body rocking to draw out the moment, clinging on like it was the last life raft before the whole ship was dragged under the waves.

I cried out, but it was nothing coherent. Just an expression of everything I felt in those moments. Heat, pleasure, perfection, bliss.

The sensations hadn't ebbed away before Tiger came hard and fast, grunting and thrusting frantically until he stilled. His eyes were open, focused on me, but his teeth were gritted in concentration and exertion. His hips rolled slowly, grinding against me, drawing out every moment, every little bit of orgasm.

He slumped over, gasping and blowing out mouthfuls of air.

"Well that was…" Bray started to say.

Whatever it was, it was interrupted by his own orgasm. He thrust into my mouth, spilling salty cum onto my tongue.

I sucked him hard, milking him for every drop. I swallowed it all down while my eyes were locked on his.

I could tell what he was thinking. *My stepsister just swallowed my cum*. He was so wonderfully dirty.

Both Tiger and Bray slid their cocks out of me, moving slow and reluctant.

Lex rolled me over and pulled me to my knees. He knelt behind me and pressed his cock into my pussy.

I was still sensitive from my orgasm and Tiger's hammering. Still, I took him in all the way, my eyes half closing at the incredible feeling of having him inside me.

No wonder Elenna and Sinclair were always so

happy. I'd never been spoiled by so many cocks before in my life. I could absolutely get used to this. Who needed to walk straight anyway? It was probably overrated.

Lex wrapped his large hands around the sides of my hips and bounced me back and forward on his cock.

"You feel like heaven," he whispered. "I want you to come again, for me." He slid one hand around to massage my clit. "Come around my cock, little birdie."

I didn't think I had any more in me until that moment. Between his hand and his cock, I was wild again in a minute or two. I rocked back against him, rubbing my clit on his fingers.

I glanced up to see Tiger and Bray watching intently. The expressions on their faces, intense looks in their eyes and their cocks in their laps were a compelling view. One I looked forward to seeing a lot more of.

I closed my eyes and bounced on Lex's cock, drawing closer and closer to coming again.

"Open your eyes," Tiger said. "Look at us while Lex fucks you."

"Yeah, look at Tiger and me, stepsister dear," Bray said.

I opened in time to see Tiger give him a look. There was no judgement, just understanding. If that was what got Bray going, he had Tiger's support.

I kept my gaze on both of them while Lex slid in and out of my pussy. My breasts swung with each thrust. My nipples were rock hard with the need to come.

Lex thrust harder, increasing the friction between our bodies. Hard enough to throw me over the edge into an orgasm that was even more intense than the first. Wave after wave washed over me, flooding me with heat and making my pulse ratchet up so hard I couldn't hear over the pounding of blood in my ears.

I cried out again at the same time Lex did. We came at the same time, in perfect unison. Thrusts, grunts, gasps and grinding, that was all that existed. All there was in the entire world. That and two pairs of eyes watching me, watching *us*. Enjoying the way we came together.

We finally slumped down on the blanket in a tangle of arms and legs, and slick skin.

"Wow," Lex said softly. "I didn't expect that when you invited us here."

"It's always best to not expect anything where Wren is concerned," Bray remarked as he finished pulling up his jeans. "She likes to keep people guessing."

"Yes I do," I agreed. "I like to keep people on their toes. It makes life interesting."

What could be more interesting than fucking three hot guys on a public beach in broad daylight? I'd almost hoped someone would walk past and see us. No one had, not this time. That was probably for the best, given who I was fucking, but I wasn't shy. A little bit of exhibitionism never hurt a girl, right?

"I think I speak for all of us when I say we knew life with you would never be boring," Lex said.

"Who needs boring?" Tiger said with a grunt. "Life is too fucking short for that."

His words brought me down to earth somewhat. He was right. Life might be short if we weren't careful. We were lucky none of our enemies found us here like this and killed us mid-thrust. That would have sucked, literally and figuratively. I wouldn't mind dying with a cock inside me, but not for another sixty or seventy years.

With that in mind, I started to search for my clothes and pull them back on. When all of this was over, I hoped to do this again.

# CHAPTER 15

## WREN

"I'm going to the post office," Dad called out.

"Okay," I called back. "I'm almost done here. I'll lock up behind me."

"Thanks, sweetie." The door closed behind him with a jingle.

I sat up and rubbed my back. I'd just finished putting the last touches on the engagement ring. I rolled my chair away from my desk and opened a drawer in a cabinet that sat against the wall.

I reached in, felt around for a moment and pulled out a ring box. I snapped it open and fitted the ring into the groove. I shut the box and pushed myself to my feet, to walk the three or four steps to the safe in the corner. Tapping the combination on the keypad beside it, I eased it open and placed the ring box inside.

It would suck to do all that work and then have it stolen.

The bell on the door tinkled again.

"I'm coming," I shouted out.

Under my breath I added, "Don't steal anything before I get there."

Everything was under lock and key, so the only way they could steal anything would be to smash and grab. I listened, but heard no sound of shattering glass.

I closed the safe, made sure it was locked and headed out to the front of the shop, where our jewellery was on display.

"Sorry I—"

I stopped in the doorway.

The shop was empty.

It wasn't big enough for anyone to hide behind anything, but I had a quick look under the counters, just in case. They were barely high enough off the floor to fit a child, but it didn't hurt to check.

No one stared back at me, nothing but wall and carpet. Clean, because my father insisted we not let dust bunnies build up anywhere in the shop.

I stepped over to the window and looked out into the street.

Cars and people passed, like normal. If anyone had pulled a 'jingle and run,' I couldn't see them watching and laughing. Maybe they just bumped against the door as they were going by. Yeah, that had to be it.

"Nothing to see here, folks," I said to myself.

Still, the whole thing freaked me out a little bit. More than a little bit, if I was honest with myself.

I was alone in the shop. If anyone wanted to abduct me, there'd be no one here to stop them except me. Well, me and the panic buttons behind each of the three counters. They were connected to a silent alarm that went to the security company that worked for the Brantley family.

They usually got here faster than the police were able to, and didn't have any limits on how they dealt with anyone who tried to break in. We hated to clutter the courts with people like that.

Also, people tended not to reoffend when they were dead, or had broken kneecaps.

Since no one was in the shop, and it was five minutes before closing anyway, I made sure the door was shut properly and clicked the locks down into place.

They say locks only keep out honest people, but these were state-of-the-art. The glass on the windows and doors was bulletproof. If they really wanted to get in here, it would take them a lot of effort.

I'd like to say that if they did, they'd be met with a barrage of poisoned darts, or a rolling boulder, but Dad said no to both those suggestions. Presumably because they might catch us and not a thief. Since I didn't want to get squashed under a boulder either, I didn't fight him on it.

As I was turning away from the door, I heard movement in the back room.

Had someone made the bell jingle to distract me

while they snuck in the back and made off with the safe? It was possible, I supposed.

I looked back at the locked door and bit my lip. If someone was out the back, did I really want the only other way out to be locked?

In the end, instinct told me to leave it and check what was going on in the workroom.

I stepped forward carefully, glad Dad insisted on carpet and not the floorboards or tiles I would have preferred. I argued they were easier to keep clean, but they might have made my footsteps audible.

I moved forward silently and peeked into the back of the shop.

What the hell?

There was no one there either. Someone was fucking with me or I was losing my mind.

Wait, there was another explanation. Someone must have moved into the apartment above us and they were walking around, flushing a toilet or something. They must have moved in during the afternoon yesterday, after Dad and I were gone for the day. We would have noticed a moving truck if we were here working.

"Stop freaking out over nothing," I told myself.

I leaned over and grabbed my bag from under my desk and slipped the strap over my shoulder. I grabbed my phone, shoved it in my pocket and tugged the back door open.

Carefully, I looked around before stepping outside.

Behind the shop was the car park, which was half full of cars, but empty of people, as far as I could tell.

I closed and locked the door behind me and walked across the car park.

I stopped to glance back, but saw no sign of anyone in the apartment upstairs. Before I moved into my townhouse, I lived there, so I knew the back window was a spare room. I'd used it as an office. If someone was in there, they'd be more likely to be in the front, where the main bedroom, bathroom and kitchen were.

I could walk around the side of the building and take a look, but they might think I was some kind of weirdo or stalker. Since I didn't feel like being arrested and thrown into a cell, I headed down the street to my townhouse.

It was a fifteen minute walk at my usual pace, but I moved faster today. Partly because the weather had changed and autumn started to settle in. Partly because I couldn't shake the feeling someone was watching me.

Every time I stopped at a traffic light to wait for the little red man to turn green, I'd look back over my shoulder and see no one doing anything strange. At least, nothing that would indicate any interest in me.

I got a couple of curious glances for my squirrelly behaviour, but that was it.

The problem was, I'd learned to trust my instincts, and they were screaming at me that something was going on. They told me to be extra careful when stepping out across the road. To stick close to the curb when

I went past a doorway or an alley. Stay out of arm's length of anyone or anything.

I pulled my keys out of my bag and held my front door key in my fist. If anyone came at me, they'd get a key in the eyeball. Or in the hand. Whatever it took.

Should I pull out my phone and call Dad or one of the guys for a ride home?

By now, I was only a couple of minutes away. I'd be there before any of them got here. The guys were at training anyway, and if Dad was finished at the post office, he would have gone home. That was on the other side of Dusk Bay. Too far if anything happened.

Now I understood why Elenna worked with Finley. Whenever her guys were at the arena, so was she. When they travelled for a game, she went with them. She was lucky she got to go to the toilet unaccompanied.

All of that sounded confining, until now.

If I was surrounded by two burly hockey gods, and a burly hockey god-coach, I'd feel a lot less anxious right now.

A block from my place, I stopped at yet another traffic light. I waited until the sign turned green. The beeping from the pole beside me sounded frantic, egging me to move quickly over the road.

I stepped out, as a black SUV came barrelling around the corner. They were going so fast, they almost ended up on two wheels. Tires screeched.

I leapt back onto the curb. The SUV missed me by less than a metre.

It whipped up exhaust-laden wind in its wake, whipping my hair around me, before racing away.

"Fucking hell." I pressed a hand to my pounding heart. That was so close. I was surprised my life didn't flash before my eyes or whatever it was that happened.

"It's just a coincidence. No one tried to kill you."

I looked down the road, but saw no sign of the SUV. If they were after me, they didn't stop and shoot me, or throw me into the back and drive away with me.

It was just a dickhead driver going too fast and taking the corner badly. They were lucky they didn't slam into something and crash. If they kept on driving that way, they would.

Excuse me if I was a little bit short on sympathy for them right now. Maybe when my heart slowed down to a normal rate. In a day or two.

By now the little electric man turned back to red and I had to wait again. When it turned back to green, I was even more careful than before to step out and hurry across the road.

I got to the end of Crane Street without anyone driving too close to me, or anything else weird happening.

I even reached and walked across the last traffic light without ending up a splat on the road.

Still, the feeling of being watched lingered. If someone was lurking on the edge of my awareness, trying to get me to unravel, they were succeeding. If they were doing it for fun, they could go fuck themselves.

If they were doing it to intimidate me, they could also go fuck themselves. I was nervous, but not intimidated. It took more than that to get to this little birdie.

That was what I told myself as I hurried up to my front door and slipped the key in the lock.

I pushed the door in and closed it behind me. I stood in the entryway for at least three minutes, waiting and listening, but hearing and seeing nothing.

The only sound was passing traffic and distant music. Maybe a bird or two. The feathered kind, that was.

I slipped my bag down off my shoulder and placed it on the hall stand. I set my keys down beside it, trying not to rattle them.

Just in case, I slipped open the drawer of the stand and pulled out the gun I kept in there after Bray surprised me. Realising I might not make it to the kitchen in time if the real enemy came after me, I bought another one and stashed it in there. I checked to see if it was loaded, and turned off the safety.

I stepped slowly through my townhouse, the gun in front of me.

There was no one in the kitchen or living area, nothing out of place. The back door was still locked. None of the windows were broken.

As quietly as I could, I made my way up the stairs to the upper level, avoiding the two creaky steps that would give me away if anyone was here. They were a good alarm system if I was alone and someone came in, but not as useful in this circumstance.

I glanced into the spare room, the bathroom, and then my room. Like downstairs, it was empty, nothing out of place. No one hiding under a bed or in the wardrobe. No one waiting behind the shower curtain to jump out at me.

Not even Bray. Lucky for him, because I was so jumpy by now, I might have shot him and asked questions later.

I lowered the gun and shook my head.

"All of this fuss for nothing. I'm just being paranoid." I headed back down the stairs and left the gun on the kitchen table. I could go for a long hot bath, with a good book and a glass of wine around about now. Something to relax me. But I couldn't relax completely.

I knew I wasn't wrong. What I didn't know was what, and why.

# CHAPTER 16

## WREN

I jolted upright at the sound of banging.

Without a second thought, I rolled off the couch and went for the gun.

Shit, I must have fallen asleep in front of the TV. The show I was half-watching had finished, replaced by some kind of action movie.

I held the gun in shaking fingers and told myself it was only an explosion on the screen that woke me.

I jumped when the banging came again. Someone was hammering on the door.

"Wren? You okay?" a male voice called out through the door. "I'm gonna break this fucking thing down in a minute." Bang. Bang.

"Tiger?" I called back tentatively.

He said what sounded like, "Thank fuck," followed by, "Yeah, you gonna open the door?"

I stepped over and unlocked it before opening it just enough to look through.

Tiger stood on my doorstep, Lex right behind him.

"What the hell?" Tiger eyed the gun I'd forgotten I was carrying.

"Wren, you're white as a sheet." Lex frowned at me, clearly worried.

"I'm a redhead, it comes with the territory." I lowered the gun and stepped back to let them in. "I don't have white sheets though."

"It's just an expression." Lex placed a hand on my forehead. "We were worried about you."

"Seems like we had good reason." Tiger took the gun from my hand and set it aside on the kitchen counter.

I shook my head at them. "I'm fine. I fell asleep watching TV."

"Was that all?" Lex took my hand and led me over to the couch. "We've been trying to call you for an hour or two."

I sat down carefully between them. "My phone must be flat."

I reached over for it and tapped the screen. It was fifty percent charged, but the screen showed notifications for six missed calls and twice as many missed texts.

"I must have slept deeper than I thought."

Since when did I sleep through anything as loud as my phone ringtone?

"You didn't accidentally switch it to silent?" Lex asked. "I've done that a time or two myself."

"That must be it." I turned my phone and glanced at the small switch on the side. It wasn't on silent.

"Can one of you try to call me?" I asked. That would be the easiest way to figure out what setting needed to be fixed.

Tiger pulled out his phone and pressed on the screen.

The device in my hand started to vibrate and play Teddy Swims' song "Broke" so loud I jumped for the third time in as many minutes. The screen lit up with Tiger's name.

He tapped his screen again and the call ended.

My phone fell silent.

"You must have some really good sleeping skills to sleep through that." Lex still looked worried. "And when you wake up, you go for a gun? What's going on, Wren?"

I shook my head. "Nothing. Not that I know of anyway." I sucked in a couple of ragged breaths.

"I had the feeling someone was watching me at the shop and following me home. I didn't see anyone. I kept the gun near me just in case. I was down here watching TV because I couldn't sleep."

It was after midnight now. "What are you doing here?"

"We both called you to see if you wanted some company, but you didn't answer," Lex said. "Tiger and I got worried. One of us should let Bray know you're okay. He needed to see the PT after training, then something about dinner with his mother."

"Yeah, they get together once a month," I said vaguely.

Usually, I'd make some comment about him being a mother's boy. I couldn't bring myself to insult him right now. Even if he was here, I didn't think I'd bother. I was too busy trying to get my head around sleeping so heavily.

Was that in any way connected to my feeling of being watched?

"Wren, I'm going to ask you something and it's only because I care," Lex said gently. "Have you taken anything?"

I responded with a double blink, followed by a wide stare. "As in drugs? Fuck no. I had friends who ruined their whole lives with them. I wouldn't touch the stuff."

I admit it would explain a few things. Paranoia and passing out, specifically.

"You don't think someone slipped me something?" I asked.

"Have you taken anything from someone you don't know?" Tiger looked ready to rip off arms. "A cup of coffee or—" He threw out his hands to either side, gesturing that he didn't know what else someone could slip something into, apart from a drink.

"I bought a chocolate chip muffin from the café near

work," I said slowly. "But I've been going there for years."

I looked down at myself, my mind jumping to all sorts of conclusions. As far as I could tell, no one tampered with my clothes. I didn't feel sticky or sore. Nothing to suggest anything happened while I was out cold.

"Any new staff?" Tiger asked.

I brought my face up to look back at him and frowned in thought. "A couple, but there always is. They have new staff there every few months. Only Leah and Nigel have been there since forever, and they own the place."

"So it's possible they have someone working for them who also works for Nicholas Fiorelli," Tiger concluded.

He pushed himself up to his feet and started to pace between the coffee table and the TV. "They could have been waiting for Wren to buy something and slipped in fuck knows what."

"Why would they do that?" My gaze followed him across the room and back.

"I can think of a few reasons right off the top of my head." Tiger pointed at his forehead. "To fuck with you. To kill you. Maybe they planned to send someone over to collect you when you were out."

My blood ran cold.

Someone could have broken into my house, thrown me over their shoulder and taken me to who knows where. I could have woken up somewhere far worse than a dirty motel room.

"This is a warning," Lex said softly. "They know we're after Nicholas. They want to let us know they can get to us. To get to Wren."

"Pack a bag," Tiger said to me, his tone allowing no room for argument. "You're not staying here."

"This is my home," I argued anyway. "They may not do anything else now. They've made their point. I shouldn't eat chocolate chip muffins anyway. I'll stay away from them, unless they're made by Finley."

Elenna's boyfriend was an exceptionally good cook. He could bake rings around everyone I knew, with his hands tied behind his back.

The guys exchanged looks.

"Tiger is right," Lex said finally. "They know where you live. This could be a one-time thing, to get us to back off, or it could be the beginning of something. I'm not going to leave you here to find out."

"If they come after me and you stay here with me, they'll get you too," I said, before anyone could suggest that. I didn't want to be forced out of my own home, but I knew when I had no further argument to make. I didn't want to be here alone if someone was going to try something.

"Okay," I said. "But only for a little while. Just until all of this blows over."

Being the mature men they were, they both tried to hold back smiles at the word 'blows.'

I rolled my eyes. "It's true what they say. Men never grow up."

"You wouldn't want us any other way," Lex said.

"I'll neither confirm nor deny that suggestion," I said. "Fine, I'll pack a bag." I eyed the gun in the kitchen, but left it there and headed upstairs.

I stepped into my bedroom and flicked on the light. "What the fuck?"

Both guys roared up the steps, taking them two at a time. They skidded to a stop beside me approximately half a minute after I spoke.

"What is it?" Lex asked.

"Someone's been in here," I said. "It wasn't like this when I was up here last."

The covers were all strewn across the floor beside the bed. One of the pillows was still in place, but the other lay right in the centre. Something wet shone on the cotton pillowcase.

I took a step closer. "Is that—"

My face twisted and my stomach turned. While I was asleep, someone came in and jacked off on my pillow. Who the fuck would do something like that?

Okay, up until a couple of days ago I would have suggested Bray might do something like that, but now…

"Was anything else touched?" Lex asked.

I hadn't thought to check. Carefully, with rising anxiety, I glanced around.

"Not as far as I can tell," I said slowly.

My room was always messy, so it would be easy for someone to rearrange things and look like it was done by me.

I stepped over to the bathroom and looked inside. "The shower is wet."

Whoever jacked off on my pillow, also took a shower before they left. How long were they here?

Long enough, apparently.

"This is twisted as fuck," Tiger said. "But it's lucky for this asshole that he came here and not inside you."

I swallowed hard. "Lucky for me too." Whatever game he was playing, this was sick. Was it Nicholas himself, or someone who worked for him? Either way, I didn't want to stay here any longer than I had to.

I stepped over to my wardrobe and pulled out my suitcase before throwing in whatever I could get my hands on.

Later, I'd probably find out I packed seventeen pairs of socks and no panties. Right now, I didn't give a shit. I needed to be anywhere but here.

If the endgame was to freak me out, they succeeded. I was well and truly freaked the fuck out.

"We can buy whatever you don't pack," Lex said. "In the morning, I'll tell Aidan what happened here. He'll send someone over to take a look and clean the place up. I'll make sure they do a good job. By the time they're done, there'll be no trace left of any of this."

I gave him a half smile of thanks and closed my suitcase to zip it up. I wasn't sure if I ever wanted to come back here. Not after this.

I felt… I felt violated.

They would have walked past me as I slept, did what they did and then walked past me again to leave. How did they get in, in the first place? I couldn't remember seeing signs of a break-in. If there were any, the guys would have mentioned it.

Unless…

No, I couldn't let myself think they had anything to do with this. Neither of them. Not Bray either. This was the work of someone who was fucked up.

More fucked up than anyone I knew. Whoever did this, they needed help. I suspected if the guys got their hands on him, he wouldn't have a chance to get any. They'd feed him his balls before they killed him.

*If* they ever found out who it was. What if they never did? What if the person who entered my townhouse and violated my privacy, walked around Dusk Bay for the next fifty or sixty years?

I could pass him on the street every day and never know. How was I supposed to live my life like that?

"Let's go." Tiger grabbed my suitcase.

Lex put an arm around me and led me back down stairs and out the door.

# CHAPTER 17

## WREN

None of us said a word on the drive to Tiger's apartment in Powell Tower, in the centre of Dusk Bay.

Lex didn't question him bringing us here. The security would be better than Lex had in his modest home.

Bray also had an apartment here. A lot of the Demons did. And the Smashers too. Not to mention a lot of the city's wealthiest residents. An apartment here would cost more than I made in several years, and then some. Times about a million.

I didn't think about any of that right now, I wanted to be somewhere no one could break in and leave their cum on my property. Or Tiger's property.

He pulled into the car park under the building and parked in one of his personal parking spaces.

"No one will touch you here," he said. "Except for us." He slid out of the driver's seat and hurried around to the passenger side.

Lex was out of his seat already, but he waited for Tiger before they opened my door and helped me out of the car.

"I can get myself out," I pointed out.

"We don't want to take the risk, even here," Lex said.

"They let some shady assholes live here," Tiger said, clearly referring to himself. "Can never be too careful."

"Exactly." Lex grabbed my suitcase and walked on one side of me while Tiger walked on the other.

We were halfway to the elevator when it pinged and the door slid open.

Bray stepped out, looking worried, his hair dishevelled like he just got out of bed.

How did he look even hotter like that?

"What the hell happened?" he barked. "Lex texted me that they were bringing you here. That was all." He looked at Lex accusingly.

Lex glanced at me, quickly realised I didn't want to talk about it, and filled Bray in on the last handful of hours.

"Fucking hell." Bray looked like he was going to slam his fist into the concrete wall beside him. Fortunately for him and his hockey career, he wasn't enough of a dumbass to follow through. "They could have—"

"They didn't." I followed him into the elevator and moved in deeper to make room for Lex and Tiger.

"They'd be dead right now if they had," Tiger growled.

"You would have had to find them first," I said.

"Was this Nicholas fucking Fiorelli?" Bray demanded.

"Probably." Tiger pressed the button for the twelfth floor. "We'll deal with him."

"Maybe you shouldn't," I said softly. "Maybe you should leave it alone. If this was a warning to back off, maybe... Maybe we should."

"I don't negotiate with terrorists, assholes, or people who take up more than one parking space with their car," Tiger said. "Nicholas is probably all of those."

"Especially the last one," Lex said. "That's an indication of how evil he actually is."

They were trying to lighten the mood, but all I could manage was a faint snort.

"That sounds like him." Honestly, that sounded like a few people I knew. Particularly those who drove cars so big that they didn't comfortably fit within one space. Why the hell anyone needed a car that big, I didn't know. Overcompensating, probably.

"Point is, I'm not backing down," Tiger said. "Not after you got abducted, and sure as fuck not after this. The minute he took aim anywhere near you was the minute he was dead. Someone should have told him never to provoke tigers. We can be cranky assholes with sharp teeth and claws."

"That might be what he wants," I said. "To provoke you into doing something rash."

If any of them got killed because of me, I'd never forgive myself.

"Then we don't do anything rash," Tiger said. "We do something cool, calm and effective. Like we do out on the ice."

"I won't rule out using my stick on him," Bray said. "Hockey stick that is. I don't want my cock anywhere near that prick."

Before anyone could respond to that, the elevator pinged and stopped at the twelfth floor. The guys hustled me out and down the corridor to Tiger's front door.

He pulled out a card and swiped it over the lock, before pushing the door open.

"Holy shit." I stepped inside.

I figured the place would be fancy, but I hadn't imagined anything this fancy.

The entryway opened up into a huge kitchen and living area, with a massive glass window overlooking Dusk Bay. The city was a carpet of twinkling lights. Beyond that, the ocean rippled in the moonlight.

The view must be stunning during the day.

The apartment was decorated in muted shades of grey, black and off-white.

A massive sectional sat in front of the biggest TV I'd ever seen. It looked more like a movie screen than a television.

The kitchen was a study in white-veined black marble, and matte brass. Even the bowls of the sink were black, as was the enormous fridge.

"This is sexy," I said.

"It's okay." Tiger tossed his keys into a bowl on the island that was so big it would have seated the whole team on the roster. "Somewhere to sleep and eat."

"It's bigger than mine," Bray remarked.

Tiger eyed him and smirked.

"I meant your apartment, not your cock, dickhead," Bray said.

"Still right on both counts." Tiger guided us to a staircase that led to another level.

Two bedrooms and a bathroom occupied one side, and the main bedroom the other. The bed in the middle of the main bedroom was big enough to fit about ten people.

"Are you *sure* you're not overcompensating?" Bray asked.

"Certain." Tiger took my suitcase from Lex and carried it into a walk-in wardrobe to the side of the room. "I've needed that much space a time or two. Before you ask, yes, everyone left satisfied." He put the suitcase down and turned to us.

"Wren can sleep in here with me." He raised his chin like that was that, the argument was over before it began.

"I'm staying too," Lex said. "If they can't get to Wren, they may try another of us. If we stay together, that will make it harder for them. And easier for us to keep an eye on each other."

Bray sighed.

"Your apartment is as secure as this," Tiger told him.

"Yeah, but Lex is right. We should all stay in one place. There's no way of knowing whether we can trust anyone that lives here or not."

"You're not filling me with much confidence," I said softly. "Can we just call Nicholas and tell him we'll back away?" Since I already knew the answer to that, I repeated Bray's sigh and rubbed my temples with my fingertips.

"I'll grab some things." Bray turned and trotted back down the stairs.

"You should get some sleep," Lex told me.

"There's something else we should do first," Tiger said. He gave Lex a meaningful look.

Lex scrubbed his chin with his hand. "Yes, we should. Is there any chance you have what we need here?"

I frowned at them both, wondering what they were referring to.

"I have all sorts of shit," Tiger replied. "I should have what we need." He disappeared into the bathroom and came back a minute or two later with a specimen jar in one hand and a syringe in the other. "Don't ask why I have these. I just do, okay?"

He handed the syringe to Lex and the small plastic specimen jar to me.

"You want to test me for whatever might be in my system?" I should have thought of that. "Shouldn't we go to a hospital or something?"

"No need," Lex said. "I've taken blood before. We

can get the team's doctors to look at the specimens and see what they can find. Whatever it is, chances are it's still in your system. Assuming we got to you in time."

He gestured for me to hold out my arm. "This would be better with a tourniquet, but unless Tiger has one lying around…"

"Right." Tiger disappeared into his wardrobe and returned with a red and blue striped silk tie. He wound it around my arm and tied it nice and tight.

"I don't want to get blood on your tie," I said, looking down at it.

He shrugged. "Plenty more where that came from. My mother gives them to me for some reason. I only wear them when we have some fancy dinner we have to go to, or to get on and off the plane."

I looked away as Lex pressed the needle against my skin. "Is it true that hockey players get naked the moment the plane doors close?"

It was Lex who responded. "It's been known to happen. They don't like to get their suits wrinkly."

"A guy has to have some vanity," Tiger said.

I suppressed a wince at the prick of pain as Lex slid the needle into my vein. It hurt for a second or two before he slid the needle out.

Tiger opened a Band-Aid and stuck it over the small wound.

"Do I get a lollipop?" I said jokingly.

"If you can fill that sample jar, you can suck whatever you want," Lex said.

That was the best incentive I ever had to do what I needed to do, and do it quickly.

I washed my hands and hurried out to give the jar to Lex. He placed it and the syringe of my blood into a Ziploc bag Tiger dug out from somewhere.

I'd have to get the story of that from him at some point. Most people didn't keep specimen jars and syringes lying around at home. Right? Maybe they did and it was me who was out of the loop.

Either way, he pressed the top of the bag closed and disappeared downstairs with it.

"Do you think they'll find anything?" I asked. "It can't have been that long, but it might be one of those undetectable drugs or something." That was a thing, wasn't it?

"The problem is in knowing what to test for," he said. "They can't just test for anything and everything until they get a hit. They'll try to narrow down the most common shit it could be. PCP, or something like that. I'll personally make sure they keep looking until they find what it is. Whatever it takes."

He slid his arms around me and pulled me to the solid comfort of his chest.

"Thank you." I leaned against him, listening to his heartbeat as I closed my eyes.

"For what? I should be saying sorry to you," he whispered. "This never should have happened. I should have insisted you come and live here before they could do anything like this. I knew there was a chance they'd come after you, but..." His tone was heavily laced with regret.

"Before tonight, I would have said no," I replied. "I would have said it was moving too fast. We're all just getting to know each other. I thought I was perfectly fine living my life. I was happy to go on doing that in my own place. Until we were ready."

"I hate that it happened, but I don't hate that you're here," he said. "I said I was an asshole, but only a massive prick would be happy you're here because of this."

"You're not an asshole," I said. "I don't think for a moment you're happy, just..."

"I got what I wanted," he said. "You know I'm not letting you leave, now you're here. Not even when this is over."

"That's a conversation for later," I said wryly.

Now I was here, I might not want to leave.

# CHAPTER 18

## WREN

"Now, someone mentioned sucking," I said slyly.

Tiger's bed looked inviting, the sheets neat and clean. Like downstairs, everything in his bedroom was white, grey or black. The mid-tone hardwood floors, side tables and wooden headboard gave it warmth, where otherwise it might have been cold and sterile. Whether it was Tiger or someone else, whoever designed the place had an eye for design and good taste.

"You should get some sleep." Tiger gave me a stern look, his back pressed against the wall, arms crossed.

"I'm wide awake right now," I protested. I gestured toward my face and smiled brighter than I was feeling. I even fluttered my eyelashes at him. This was sucking cock were talking about. Sometimes a girl has to fight for what she wants.

Besides, I'd slept soundly for enough hours that I

wasn't ready to sleep again. Not for a while. Added to that, my lingering anxiety about what happened when I was asleep. I needed to unwind first.

Tiger looked tired, but at the same time, as wired as I felt. I wanted to unwind him too.

In spite of it almost being four o'clock in the morning, rest wouldn't happen easily.

"I could sleep better after an orgasm or two. Unless you'd rather turn in? I could use my fingers I guess." I started to turn away.

Predictably, he dropped his arms and stepped forward. His eyes were both dark and stern. "There's no need for you to give yourself orgasms. That's what I'm here for."

"Me too." Lex stepped through the doorway. He must have reached the top of the stairs just in time. "Unless you want to—" He gestured back the way he'd come.

"Stay," Tiger told him. "Between us, we'll wear her out." Apparently he'd come around to my way of thinking.

I liked the sound of that. I could do with some nice, hard wearing out.

Tiger slipped the tie off my arm, down to my wrist. He grabbed the other one and bound them both together in front of me. "I knew there was a good use for all of these ties."

"You look good wearing one," I said.

"It looks better on you." Tiger guided me over to the

bed and helped me down so my arms stretched up above my head. "What do you think we should do to her?" he asked Lex. His voice was husky, making my skin pebble.

Lex eyed me. "What does she *want* us to do to her?"

I eyed him back. "You mentioned something about CNC?" I hadn't stopped thinking about it since. As an avid reader of dark romance books, I had my share of fantasies. That was high on my list. That and being fucked on a throne somewhere. Since that didn't seem likely, I'd stick to this for now.

His eyebrows twitched upward. "You're sure about that?"

"You said you'd stop whenever I asked you to," I reminded him. "I felt violated by whoever broke into my place. I want to take back the power they tried to take from me. I want to be in control." To do that, I had to surrender to them. And trust them to respect my boundaries.

I glanced from one to the other, taking in their expressions. They both seemed reluctant at first but then, when they realised I was serious, they looked eager, excited.

"As long as you don't try to stick a gun in my pussy, then I trust you," I added.

They both gave me a funny look and Tiger shook his head. "Don't even get me started on how dangerous that shit is. Even if you asked, I'd say no. Not with a real one anyway."

Lex grimaced and nodded. "We need a safe word, so none of this gets out of hand."

"Highland cow," Tiger said. His mouth twisted to the side, but he managed to hold back a smile.

Lex responded with a double take and a surprised smile of his own. "Highland cow?"

Tiger shrugged. "They're cute. No one is going to mistake it for any other word. Do you have a better suggestion?"

"Highland cow works for me," Lex said.

"Good." Tiger disappeared into his walk-in wardrobe.

He returned a minute later with another tie. This one, he placed over my eyes before knotting it behind my head.

Without further warning, he flipped me onto my stomach and shoved me face first into the mattress. He pushed an arm under my stomach and hauled me up high enough to tear open the fastenings of my pants. He shoved me back down and grabbed the waistband.

"Hold her still," he barked.

The mattress dipped as Lex sat down beside me. He wrapped his hands around my waist and held me while Tiger dragged my pants and panties down my body and off over my feet.

I was already panting and wet as hell. I didn't mind being thrown around a bit, and by two hot guys who cared about me? Fuck yeah.

Tiger grabbed my knees and bent them, opening me

out to him. He sat on the other side of me and rammed his fingers straight into my pussy.

I gasped out loud with shock at the suddenness of his penetration. "Holy—"

He slapped my ass cheek hard. "I didn't say you could talk. Shut up while I fuck you with my fingers."

He rammed them in and out several times, increasing my excitement.

I couldn't contain myself. Didn't want to. "That feels so good," I groaned.

He slapped me again, harder this time. "You know what happens to girls who don't keep their mouths shut."

Oh yes, I certainly did.

The sound of his zipper sliding down was followed by the rustle of fabric before something hot and hard was shoved against my lips.

"Are you going to keep talking?" he growled.

"If you're going to keep making me feel good, I am," I said. Let him punish me. I couldn't wait.

"Then shut the fuck up and take my dick like the brat you are." He shoved his head right between my lips. When I opened further, he rammed his cock all the way down to the back of my throat.

I gagged, but his hot, pulsing cock tasted like heaven. Knowing I made him hard like that, that it was my mouth he was fucking, all went a long way to helping me regain my confidence. He didn't need to come on a stranger's pillow. He had me. Would he do this with Lex or Bray? That was a question for later, but I would be asking.

"That's better," Lex said. "She looks good with your cock in her mouth. She takes it so well."

The mattress rose on his side and dipped again a couple of moments later. He poked his naked cock into my ass cheek.

I shifted away from him as though I didn't want him inside me as deep as he could go. Pretending to fight against him so he'd have to use force to fuck me. I enjoyed this game, but I was aching to have him inside me. He'd be worth the wait and all the effort.

He gripped my hips and hauled me back.

We did that dance a couple of times before he straddled me, holding me in place with his knees. He slid the tip of his cock up and down my crack, poking around near my rear hole and sliding up and down my arousal.

I forced back a groan, along with the urge to insist he fuck me right now. The longer we both waited, the better this would be.

I wriggled and writhed, but couldn't have pushed him off me if I wanted to. He was too heavy and too strong for me.

Knowing all I had to do was say two words and he'd get straight off made me feel powerful beyond words. This was exactly what I needed.

He pushed my legs farther apart and pressed his cock into my pussy.

I groaned around my mouth full of Tiger's delicious dick.

"Quiet." That was Lex this time, his tone softer than Tiger but no less authoritative. He slapped a hand down on my ass cheek. "Tiger, I don't think your cock is in deep enough."

"I think you might be right." Tiger thrusted deeper and harder, making me gag each time.

I realised then how clever the safe words were. Even with my mouth as full as this, I could say them and be understood. Tiger knew how important it was for me to be able to stop this at any moment. If he wasn't careful, I'd start to think he really was sweet.

Contradicting that thought somewhat, he grabbed a fistful of hair. He leaned in and spoke in my ear.

"Listen up, woman. I'm going to come in that smart mouth of yours. You're going to swallow down every single drop. Understood?"

I made a sound of agreement in the back of my throat, knowing it would earn me another slap from Lex. The sharp sting almost made me come then and there.

Tiger beat me to it, thrusting vigorously into my mouth until he came between one gag and the next.

I almost choked on the mouthful of cum he squirted into my throat. I managed to cough slightly, then swallow it all down after he pulled out of my mouth.

Lex slipped out of me and flipped me over onto my back. He wrapped a hand lightly around my throat and parted my legs so he could ram back into me. Like Tiger was with my mouth, he was relentless, slamming into me over and over, his grip on my throat gradually becoming tighter.

I was becoming lightheaded, but before I could stop myself, I came hard, my lips pressed together, body rocking to meet Lex's rhythm.

"I don't remember saying you could come," Tiger snarled.

His tone made me come again when I was halfway down from the first orgasm.

"She's very disobedient," Lex said. He pounded into me harder.

"Fuck her so hard she can't walk tomorrow," Tiger ordered. "Then maybe she'll learn."

I didn't think Lex could slam into me harder, but he did. Over and over until I was ready to cry out in pain. At the same time, it felt incredible. So full and wild, holding back nothing. He gave me everything he had.

I took every bit of it and more.

I came for a third time, so hard I couldn't contain a scream. I didn't care if they heard me on the other side of the city.

Lex came a moment later, shouting his own release as he came inside me.

We both flopped down hard, panting and sweating like crazy.

"Holy fuck." I winced as he slid carefully out of me. That was going to hurt like a bitch tomorrow. Well, later today. I couldn't bring myself to regret a moment of it. I was a lot less freaked out and a lot more tired.

"Let's get you cleaned up," Lex said gently. "Then you can try to get some rest."

They took the ties off me and helped me to the shower.

# CHAPTER 19

## LEX

"Did they find anything?" Tiger looked up from where he was taping up his favourite stick. Every wind of his hand around the shaft was more violent than the last. He worked like a man ready to use the stick on someone's head.

I eased myself down to the bench beside him. "What we suspected. Minute traces of a known hallucinogen. Enough to give her a dose of paranoia before putting her to sleep."

Tiger voiced my annoyance eloquently by growling from deep in the back of his throat. He gripped his stick so tight his knuckles turned white. "If I get my hands on whoever did that—"

I ignored the way my dick twitched in response.

"You'll tell me about it first," Aidan stopped a metre or two away. He gave us both a stern look, as though we had a history of keeping secrets from him. Some of the guys on the team did, but we'd done our best to keep him in the loop.

"Unless they accidentally get shot in the head before we say anything," Tiger said, unapologetically. "Don't say you wouldn't act first if it was Elenna they drugged."

"I'd absolutely act first, but I'm already in charge here, I don't have to report to myself," Aidan said. "You have a list of all the employees at the bakery?" He directed the question to me.

"You should have it on your phone." I nodded toward him. "None of the names stand out, but that's what we expected. They wouldn't have anyone high-profile pull something like this."

"Anyone high-profile would stand out like dog's balls," Aidan agreed. "The minute they stepped foot in Dusk Bay, we'd know about it."

He sounded confident. I wished I felt the same way. Dusk Bay was a big place. Hiding wouldn't be difficult. Although, people like that had contacts and if you use enough of those, word eventually gets out. Rumours. Whispers.

That was too much risk to pull off something like this. Wren was important to us, vital, but not so much to Nicholas Fiorelli.

At least, she didn't used to be, until Tiger started sniffing around. I didn't blame him, not really. He was doing everything he could to protect her *because* of Fiorelli. The point was, if Nicholas put in that much effort, he'd go for a bigger target. Why, then, did he have someone drug Wren?

"We could kill them all. Then we'd know we got whoever messed with Wren," Tiger said.

"As tempting as that is," Aidan drawled, "I can't condone the murder of innocent people. And it wouldn't assure us of anything. Whoever drugged the muffin might have been someone passing by. Someone else might have been the intended target. They might have expected Caleb to drop in for a muffin."

Tiger looked disbelieving. "Seems more likely someone like Wren or Elenna would have bought it."

"Men eat chocolate chip muffins too," I told him. "It could have been meant for me."

Under other circumstances, I might have craved chocolate cake after this conversation. Seeing what it did to Wren, I was much less inclined to touch any of it unless I made it myself. Since I couldn't bake for nuts, I wouldn't be eating it any time soon.

"It could have been meant for anyone, but Wren was the one who ate it. I'd rather find out if she was the target and why, than go off half-cocked and spill blood," Aidan said calmly.

"Who are you and what have you done with Aidan Draeger?" I asked.

He rolled his eyes at me. "When have I ever advocated for killing innocent people?"

"Never," I agreed. "But if an innocent person was

standing between you and Elenna, all bets would be off."

"No one with half a brain would stand between me and her," he said darkly. "If they did, they wouldn't qualify as innocent." He pulled out his phone and tapped on the screen. "I'll run a check on these people and see if we can find anything."

"From what I found so far, they're all squeaky clean," I said.

"Clean like a murder scene when it's been scrubbed to remove all evidence?" Tiger asked. He tore the end of the tape off the roll and pressed it down to his stick.

"Exactly," I said. "Not even a speeding ticket."

"I've never had a speeding ticket," Tiger said.

"The point is, on paper all of the bakery employees are perfect. That's as suspicious as fuck," I said.

"Like I said, if we just kill them all, we know they're dealt with." Tiger shrugged. "They all sound guilty as shit to me."

"By that logic, someone should kill all of the Demons," Aidan said dryly. "Should we start with you?"

Tiger glanced up at him and smirked, but didn't respond. Probably just as well. Swearing at the head coach, or flipping him off, tended to be a bad idea. Aidan had a hair-trigger temper at the best of times.

"If it turns out they were all involved," I started slowly.

The idea of anyone coming after my woman in any way, even accidentally, made my blood boil. On the surface, I kept my temper even, but underneath I was as ready to do violence as Tiger was. When we found out exactly who did this, he might have to get in line behind me to deal with them.

Seeing Wren as scared as she was when she opened the door to us... The thought of it made me crazy. She didn't deserve to be caught up in any of this bullshit. The fact they got to her so easily, that was something that would keep me awake at night. She could have died.

"We'll deal with them," Aidan said. "Assuming it was the muffin in the first place. Someone could have slipped something in her coffee."

I shook my head. "She said the only one that made her coffee was her and her father. She and he are close. There's no way he'd do that to her, and she wouldn't do it to herself."

"Are you sure about that?" Aidan asked. "People who use drugs—"

Tiger shot to his feet, but stopped short of lunging at Aidan. "Wren is *not* doing drugs. She's not that fucking stupid." His face was red with anger. He sucked in a ragged breath.

"I know what drug use looks like. She had no track marks or anything like that. Someone did this to her, she did *not* do it to herself."

Aidan nodded. "Fair enough."

Tiger's brother overdosed twice, that was no secret. If it wasn't for his bandmates finding him, he'd be dead now. Tiger was understandably touchy on the subject.

He did his best to hide the fact, but somewhere deep down, he cared for his brother.

"It's okay, Tige," I said softly. "Aidan is just thinking through potential scenarios. No one thinks she took something on purpose." I glanced at Aidan meaningfully until he nodded again.

"They fucking better not," Tiger said with a grunt. He gripped his stick in his fist like it was a club.

"Get warmed up," Aidan said. "Practice starts in ten." He gave us both a last glance before turning and walking away.

"Where does he fucking get off?" Tiger said under his breath.

"Don't let him get to you." I put a hand on Tiger's bicep.

I couldn't keep a mental image of him naked the night before, from popping into my head. Seeing the way his cock…

I swallowed hard. "You know what Aidan is like. He doesn't beat around the bush. So to speak." I smiled.

Tiger snorted. "I don't want to think about him beating." For a heartbeat or two, our eyes met.

Heat roared through my body. I knew the same thing happened to him, I saw the way his eyes darkened.

He was a fascinating guy. A hard, angry shell on the outside, but a regular guy with a soft side underneath.

One he'd never admit to, but I saw flashes of it here and there. Particularly when he looked at Wren. He wanted to possess and own her, but he loved her and wanted her to love him.

I felt the same way about her. Could I feel the same about him too? I'd never been around people before who didn't judge me. They accepted me for all my flaws. Fuck knows I had plenty of those. They wanted me to be a better version of myself.

That was exactly what I wanted for them too. I knew things would be interesting, getting into a relationship like this, but I never expected it to be the support system it already was.

"Me either," I said softly, when I realised neither of us had spoken for at least a minute or two. I lowered my hand and stepped away, but my palm immediately felt colder without the connection.

"I should start warming up before the strength and conditioning coach kicks my ass," Tiger said.

I grinned. "Right. I still get to do that, don't I?"

"Not if you want to keep staying at my place." He sat back down and started to lace up his skates.

"You've never got a speeding ticket, but you don't mind a bit of casual blackmail," I said.

He glanced up and grinned. "Nope. Whatever gets the job done."

His smile made my heart do a somersault.

"Since there's no chance I'm leaving you alone with Wren, I'm going to say good luck with trying to kick me out. I'm going to keep doing my job. If that means kicking your ass, then your ass gets a kicking."

I might kiss it better afterward, but I'd do what I had to do to keep him on track. The Demons were going to take the cup this year, whatever it took to get there.

"She's not alone with me, Bray is there too," Tiger pointed out.

"There's even less chance of me leaving her alone with him," I said.

He knew her better than anyone. I wasn't jealous of that past and the connection between them, but it would take time for us to get to know each other as well as that. Time I was more than happy to spend.

"If he starts anything, we can throw him off the balcony," Tiger said as Bray walked past on his skates.

Bray stopped to smirk. "You wouldn't do that. Wren would never forgive you."

"If we don't, that would be the only reason for it," Tiger said. He smirked at Bray, then went back to lacing his skates.

"Deep down, he really likes me," Bray said.

"Keep telling yourself that," Tiger said without looking up.

I shook my head at them both and laughed. They might end up closer than Tiger was to his brother. The pair were a lot alike, even if they wouldn't admit it right now.

"Remember, team unity," I told them. "The Demons and us. Unified, no one can get to us or beat us."

"Did you get that off a motivational meme?" Bray asked.

"No, it came out of my own brain," I said. "The only motivational meme I've seen today said, 'life is like the human body. You get out what you put into it.'"

"So you put in food and get out shit," Bray concluded.

I chuckled. "Something like that."

"Motivational memes are full of crap," Tiger said. "Like the fortunes you get out of fortune cookies. I once got one that said, 'the next person you see will be the love of your life.' The next person I saw was my reflection in the mirror."

"Sounds accurate to me," Bray said, grinning.

Tiger flipped him off. "Fuckwit."

"Get your asses out on the ice," Aidan shouted.

"You heard the man." I waved them both out and followed behind.

# CHAPTER 20
## WREN

"This place is amazing." Sinclair looked around Tiger's apartment, her lips slightly apart. "That view. I thought Coast's old apartment was impressive, but this is something else."

Like I suspected, the view of the ocean was stunning during the day. The sun glinted invitingly off the water. A cruise ship slowly sailed past. It was better than a postcard, or holiday photos from social media.

"Tiger has good taste." Elenna seemed more impressed with his kitchen than the view. She might have been picturing Finley cooking in it, even though their kitchen was almost as beautiful.

"Of course he does." Sinclair slipped an arm around me and gave me a squeeze. She even managed to tear her eyes away from the window to do it. "Wren is incredible. How are you feeling? You must have been terrified."

My arm around her, we made our way to the couch and sat down.

"It was strange," I said slowly. "I wasn't scared at the time. What really scares me was thinking about what might have happened. That someone would actually do something like that to me. Drugging me and then breaking in." I shuddered. "Who does shit like that?"

"Someone with a death wish." Elenna sank down in one of the armchairs. "Did they really think they could pull something like that and get away with it? They must have no idea who you are and who you know. And who cares about you."

"I think they know exactly who I am," I said. "That's the point. They could get to any one of us. I'm scared they'll try to come after all three of us."

"They'll have to come through a wall of nine guys," Sinclair said. "Not to mention the rest of the team."

"I wish I could say I thought that would deter them, but I can't." I leaned against the back of the couch and pulled my feet up beside me. "They came after us before. What's to stop them from trying again?"

Elenna's eyes glazed, clearly thinking back to that night. "Everyone who took part in that is dead."

"That's a very good way of stopping people from doing things like that again," Sinclair said. "Unless they're zombies."

I stared at her. "Why would you even suggest something like that? Now I'm going to have nightmares about zombie Sawyer Mancini. It's bad enough knowing Roach, Otis and Gus are out there still."

I had recurring nightmares about the three men holding Sinclair and I at gunpoint. She didn't say anything, but I was sure she had them too.

"Zombies aren't real," she said. "No more than vampires and wolf shifters."

"Wolf shifters aren't real?" Elenna asked sarcastically. "There goes that fantasy." She punctuated her words with a sigh that was both heavy and playful.

"I'll never believe they aren't," I said. "Women every-where deserve hot guys who can change into wolves. Or dragons. Or gargoyles."

"One hundred percent." Elenna smiled and added, "Listen to us. You'd think we weren't all in relationships with gorgeous men who are crazy about us. Who would do anything for us. I wouldn't trade them in for a wolf shifter."

"Of course not, but a shifter could be a fourth boyfriend," I said with a grin. "They'd keep Aidan, Finley and Orion on their toes."

"When you put it that way…" She grinned.

"You guys are crazy," Sinclair said. "My ideal book boyfriend is a billionaire. Although the players in hockey romance are hot too. Not as hot as the real thing, but they're fun to read about." She fanned herself.

"So, you'd be here for a billionaire, hockey playing wolf shifter?" Elenna asked. "Just in case someone was going to write that."

"If you wrote it, I'd read it," she said. "You know I'll read everything you write."

"Me too," I said.

Elenna was a very talented author, even if she didn't believe in herself and her own writing too much of the time. From what I could gather, that was typical of most authors. They were never sure if what they were doing was good enough.

"That's very sweet of you," she said modestly.

"I just realised I haven't offered you coffee." I grabbed my phone from the coffee table, opened the app and started the coffee machine in the kitchen.

"Tiger has a voice or app that activates everything around here. The toilet is even one of those that flushes automatically when you stand up. It scared the shit out of me the first time. Figuratively."

"I wouldn't have picked Tiger as a tech geek." Sinclair watched the machine over the back of the couch.

"He's full of surprises," I said. "The more I get to know him, the more interesting things I uncover. Same with Lex. There's more to him than a superhero nerd."

"What about Bray?" Sinclair turned back to me, an eyebrow raised.

"Don't tell him I said this, but he might not be as big an asshole as I thought he was," I said in a loud, dramatic whisper. "Close, but not *quite* that big."

"You look smitten to me." Sinclair smiled softly. "With all of them."

"I am," I said. "I'm falling for them. And I think they're falling for each other. Lex and Tiger anyway. I don't think Bray swings that way."

I was almost certain he didn't, but up until recently, I didn't think he swung my way either. Whatever made him happy, I was here for it.

"That's adorable," Elenna said. "It's nice to see guys like that embracing their true selves. Orion and Finley are the same. Orion is such a masculine man, but when they're together they get along so well. It's sweet and hot at the same time."

"Amen to that," Sinclair said. "Coast, Javey and Phoenix… I don't know how they haven't set the house on fire." She fanned herself again.

"Better than a wolf shifter any day," Elenna said.

My phone pinged and the coffee machine filled three cups of the steaming brew.

I pushed myself to my feet. "The only thing we don't have here is coffee cups that bring themselves to you."

I hurried over to the kitchen and carried their cups to them before grabbing up my own. In my other hand, I grabbed a box Elenna had left on the island. I carried it over to the coffee table and placed it where we could all reach.

"It's sweet of Finley to bake us biscuits." I picked one up and nibbled on the side.

"We figured it was safer than buying any," Elenna said. "Besides, they always taste better when he makes them." She picked up one of her own and dipped the side into her coffee before popping it into her mouth.

"I love his baked goods, but it sucks that we can't trust anyone enough to buy them, until they find out who drugged you." Sinclair sighed. "Even then, I'll be suspicious of anyone selling muffins."

"Me too," I agreed. "I'll be working from here for a while. Dad said he can manage the shop, if I can do the jewellery-making. Bray has already brought everything I need. I've taken over Tiger's office. Not gonna lie, the view makes it difficult to work. I keep stopping to stare at it."

"I can't blame you," Sinclair said. "I wonder if I can convince the guys to buy an apartment in this tower." She looked out the window thoughtfully. "We could be neighbours."

"I wonder how long it would be before the guys turned the helipad on the roof into a practice rink," Elenna mused.

I laughed. "I'm surprised Tiger and Bray haven't thought of that already. They could have all the guys over for a practice and a few beers afterwards. With a barbecue up there and everything."

"The ultimate party space." Sinclair grinned. "I'm so in. I might have to work on them. After all, isn't Powell Tower basically the most secure place in the entire city? Where better to live?"

"You just want to pretend you're Rapunzel," I teased.

She laughed. "Nah, I want to wake up to that view

every morning. The guys would love it. Especially Javey. He could watch the whole city go by."

"I think you might find it difficult to tear them away from the big-ass mansion you currently live in," I said. "If they want their own rink, your house is big enough for one."

"It is, but I'm not going to suggest it," she said. "If I did, I'd never see them again. They'd spend all their time skating."

I laughed. "That's probably true. No rink on the roof then." The barbecue sounded nice though.

"Are you okay with spending all of your time here?" Elenna asked gently. "We know you like your independence."

She wasn't wrong about that. It was nice of her to worry about me. I'd worried about her plenty of times in the past. Especially when people were after her, wanting her dead. Lucky for us, they were dead now, not her.

I sighed. "Yeah, this birdie likes to spread her wings and fly, but until all of this is over, it's better that I'm here. It's not permanent."

In spite of what Tiger said about not letting me go, I wanted to get back to work in the shop at some point. Or work on expanding Danglies.

I might go on living here, but I couldn't conduct every day for the rest of my life within these walls. As big and beautiful as the walls were. Sooner or later, they'd start to feel like the bars of a cage. Like my wings were clipped. I couldn't let that happen.

If I did, then whoever drugged me ultimately won. Fuck that. I wasn't going to let anyone do that to me. No way.

"We'll come and visit you as often as we can," Elenna said. "I'm thinking of concentrating more on my writing than working with the Demons."

"Yes!" Sinclair pumped the air in excitement. "More books from you."

Elenna smiled. "That's what I'm hoping. Aidan keeps saying he'll find someone to turn one of my books into a movie, but I want that to happen on merit, not because of someone he knows." She wrinkled her nose.

"He has enough faith in you to know that'll happen without his help," I said. "It is sweet of him to suggest that though."

"It is," she agreed. "He only wants what's best for me. I told him that's for me to keep working my own way and write something readers will love enough that a studio will want it."

"You're so nice," Sinclair said. "I would have told him to back the fuck off." She grinned.

She'd do that if one of her guys tried to get too pushy about something she was working on. Although, considering she tended to arrange photo shoots for calendars, and ice dancing dance-offs for charity, they might be justified in keeping an eye on her and her work. Who knew what she might come up with next?

Elenna laughed. "I might have done that too. The point is, he respects me and he's giving me space. Finley and Orion too. The support they give me is everything."

"You deserve it," I told her. I meant that. They both deserved a butt load of happiness. I was genuinely pleased they both found families that adored them as much as I did.

Didn't everyone deserve to feel that kind of love?

"So it won't be long until we see a movie about a billionaire, hockey playing wolf shifter," I said. "I can't wait. Maybe they could cast one of the guys as the lead role."

"Or three guys," Sinclair said. "The world needs more reverse harem movies. I'm sure Coast would be more than happy to be in it."

Elenna laughed. "I don't think I'd have that much say in it, but I can suggest them if it ever happens. It could be fun to make a movie with half the team."

"You should write a hockey reverse harem," I said. "Then the whole team could be in the movie. They could play themselves."

We all laughed at that. If they made our lives into a movie, no one would believe it.

# CHAPTER 21

## WREN

"I don't like it," Tiger said.

"You said that at least a hundred times already," I pointed out. "I'll be all right here by myself. You were the one who said this place was secure. I'm not planning to let anyone in. None of you guys can stay back while the rest of the team plays away games. And anyway, it's only for a few days."

Honestly, I was nervous as hell being here by myself, but at some point it had to happen. They couldn't put their entire lives and careers on hold for me. They'd do it if I let them. Which I wouldn't and we all knew it.

"They could break in," Tiger said stubbornly.

"How?" I asked. "Land a helicopter on the roof and rappel down to the balcony?"

He looked towards the balcony doors, lips parted,

clearly picturing that in his head. "They might. I wouldn't put anything past these assholes."

"Nothing says subtle like landing a helicopter on the roof," Bray said. "Half the city would see them."

"No one wouldn't be able to act in time to stop them from grabbing Wren and flying away with her." Tiger slid his arms around me as though he could hold me in place if that happened.

"It's not Fiorelli's style," Lex pointed out. He was busy slicing vegetables to make a salad for dinner. "Not to mention, hiring a helicopter would be expensive. I'm not saying Wren isn't worth the expense, but I can't see him doing something like that. Not with the limited resources he has. When Dante was alive, that would totally have been his jam."

"Lucky for us he's long gone," Bray said. "I hate to agree with Tiger on anything, but I don't like the idea of Wren being here alone." He looked over to me. "Can you go and stay with Mum and Martin?"

"And risk them getting caught up in all this shit?" I asked. "You don't want that any more than I do."

"They could stay here." Bray's stubbled chin jutted out, as stubborn as Tiger.

"They wouldn't want that. They've done well so far to stay under the radar. If they stayed here, that could change. The last thing in the world I want is to risk either of them."

"You could come with us," Lex suggested. "Elenna and Sinclair are."

"They both work for the team," I pointed out. "I don't."

"We could get you a job as a Demon Girl," Bray said, half teasing. "Or a mascot. You'd look cute dressed as the Demon."

In spite of its name, the mascot was a cute version of a demon, with a bright red face and bright blue horns, dressed in the red and blue of the team.

"The team doesn't need either of those things," I said. "Those positions are taken by other people and I'm not going to take their jobs from them."

"I could speak to Caleb and see if there's any…work he needs done while we're travelling," Lex suggested.

"Like taking delivery of stolen gems and bringing it back to Dusk Bay with the team?" I asked. "He has Finley and Elenna to do that. Seriously, I'll be fine. I'm sure you guys will call and text three million times a day, until I tell you to stop because you're interrupting my work." I eyed them all, because they all knew it was true.

"Only because we care." Tiger squeezed me a little harder. "None of us want anything bad to happen to you."

"I don't want anything bad to happen to me either. Or any of you." I placed my hands on his arms.

I didn't want to be the one to bring it up, but there was always a possibility Nicholas would go after him when they were on the road. They'd done it before, when Dante was alive. Not chasing the team, but chasing the band Tiger's brother was a member of. If they could pull that then, fuck knows what they might pull now.

"I'm starting to think the only answer to all of this is to stay home," Tiger said.

"The only answer is for you to do your job and stop worrying about me," I said. "The worst thing that could happen to me while I'm alone here is that I'll get bored. I mean, your TV is so tiny I can't even watch a movie on it."

He chuckled. "You won't be watching movies on that anyway. You'll be too busy watching us play."

"And answering our text messages," Lex said. He piled the vegetables into a bowl and started to toss them with his hands.

"And making pendants shaped like dicks," Bray added, looking smug.

I sniffed. "I told you I don't do those."

"Yeah, but you were lying," he said. "What's the problem, stepsister dear? Do you think I'm going to give you shit for it?"

"You absolutely will," I agreed. "Just like you've been doing for the last fifteen years. If you weren't any good at hockey, you would have made a career out of it somehow."

"There's a career where I get to give you shit and get paid for it?" He cocked an eyebrow at me. "Because I want in. I can't play hockey forever."

"If there's a way to do it, you'll figure it out." I rolled

my eyes at him. "In the meantime, you'll have to keep practising those mediocre stick skills of yours and hope the Demons don't realise they don't have to keep feeling sorry for you, and keep you on the team."

He laughed. "At least I didn't have to rely on my daddy for a job."

Resting the back of my hands on Tiger's arms, I turned my wrists to stick both my middle fingers up at him. "You would have if people realised you actually suck at hockey. You could have learnt to make cock bars."

"If I did, I'd make fucking good cock bars," Bray said.

"You *are* a cock bar," Tiger told him.

"I belong at the end of a dick?" Bray asked, pretending to misunderstand.

Tiger shrugged. "Probably. It sounded like a good insult."

"I like it," I said. "It's perfect for Bray."

Bray smirked. "I love you too. With a stepsister like you, who needs enemies?"

"Probably still you," I said. "Since I'm amazing. Maybe if you weren't such an asshole, you wouldn't have enemies."

"You're the one who got drugged by a chocolate chip muffin," he pointed out. "It seems to me you're the one with the enemies."

Tiger growled. "Don't fucking go there. There's nothing funny about what they did to her."

Bray was undeterred. "This is how Wren and I are. We snipe at each other, but we don't really hate each other too much. Right, Socks?"

"Not too much," I agreed. "We don't hate each other enough to want to kill each other. Just enough to want to give each other hell as much as possible."

Tiger grumbled something but didn't continue the line of conversation.

"Dinner is ready," Lex said. He was placing pieces of grilled chicken onto plates already piled with salad.

"Since when do you cook?" Tiger asked.

"Since I've lived by myself for the last decade," Lex said. "This is about all I know how to make, but it fits in with your diet and Bray's."

"It looks delicious." I picked up a plate and a fork and sat down on one of the stools at the edge of the island. I should eat more food like this, especially after eating so many of Finley's biscuits. Having someone like him around would be dangerous for my waistline.

"I've always meant to hire a personal chef," Tiger said. He slipped into the stool beside mine and started to eat.

"That can go on the list of things we can think about after we've dealt with Nicholas Fiorelli," Lex said. "I wouldn't trust anyone to come in here and make food unless it's the four of us, or someone we know really well."

"Let's not give anyone the opportunity to drag or

poison us all," Bray agreed. He slipped into another seat. "I hear that happens a lot at Brutham Academy."

"I heard the same thing." When I was growing up, the only thing I wanted to do was study there. I didn't know what I'd study, but something, in spite of the University's reputation for being the only one in Australia with a higher mortality rate than dropout rate.

At the end of the first year, they held trials, designed to weed out the weakest. It's one of the things that gave the place its nickname— Brutal Academy.

"They're opening a campus of Brutham here in Dusk Bay soon," Lex said. "I'm hoping they'll add a hockey program, to transition more players to the professional level."

"That's just what we need," Tiger said. "A whole new generation of Dusk Bay Demons happy to kill their competition to get them out of the way."

"That would be different to the way it is now, how?" I asked.

He stopped with his fork half way to his mouth. "I never killed anyone to get where I am." He pushed the chicken into his mouth and chewed.

"You might not, but Bray might." I couldn't resist the tease. "That would explain how he got his spot on the team."

Bray snorted. "Why would I kill them and leave you alive? I could have done us all a favour."

I put a hand on Tiger's arm before he lunged at Bray

to embed a fork in his eye. "There's as much chance of him killing me as him killing anyone to get a spot on the team."

"Did you just say I'm talented, Socks?" Bray asked.

"First of all, if you keep calling me that, I'll let Tiger stab you with a fork," I said. "Second of all, let's not go crazy here. If I said anything that nice, you might think I'm sick." Before he could take a dig, I added, "I mean the unwell kind of sick, not the fucked up in the head kind."

"You say fucked up in the head like it's a bad thing." Bray grinned.

"Only you would respond that way," I said.

"I like to be original." He bit into a slice of cucumber.

"That's one word for it," I said.

"Unique. Different. Special." He ate the other half of the cucumber.

"Weird. Odd. Peculiar." I smiled.

"Amazing. Handsome. Irresistible." He wiggled his eyebrows at me.

"Delusional. Crazy. Frustrating." I was having too much fun with this.

"All just words to say how much you care about me," he concluded.

"You two are adorable," Lex said. "I can see why you both gave in after all those years. Lucky for me and Tiger you waited. Otherwise we might have missed out on being with Wren."

He gave me a look full of affection and heat. My

heart flipped and my nipples perked up. I couldn't imagine a time when my body didn't react to them that way.

Amazing, handsome and irresistible were perfect words for the three of them. And here I was. Wren Valentine, who was never a model student, but makes pendants shaped like cocks, and engagement rings for people who could afford something extra special. And has three boyfriends.

"I wouldn't have missed out," Tiger said. "I would have ended up with her either way. Whatever I had to do to make that happen."

"Awww, did you just say you'd kill Bray for me? That's so sweet." I leaned my head against his shoulder.

"As if he could," Bray muttered.

Hopefully it never came to that.

# CHAPTER 22

## WREN

I peered at the finished cock pendant through my loupe.

Sinclair had requested rose gold with a magic cross in silver at the end. I hadn't asked for details about who inspired the design, and she hadn't offered any. The guys could probably tell me, but I wasn't going to ask them either. I was happy to let which of her guys had the piercing remain a mystery. Whoever it was, the pendant looked amazing, if I said so myself.

I set it aside beside the half finished pendant of a cock with a Jacob's ladder. Before I could pick it up to start working on it, my phone rang.

I startled at the sudden loud ringtone, my pulse racing like crazy. I was safe here in Tiger's apartment, but I was still on edge most of the time. Nowhere was impenetrable if someone wanted to get in badly enough.

"It's just the phone," I reminded myself. Which of

course stopped ringing when I went to answer it. I picked it up and tapped on the screen.

One missed call from Tiger. Before I could call him back, the phone vibrated in my hand and the ringtone started again.

I pressed on the screen to answer and put it on speakerphone.

"Hey," I said lightly. "How are things—"

"Why didn't you answer the first time?" Tiger demanded.

"You hung up before I could." I frowned at the device. "Did you call to yell at me?"

His response was a weighty sigh. "No, I was worried when you didn't answer. Are you all right?"

"I'm fine. Busy working on… Work." Very articulate, Wren.

Tiger chuckled. "Sounds like a good time for a distraction." He ended the call, but a request flashed up a second later for a video call.

I hit accept and held the phone out in front of me, trying not to cringe too much at the angle of my face, and the hair trying to escape from my messy bun.

He appeared on the screen, blue eyes so intense they could have bored a hole through the distance between us. He hadn't shaved in a couple of days, giving him a more dangerous appearance.

"You look beautiful," he said softly. "Good enough to eat."

"Funny, I was going to say the same about you." I

hadn't realised how much I missed him and the other guys until right now.

I assumed Lex and Bray weren't in the room, or they would have been elbowing each other out of the way to say hello. Or Bray would have been offering some smartass observation about me or the world.

"I was hoping you'd be naked," he said with a smile.

"Once again, I was about to say the same thing." I grinned.

"Easily done." He propped the phone against something and stepped back. He grabbed the hem of his T-shirt and pulled it up over his head with one hand.

"That will never not be hot," I remarked. Not to mention the sight of his abs, the flat plane of his stomach and the hint of a V peeking out above his track pants.

"You like that, hmmm? Your turn." He raised an eyebrow at me.

"Like that is it?" I looked around for something to lean the phone against, before propping it up on the side of my empty coffee cup.

"Yes, take it off," he ordered.

That gave me a full body shiver and made me wet between my legs.

I gripped the hem of my shirt the way he had and tried to pull it up over my head. It snagged on my messy bun, forcing me to use both hands to free it and toss it aside.

I expected him to laugh at my clumsy attempt to be

sexy, but even through the phone, I saw the way his track pants tented.

"Bra too," he ordered.

This I could take off with some finesse. Eyes on the screen, I unhooked it and let the straps slide down my arms and off my wrists.

"You have the best breasts," he said. "Touch yourself."

I hesitated for a moment.

"Go on," he said, his voice husky. "Touch your breasts for me."

My tongue swiped over my lower lip. Tentatively, I raised both hands and ran them around my breasts, pinching and rolling my nipples until they were hard peaks.

"Just like that," he said approvingly.

"Your turn," I told him. "Take off those pants and let me see your dick."

"You're the bossy one now." He hooked his thumbs into the waistband of his track pants and pushed them down his hips until his erection sprang free.

"What can I say, I like looking at your cock," I said unapologetically.

Tiger wrapped his fingers around his length and slid them up and down a couple of times. "He likes you too. Your turn; let me see that pussy."

I shimmied out of my leggings and managed to step out of them without falling on my face. I did a slow turn around and danced, wiggling my ass in my panties before removing those too.

I looked back over my shoulder at Tiger and smiled teasingly.

"If I was there, I'd smack that ass," he growled playfully.

"Do you want me to smack it for you?" I asked. Before he could answer, I brought my hand down on my ass cheek a couple of times. Not hard enough to hurt, but it made a satisfying slap.

"Turn around," he ordered. "I love that cute little ass of yours, but I want to see your pussy."

I turned slowly, feeling my face heat.

Being naked in his living room, with him able to see all of me, felt strange, awkward. At the same time I felt pretty, empowered. He wanted to see me like this. Naked for his eyes, in spite of the kilometres that separated us.

"Do you have any idea how gorgeous you are?" he asked softly. "I want to touch you all over." He pumped his cock again. "Are you wet?"

I slipped a hand down between my thighs and ran a finger over my seam. "Very wet."

"Don't stop," he ordered. "I want you to make yourself come."

"I will if you will," I said. "Are you imagining fucking my mouth or my pussy?"

"Neither," he pumped slowly. "I'm imagining

fucking the space between your breasts and coming on your face."

I rubbed my clit with my pointer and middle finger, tracing circles around and pressing a finger inside myself every few passes.

"I'm going to imagine the same thing. You rubbing against my chest." I placed my other hand between my breasts, and ran it up and down slowly, simulating the way he might feel on my skin.

He groaned. "I'm going to last about a minute if you keep doing that. I want you to come first."

"Always a gentleman," I said appreciatively. I rubbed my clit a little faster while running the heel of my hand over my nipple.

"There's nothing gentlemanly about me," he said. "Hearing you come is my favourite song. One of these days, I'm going to record it so I can listen to it over and over. If I released it, it would get more downloads than any other sound ever made. But I wouldn't release it. It would be for me and me only."

"Not even for Bray and Lex?" I asked.

"They can record their own," Tiger said. "I don't mind sharing some things, but others, no fucking way. When I record you, it will be a time I make you come. Whenever I listen, I'll know I did that to you. Me, with my tongue, fingers or cock."

"I should record you too," I said. "You make special sounds when you fuck my mouth."

"I wish I was fucking your mouth right now." He

pumped a little faster. "You have the most perfect, fuck-able mouth."

"You have the most talented tongue." I rubbed myself faster. "I'm so close."

I would have liked to close my eyes, but I needed to see him on my screen, his hips moving back and forth, in rhythm with his hand. What in the world could be hotter than a gorgeous hockey player with his thick cock in his hand, thinking about fucking me while he got himself off?

"Come for me," he said breathlessly. "I want to see you come on your hand."

I dropped my head back slightly, my eyes still on my phone. I pinched my nipple hard and came on my fingers, rocking my own hips back and forth.

Blood pounded around my body, pooling in my pussy, making my clit throb. Everything around me went dark except Tiger. He went slightly blurry for a few moments while a tide of pleasure washed over my body.

When I was finally able to focus again, he looked sharper than ever, his hand working his cock vigorously until he came, spilling cum over his hand.

"Fucking hell," he grunted. "I wish that was your face. I wish you had my cum dripping off your face and hair. Dripping onto your shoulders and sliding down onto your tits."

"We can do that when you get home," I assured him.

I dropped my hands from my breasts and pussy. "Until then, we can do this again."

"We will do this again," he said. "Soon. You might as well stay naked."

"I will, if you will," I teased.

He chuckled. "That would raise some eyebrows on the ice."

"You could start a new trend or a new sport," I said. "Naked ice hockey." I grinned.

"That sounds like a danger to my balls." He grimaced and reached for a tissue to wipe his hand.

"Probably. The fans would love it, but I'd prefer you don't freeze your cock off." I bobbed down to pick up my panties and bra.

"Take a couple of photos of yourself and send them to me before you get dressed," he said. "If you won't stay naked, I can look at those and pretend."

I hesitated for a moment.

"I won't show them to anyone," he said quickly.

"I know you won't, I just… I'm a bit self-conscious." I wasn't drop dead gorgeous like Elenna and Sinclair. Or my three guys for that matter.

He picked up his phone and brought it up to his face. "What you are is fucking gorgeous. I'm going to keep telling you that until you believe it. However long that takes, I'll do it."

"You're good for my ego," I said. "If I'm going to take photos, I need to swap out of this app."

"I need to get ready for warm up anyway," he said.

"I'll keep an eye on my phone. Goodbye gorgeous. I love you."

"I love you too." I ended the video call and opened the camera app. I chose the time option and started a ten second timer. I took a couple of steps back and posed for the camera.

I took a few photos and picked up the phone to flick through them. Okay, maybe they weren't so bad after all. I deleted a couple, then went to contacts, tapped on Tiger's name and pressed send.

I didn't wait for his response. I put my phone down and hurried to get dressed again.

# CHAPTER 23

## WREN

"Bray sent you to check up on me." I opened the door to let Dad and Jenny into the apartment.

"Believe it or not, he's worried about you." Jenny gave me a hug and a kiss on the cheek as she stepped past. "So are your father and I."

"As you can see, I'm fine," I said. I tried to smile, but my work tools were spread out on the kitchen island. Including several half made cock pendants.

I closed the door, locked it and moved to stand in front of my workspace. "Totally okay. It's really sweet of you to worry about me." I cleared my throat. "Would you like a coffee?" I reached for my phone.

"I'd love one," Dad said. He sighed heavily, his expression serious, concerned. "You'd worry too if your child got drugged and could have died. I shouldn't have left you in the shop alone. If I hadn't—"

"It wouldn't have changed anything." I activated the

coffee machine with my phone. "We think it was from the muffin I ate for afternoon tea." I couldn't meet his eyes for a couple of reasons. Mostly because of the pendants, but also the suggestion he drugged my coffee. I didn't want to see that on his face and I didn't want him to see the accusation on mine. I wasn't entirely sure I could keep it from showing.

"I could have driven you home," he said. "I would have seen something was wrong and insisted you stay with us or go to the hospital. You wouldn't have been alone when someone broke into your townhouse."

His tone forced me to look right at him. I'd never heard or seen him like this. Regretful that he could have prevented all of this and didn't. Like somehow he'd failed his little girl.

"They might have done something else," I said. "They might have gone after Jenny because you were with me. This was a warning. It's possible they didn't care who they messed with, as long as they made their point."

He clearly hadn't considered that. He moved closer to her and put a protective arm around her shoulders. "I've made some choices in my life I'm not proud of. I've often wondered if working for Caleb was a bad idea. In the end, it's lucrative, that's why I do it. Not to mention how difficult it is to walk away. You know what the Brantley family is like with people like us."

"Trying to walk away could get you dead," I said bluntly. "I don't blame you for anything you did. None of this was about you." I didn't think it was anyway. "This is about Tiger going after Nicholas Fiorelli."

"Which he wouldn't need to do if it wasn't for Fiorelli abducting you." Dad's jaw clenched with fury at the memory. "Which wouldn't have happened if Sinclair wasn't associated with Coast Riggs."

"She can date whoever she wants to," I started.

He rested his other hand on the top of the island. "Of course she can, but is it wise for you to associate with her?"

"She's one of my best friends," I said, more snappy than I intended. "Are you going to try to tell me I can't see her or Elenna anymore? Because in case you hadn't noticed, I'm a grown woman and I can be friends with whoever I want to."

Jenny reached out and put a hand on my forearm. "Of course you can, sweetie. We're just worried about you, that's all. Your father is right. You never would have been abducted if you weren't with Sinclair that night. Tiger would have had no reason to start searching for Nicholas."

"I have a feeling he would have found a reason," I said. "He was right there when Nicholas attacked Sawyer. He was held at gunpoint by Geneva and her goons. He wants to put an end to all of it."

"Even if it means putting you at risk?" Dad asked. "If he really cares about you—"

"He does," I interrupted. "Everything he's doing is because he cares about me." I spread my hands to gesture around the opulent apartment. "If he didn't, I'd still be living in my townhouse, not here."

"If he left it all alone, you'd still be living there," Dad said.

I was saved from having to respond by the coffee machine beeping. I forgot all about the cock pendants and stepped around the island to pick up the steaming mugs.

"Tiger has the best—" I turned around to see Dad eyeing the pendants lying out in front of him. "Um."

He looked up at me, completely unamused. "Um? I presume you have an explanation for..." He waved his hand over them. *"These."*

Jenny leaned in for a better look. "Are they— Oh!" Her hand flew up to her mouth. She pressed the tips of her fingers against her lips. "Golden penises. How adorable."

Dad looked at her in surprise. "Adorable?"

She lowered her hand and laughed at the expression on his face. "You don't think so?"

She picked up one that had a Jacob's ladder piercing on the underside. "Look at the craftsmanship. It's absolutely charming. How much?"

Dad snatched it out of her fingers and placed it back on the island. "That's not something you need."

She huffed. "I'll decide if it's something I need or not, Martin."

I couldn't help saying, "Your birthday is coming soon."

Dad looked outraged. "Don't encourage her. It's bad enough you're making those."

"I make pussies too," I said. What the hell, I was in enough trouble as it was. I might as well dig myself a deeper hole. "I can make one with a piercing in the clit hood if you like."

Jenny stifled a giggle, but Dad looked just this side of disgusted.

"No thank you. This is what you've been doing when you're supposed to be making jewellery for my business?"

"I've been working on them once my work for you is finished," I said, my irritation rising. "In my own spare time. I'm making hockey sticks and pucks too." I hadn't even thought about doing that until the words were out of my mouth. Now I said them, I'd have to do it. Fortunately, I wanted to. Little personalised sticks and pucks would be too cute to resist.

"Have you been selling them on our website?" Dad asked.

"Of course not, I set up my own. I figured they wouldn't match our brand, so I kept it separate." If I hadn't, I could potentially look forward to a one-way trip off Tiger's balcony, courtesy of my father. If he was possessive of anything apart from Jenny, it was his business. I knew better than to fuck with it.

"Does anyone know you're doing this?" he asked.

"My guys and my friends," I said. "Bray knows. I guess he didn't tell either of you."

"Leave your stepbrother out of this," Dad said. "This is about you and me. It's nothing to do with him."

Okay, I was about to make this a thousand times worse or… No, there might not be a second option.

"Those guys I mentioned," I said slowly. I swallowed hard. "Bray is one of them."

I placed Dad's coffee on the island and pushed it towards him, like someone might do if they were scared of getting bitten.

I winced and waited.

Jenny looked unconcerned, but my father stared at me like he wasn't sure he recognised me.

"You're seeing your stepbrother?"

"Yes."

"Romantically?"

"Yes."

Dad grimaced. He looked like he had a question on the tip of his tongue that he didn't want to say or know the answer to.

"If you're wondering if we're sleeping together, the answer is also yes," I said. "Although, not a lot of actual sleeping takes place. At this point, I'll remind you we're both grown adults. And we're not related biologically."

"Thank fuck for that," Dad said. He picked up his coffee and swallowed half of it in one gulp.

"Would you like some alcohol in that?" I asked dryly. "Something to numb the pain of having a daughter who's such a disappointment." I didn't try to keep the bitterness out of my tone.

Dad set the mug down on the island with a thunk. "Wren Elizabeth Valentine, you are not a disappointment. I'm just surprised. This is a lot for an old man to process. Penis pendants and dating your stepbrother. And the whole drugging thing on top of that."

"It's a lot to have gone through," I said quietly. "But I'm happy making these." I jerked my head towards my pendants. "And I am happy spending time with Bray and the direction our relationship has gone. Don't worry, we still give each other hell."

We just gave each other orgasms now too.

"Do you want to keep working for me?" he asked. There was something intense in his eyes. He wanted a straight answer with a firm decision behind it. He didn't like to have conversations about things more than once if he could help it. One and done, that was him.

"Is this where you tell me I have to choose between you and making genitals out of metal?" Because that would be an impossible choice.

He flinched. "No. I want to know if I need to train someone to replace you. I don't want to lose you. You're my daughter and I love you. You're good at what you do. I don't want you sneaking around behind my back anymore though. If you want to keep making these, and doing that doesn't affect your work for me, then you have my support."

He hesitated for a moment before, with some reluctance, he added, "I might even be able to give you some tips to make them better."

"No pun intended," Jenny teased.

He turned a droll expression on her and shook his head. "I never thought I'd have this conversation. Let's maybe keep it to a minimum until I get my head around it." He closed his eyes, shook his head and groaned. "No pun intended there either."

"That's good, because I don't really want to think about my father's bits," I said.

Ewww.

"No more than I want to think about yours or anything you might get up to with Bray or anyone else," Dad said.

He picked up the rest of his coffee and swallowed it in two gulps. "Alcohol might be a good idea next time, but we all need to be on our guard right now. We don't know what move they'll make next. The minute we get complacent will be the minute they try something. We can't afford to be impeded by alcohol."

"Unless you're locked away in a tower like a princess," Jenny said.

She moved over to the window and looked outside. "This is incredible. Martin, do you think we could—"

"No," he said immediately. "We couldn't afford a place here." He rolled his eyes towards the ceiling, as though he'd expected the question at some point. There was something about this apartment that seemed to provoke that sentiment.

She clicked her tongue in disappointment, but the smile on her face suggested she knew exactly what his answer would be before she spoke. "I guess we'll be content visiting once in a while. You can show us more of your little, precious penises."

"That's not a sentence you expect to hear every day from your stepmother," I said with a smile.

She laughed, lines around her eyes crinkling with humour and warmth.

Jenny was an easy person to love. Dad was lucky he found her. So was I.

I used to wonder exactly where Bray came from. The more I got to know him, the more of her I saw. They both had a wicked sense of humour and generous spirit. They kept the people around them on their toes.

"We should get going," Dad said. He pushed his empty cup back across the island.

"Yes, we should—" Jenny took a step towards me when something slammed into the window behind her, cracking the wall of glass.

# CHAPTER 24

## TIGER

I slipped out of the back of Lex's SUV and walked around to grab my bags. One by one, I dumped the other guy's bags down on the ground and shut the hatch. Lex pressed the button on his fob to lock it.

Silently, I grabbed the handles of my bags and carried them toward the elevator.

None of us had much to say to each other right now. If we did, it would have consisted of 'hurry up.' Maybe 'hurry the fuck up.'

The last few days were both a blur and had dragged on forever. We won three out of four of our games, smashing the opposition by a handful of goals. One of the games was a shutout. No one could say we weren't focused when we were on the ice. When we weren't— That was another story.

Personally, my mind kept returning to Wren and her being alone here.

Knowing she was fine, and seeing her with my own eyes were two different things.

All I could think about was touching her. Holding her. Feeling the warmth of her body and hearing her heartbeat. And yeah, fucking her.

The woman made me feel things I'd never felt before. Things I never thought I'd feel for anyone.

And Lex… If it wasn't for him along with me the last few days, I would have caught the first flight back to Dusk Bay. He seemed to understand what I was thinking and feeling without me saying a word.

Once Bray followed Lex and I into the elevator, I pressed the button and waited impatiently for the doors to close and the car to start moving. I was tempted to step out and bolt up the stairs, but before I could, the doors slid shut.

"I'll leave my stuff in my place and come up after." Bray pressed the button to the fifth floor.

I smirked.

"What?" He caught the expression on my face.

"No wonder your place is smaller than mine," I said. "All the way down there."

He shrugged. "My place might be smaller but my cock is still bigger." The elevator dinged and the door slid open.

"Keep telling yourself that," I said just before the doors closed. I caught a glimpse of him flipping me off before he was cut off from view.

Lex chuckled. "It's a good thing you're both on the

same side. If you weren't, you two would kill each other. Possibly literally."

"If we weren't on the same side, I'd have to, to keep him away from Wren," I said.

"That's a good point," he conceded. "I'd have to help you."

The look he gave me made me want to pin him up against the wall of the elevator and kiss him. Only the fact we were a couple of floors from mine, and both of us needed to see her, stopped me. Any other time—

"We'd make quick work of him." I gripped my bags tighter as we reached our floor.

The doors slid open, followed by a series of loud cracks, and voices shouting and screaming.

I exchanged a brief glance with Lex and released the handle of my bags. I sprinted to the front door of my apartment and pushed. It didn't budge.

"Fuck." It was locked. Of course it was. It was *supposed* to be locked.

I fumbled to pull my wallet out of my back pocket and pull out the key card. Every single finger on my hand suddenly turned into a thumb. Nothing worked.

"Fucking hell." I finally managed to get a grip and yank it out. I swiped it and shoved into my apartment.

"What the…"

The windows overlooking the city were cracked in several places, indented with what looked like bullets embedded in the glass. Cracks flared out in every direction, a few centimetres each.

Wren and her father were huddled in front of the kitchen island, his arm around her. Her stepmother, Jenny, was in front of the window, her arms wrapped around her head, as if they'd save her from more bullets, or shards of glass.

"Everyone okay?" Wren rose slowly. Her eyes were wide, skin paler than usual. Typical of her, she was worried about her parents first, not herself.

"I'm okay," Jenny said in a shaky voice. "If one of those came through…"

Martin stood and staggered over to gather her up in his arms.

"Bulletproof glass," I said.

While Lex trotted over to comfort Wren, I stepped over to the window. I couldn't see anyone in the building across the road. If they had half a brain they would have ducked down and fucked off by now.

"How?" Wren had come to stand beside me. She and Lex both stood close enough to touch.

I pointed. "There's a residential building opposite this." As tall as this one, it was positioned so it didn't block off the sea view.

"They must have put someone there to wait until one of us stood in front of the window. Joke's on them. As if I wouldn't have bulletproof fucking glass." Which was going to cost a small fortune to replace, but it was worth every dollar.

"I'll let Aidan know." Lex stepped away to make the phone call.

"Maybe they knew it was bulletproof glass," Wren suggested. "This could be just another warning."

I was finally able to put my arms around her and pull her to me. Her body was warm but trembling.

"I doubt they would have factored in bulletproof glass. Considering we should have been back half an hour ago, I think we can safely assume the asshole was after me."

Just in case they were still out there, watching, I raised two fingers at them.

"Or me," she said softly. "If that was regular glass, Jenny would be dead right now. Maybe the rest of us too."

"Jenny would what?" Bray demanded. He stood in the doorway, staring at the scene in front of him. He took in the bullets in the window. "What the ever loving fuck?" He looked like he didn't know which he should do first, hug his mother and Wren, or track down who did this and put a bullet in them.

"They might still be there," Bray said.

"Bray—" Jenny said in warning, but he'd already turned and headed back down.

"Fuck," I said under my breath. "Lex, stay here with Wren and her parents."

"Tige—" Wren started to say.

I grabbed her, a hand on either side of her face and kissed her roughly. "Stay here. I'll be right back."

Before I could rethink my life choices, I bolted after Bray. We didn't wait for the elevator, we hurtled down the stairs so fast it was a miracle we didn't fall and break our necks.

We shoved out of the door at the bottom of the stairs and ran out into the alley behind the building.

"This way." I headed towards the street, scanning the area for anyone looking more suspicious than usual.

Cars zipped back and forth along Myers Street, in front of Powell Tower. Pedestrians walked without looking anywhere but the direction they were headed. Except the few who were staring at their phones as they went. No one hurried. No one looked like they saw or heard anything out of place. No one even looked shifty, which was strange in itself for Dusk Bay.

"Let's head around the back of Luchesi Tower," Bray said. "If they went down the stairs too, they might have ended up there."

"Right." We crossed the road, both trying to look like we were behaving as normal as possible. For two men over six foot tall, and well-built, to blend into the crowds, it wasn't easy, but we could pretend we weren't looking for a gunman.

The back of the tower was fenced off. We followed the fence down to the end of the block and around. A heavy lock hung on the gate, keeping it firmly shut.

There was no sign of anyone. No getaway cars. No one vaulting the fence to make a run for it. Nothing to indicate anything strange at all.

"Whoever it is, they're gone," I said. Frustrated, I

kicked at some grass that grew up from a crack in the footpath.

"Unless they're still inside." Bray stood back and looked up at the dark façade of the building. "Waiting for us to leave."

"Or waiting for us to come to them." I rubbed my chin. I could do with a shave.

"We could—"

Whatever he was about to say was interrupted by a black SUV pulling up right in front of us, the windows wound down. Aidan was inside with Finley. Orion, Coast and Phoenix looked squashed in the back seat.

"We could wait for the cavalry," I said as if that was what Bray was going to say.

"Looks like we're just in time," Coast said with a smug grin. Which, considering it was Coast, was his usual expression.

I ignored him and rested my forearms on the driver's side door to lean in the window. In as few words as possible, I told Aidan what happened.

"There's no sign of anything suspicious out here." I shot Coast and Phoenix a look, daring them to say the only suspicious entity in the area was me. If they were going to start that, they could fuck off right now. "We were thinking of going inside to take a look."

Aidan nodded and killed the engine. He waited until I stepped back to open his door. "Me, Orion and Finley will go in through the front. Coast and Tiger, take that back entrance. Bray and Phoenix, stay here and watch the back gate."

We all nodded and separated, Coast and I climbing the fence and dropping over the other side before heading to the back door.

"Sucks when they come after you," Coast said.

I was about to give him a sarcastic response—something about sucking—when I glanced over to see his expression.

For once, he was actually serious and sympathetic. I'd forgotten he was attacked in his own home and Sinclair, his girlfriend, was abducted along with Wren. If anyone understood what we were going through right now, it was him.

"Yeah, it does," I agreed. "Bad enough if it involves us. When they come after our women…"

"They're asking for trouble," he said. He sounded like an action hero out of a movie, with all the snappy lines delivered before everything went to hell.

"Then trouble is what the assholes are going to get." I could deliver a snappy line too, when I wanted to.

"They messed with the wrong dudes." Apparently Coast caught the vibe.

"I hope they like eating balls for breakfast, because that's what they're getting," I added.

Coast chuckled. "With a side of their own left toes."

"That's very specific," I observed. "But I like it."

"I thought you might," he said. "It's one of my personal favourites."

We reached the back door. I grabbed the knob and gave it a twist. Not surprisingly, it didn't open. "Locked."

Coast rubbed a hand on the back of his neck. "Doesn't look like much of a lock to me. Stand back." He raised his gun.

I took a couple of steps back and held up a hand in front of my face, just in case. Coast was a good shot, but I preferred not to get shrapnel in my eyeballs.

The shot sounded painfully loud in the otherwise quiet alley. Loud enough to make me wince. The door around the lock splintered, and the whole mechanism fell out, dangling by a long screw.

"Huh, that was shittier than I thought it was," he admitted. "We probably could have kicked it in."

"Kicking it in would have been quieter, but it's done now." I twisted the knob again and pushed the door in.

Coast followed me inside.

"I don't like any of this," I said.

We'd rescued Tiger's and Lex's bags from the elevator. Tiger's was wedged between the doors, stopping it from closing. Lex's were lying on their sides where they'd fallen before he ran.

We carried them into the apartment, closed the door behind us and stashed them off to the side.

I made us all coffee for something to do, while we waited.

"Me either." Lex laced his fingers in mine. "I should be helping."

"You *are* helping," I told him. "You're stopping me from losing my mind."

An hour or two had passed since the shooting. The reality was starting to seep into my brain.

Jenny could have died. One of those bullets could have lodged right in her head. She wouldn't have even known it happened. She would have been alive, admiring the view one minute, gone in the next.

The others could easily have taken out Dad and me. The guys could have come home and found us lying in pools of blood. The gunman could have waited to kill them too. If it wasn't for Tiger's foresight in having bulletproof glass in the windows, we'd all be fucked right now.

Bray's suggestion about people rappelling down from the helipad, didn't seem so funny now. Or even so outrageous. In this place, where I felt safe being alone, I was now on edge. Was there nowhere we could go that they wouldn't strike out at us?

"You wouldn't lose your mind if I wasn't here," Lex said. "You're stronger than you think you are."

"Lex is right," Dad said. "You've always gotten past every roadblock that's been put in front of you. You've never let anything hold you back or down. You'll get past this too. I'm not sure I will though." His arm was around Jenny. He was stroking her hair.

The look of fear in his wide eyes, suggested he was terrified someone would burst in through the door and take her from him after all.

"Martin Valentine, you're the strongest man I know," Jenny told him. "No one was hurt. I'm sure Aidan will take care of this. Reuben and Caleb might even send in some help."

"Reuben wanted us to deal with the Fiorellis on our

own," Lex said. "But he owns this building. He might consider the attack to be personal."

I snorted. I'd met Reuben a couple of times. He seemed like the sort of man who cared more about his property than he did people.

If he was shot in the chest, I wouldn't be surprised if he went on existing, barely noticing the hole. He was good at keeping it a secret, if he actually had a heart.

For a girl who was into assholes, he was perfect. He was rich and good looking, and would probably kill anyone who looked the wrong way at any woman of his.

"I don't care what it takes, I want this to stop," I said. If I was alone when this happened, I would have freaked the fuck out. The fact they almost killed the woman who was the closest thing to a mother I had, that made it more fucking personal than any stupid building.

"It will." Lex put an arm around me and tucked me against his side. "We'll deal with it." He squinted at the window like he could aim laser vision at the shooter and blast them into oblivion.

My phone rang, startling me violently. That had to stop too. I hated jump scares at the best of times.

I picked the device up from the table and glanced at the screen. I half expected a number I didn't recognise, with someone on the other end to taunt me at how close they came to killing us.

Instead, Elenna's name was on the screen. I tapped to answer the call and pressed it to my ear.

"Hey."

"Are you okay?" Elenna's voice came down the line. "Aidan told me what happened."

"Where are you?" I frowned.

"I'm at Sinclair's. Aidan told me to come here and stay with Sinclair and Javey while they look for whoever shot at Tiger's window. We're all fine. Did you see anything?"

I exhaled softly, relieved my friends were safe. "I didn't see anything. I wasn't near the window at the time. Jenny didn't see anything either, she was facing the other way, looking at the ocean."

"Thank goodness." That was Sinclair's voice. They must have me on speaker phone. "When Aidan called and said he was picking up Coast and Phoenix, I was terrified. I thought—"

I could just imagine what she thought. "I'm not going anywhere that doesn't have bulletproof glass, ever again. In fact, I may never step foot out the front door." I could get everything delivered. I might go crazy staring at these walls all day everyday, but it could be worse, right?

"You will," Elenna said. "You've never let anyone tell you how to live before. You're not going to do it now."

"I guess not," I said, unconvinced. She was right though. I had a life outside this apartment and sooner or later I had to go back to living it. Not tonight. Maybe not tomorrow. But eventually.

"Hold on a moment, Aidan sent a text." Silence fell for a few moments. "He said they didn't find anyone. Just an open window on the twelfth floor that looks straight across to where you are."

I wasn't sure if I was relieved or not. If they found and dealt with the shooter, they couldn't try again. On the other hand, they could have walked into an ambush and be lying dead right now.

"Phoenix said they're heading back," Sinclair said. "Do you want us to come over?"

"No," I said quickly. "That's okay. Like I said, I'm fine. You haven't seen your guys for a few days either. Enjoy it. But not too much." I managed a smile. "I'll catch up with you both in the next few days."

"If you're sure?" Elenna sounded uncertain.

"I'm sure," I said. "Do me a favour and stay safe, okay?"

"We will if you will," Sinclair said. "Love you."

"Love you both too." I ended the call and tossed the phone back onto the table.

"They sounded worried," Lex said. "They're good people."

I nestled into him. "They're very good people. I seem to attract the best people."

I might question how or why, but I didn't question their loyalty or that they cared about me. Not for a moment.

"That's because you are one of the best people," Lex said. "Birds of a feather and all that."

I laughed softly. "So, you're all birds now?"

"I don't know about any of you, but I'm an old bird," Dad said. "Too old for all this excitement. I'm going to take Jenny home."

I sat up halfway. "Are you sure? There's enough space here for you to stay if you want to."

"I'm sure." His expression was very familiar.

I've seen that stubborn look on my reflection in the mirror all my life. There and on his face. That stubborn I'm-not-going-to-budge expression. The one I knew not to bother fighting, because I wouldn't win.

I slumped back down. "Okay. But wait until—"

We all jumped as the door clicked and opened. Only to relax a moment later when we realised it was Tiger and Bray returning.

"No sign of the motherfucker," Tiger growled. "They won't be so lucky next time."

His expression softened when he looked at me and Lex. "Next time, you come with us when we leave town. If Aidan doesn't like it, he can kiss my ass."

"That's our cue to leave." Dad helped Jenny to her feet and started towards the door.

Before they could step out, I rose and gave them both a tight hug. "I love you both."

"We love you too," Jenny said. She squeezed me back, then hugged Bray. "Keep each other safe."

"What your mother said," Dad said. He realised his

own wording and shook his head. "You know what I mean."

Bray grinned. "Yeah, we do." He clapped Dad on the shoulder, then gave him a bro hug before slipping an arm around me and pulling me to him.

Dad grimaced, but hurried out the door when Jenny all but dragged him.

"That wasn't weird at all," I said.

"Welcome to the new normal." Bray leaned down to kiss my hair. "In which my stepsister is also my girlfriend."

In spite of everything that went on in the last couple of hours, his words made my heart flip and my pussy throb.

"Who says I'm your girlfriend?" I retorted. "I don't remember anyone asking me about that." We'd talked about a lot of things, but always skirted around words like girlfriend and boyfriend.

He turned me to face him, slid his hands down my back and grabbed my ass. "I say you are." His fingers dug into my flesh in a way that hurt and aroused me at the same time. In a way that said he was claiming me.

His voice was a low growl when he added, "I'd ask if you're going to argue with me, but I know the answer to that. Arguing with me is your favourite hobby."

Actually, having orgasms given to me by these three guys was my favourite hobby, but arguing with Bray was a close second. His growly, possessive tone got me going like crazy.

"I consider arguing with you to be an art form," I said. "One I keep trying to perfect. If I stop now, I'll never know how good at it I get."

"You're such a brat." He kissed my forehead.

"I learnt it from you," I said.

He snorted. "You surpassed me a long time ago. Probably before we met. In fact, I seem to recall you teaching me. I used to be sweet and innocent. Butter wouldn't melt in my mouth, whatever that means." He made a 'fucked if I know' face.

"Your memory is faulty," I teased. "It was definitely you teaching me. After all, that is what big stepbrothers are for, right?"

He leaned in until he was whispering in my ear. "I'm almost certain big stepbrothers are for corrupting their smoking hot stepsisters."

"What a shame you only got stuck with me, then." I placed my hands on his chest. "No wonder you were so angry for so long. You were hoping for someone cuter than me."

He kissed my nose. "There is no one cuter than you. No one is a bigger pain in my ass, but you're adorable."

"No, you." I smiled.

"Yes, me as well." He smiled his best smug-as-fuck smile. No one should be allowed to be as hot as he was, with an expression like that on his stubbly face, but here we were. He was owning every moment of it.

I slapped a hand against his chest. "See, you're one

hundred percent a brat." It felt good to stop thinking about shooters or drugged muffins for a while.

"Guilty. What are you going to do about it?"

It didn't take him long to go from worried, hunting down a gunman, to horn dog.

Not that I could talk. I went from scared, to wanting to get naked with these guys in a blink. There was nothing like being shot at, to make you appreciate life and wanting to live it as much as possible.

Elenna was right. I had to go on living and enjoying myself, whatever that took. Hiding away from the world would mean the assholes won. Fuck that. I was going to take life by the balls and live every moment of it.

Although, I might invest in some Kevlar.

# CHAPTER 26

## WREN

"Fucking dog's balls." Tiger looked up from his phone screen. His face turned towards the door, irritation etched on his face.

"What is it?" I sat up, my palms pressed hard against the butter soft leather of the couch. Every centimetre of me was tense, ready. The moment he gave the word, I'd grab a gun and join in the fight.

"We have visitors. They're on their way up." He looked like this was the last thing in the world he wanted.

The guys all had a rare day off and, so far, we'd almost managed to relax. The window was a constant reminder of what happened. Tiger would get it fixed when this was over. We couldn't risk having no glass in the windows, even for a short time.

"I got the same message," Lex said with slightly less annoyance than Tiger displayed.

"I'm starting to feel out of the loop." Bray checked his phone and shook his head. "Nothing. Just annoying spam I keep responding *stop* to, but they never stop."

"I didn't get one either," I said. I forced myself to relax back down, and not feed off Tiger's irritated vibes. "Who—"

I was interrupted by a rhythm of knocks on the door.

"Since when did we have a secret knock?" Bray asked.

"We don't." Tiger rose reluctantly and stalked over to the door like the big cat he was nicknamed after. It suited him better than Tiberius.

He unlocked the door and opened it slowly.

"Tige, dude!" A man in his early twenties, dressed in black jeans and a dark red Henley, stepped inside. He was followed by an identical man, dressed in dark blue jeans and a dark green button down.

"Hunter fucking Brantley," Tiger said as he was pulled into a hug. "Parker."

I'd met the Brantley twins, or as they were affection-ately known, the evil twins, a couple of times before, but not recently.

"Long time no see," Parker said. He rubbed a couple of fingers over his crooked nose. "The only man we know who dislikes his brother as much as we do. Maybe more." He hugged Tiger once his twin stepped aside.

"Lex," Hunter greeted. "How's it hanging?"

Lex grinned. "A little to the left, as always. Still works as well as ever."

"That's what I like to hear." Hunter's gaze grazed over Bray and me. He was young, but he took in everything, clearly making mental notes for later. Only a silly person would underestimate the twins. From what I understood, they more than lived up to their nickname.

"This is Wren and Bray." Tiger gestured to us in turn. "Keep your fucking hands off my girlfriend."

Parker smirked. He didn't take orders from Tiger and obviously wasn't going to start now.

Hunter grinned and stepped towards Bray. "Braylon Ellis." He held out his hand. "I'm a big fan. We've been trying to talk Caleb into handing the team over to us, so we can hang out with all of you more. So far, he's holding out. Luckily Parker and I are patient."

Bray shook his hand, still cautious. "Why are you here?"

"This." Hunter moved over to the window and inspected the bullet holes. "Reuben isn't impressed that people shot at the building. He wants to know why anyone would do that and what we need to do to end them."

He turned around and leaned his back against the glass. "Not in those exact words. You know Reuben, he likes to sound educated, like somehow that makes him more legitimate. But he really wants to know what the fuck is up with this." He jerked a thumb over his shoulder, tapping the tip on the glass.

Tiger explained in a handful of words. He concluded by saying, "If Reuben wants to help, he can find Fiorelli and put an end to his breathing."

"Reuben doesn't consider Nicholas Fiorelli a threat anymore," Parker said. "Something about him being as big as an ant. Metaphorically speaking. Nicholas is about as tall as we are."

"I think they guessed you didn't mean it literally, Park," Hunter said.

"Evidently he is a threat," Lex said. "Enough of one to hire someone to shoot at a building and enough of one for Reuben to send you two here."

"Yeah, this changed the game a little," Hunter agreed. "He's not a threat to Reuben's business, but he pissed Reuben off. That doesn't usually end well. I'm sure you won't be surprised at how little sympathy I have for dear Nicholas."

"About as much as I do," I said. "I think we're all on the same page on that."

Parker stepped over to sit down beside me. He draped his own arm over the back of the couch. "We heard a rumour about drugged baked goods."

"You heard right," I said. "Nicholas started subtle and then escalated to that." I tilted my head toward the window.

"That tends to be how it goes," Parker said. "It starts with harmless drugging and ends up with gunshots and car crashes."

"Harmless drugging?" Bray snapped. "She could

have died."

"In my experience, if someone wants someone else dead, then they give them something worse than what he gave to Wren. They don't mess around with hallucinogens." Parker spoke casually, unconcerned about what might have happened.

Bray bared his teeth. "If it was your girlfriend—"

Parker's eyes narrowed dangerously, but he didn't stop smiling. As though he was talking about the late autumn weather, he said, "They'd end up fucking dead. Just like Fiorelli will."

"What Parker said," Hunter agreed. "We don't condone the drugging of *innocent* women."

I wondered if his emphasis on the word innocent had anything to do with the competition between the twins' girlfriend Lila and her sister Chloe. From what I gather, things got ugly between them. When people had few boundaries to start with, they tended to come out swinging hard, and often didn't mind who got caught up in the crossfire.

"So are you here to help us, or ask questions?" Lex asked. "Better yet, give us an address for Fiorelli's present whereabouts."

"We gratefully accept the location of a shallow grave," Tiger said. "I don't have to kill the fucker personally to feel satisfied."

"As far as our sources know, he's alive," Hunter said. "Alive and well somewhere here in Dusk Bay. Congratulations on such a good season, by the way. Although, that may make it harder for us to convince Caleb to give us the Demons."

His sudden change of topic was almost swift enough to give me whiplash.

"Where in Dusk Bay?" I asked.

Hunter ignored Tiger's warning look and sat on the coffee table. "If we knew that, we wouldn't be sitting here having this pleasant chat."

"No, we'd be tearing Nicholas a new one," Bray said.

Hunter slowly swivelled around to face Bray. "If we were inclined to tell you. Which would depend on a lot of factors, including Reuben."

"Still haven't learned to think for yourselves," Tiger said.

Parker chuckled. "There's that Pennington wit."

Tiger glared at him. "At least I don't share a brain cell with my brother."

His tone suggested he liked the twins more than he let on. Maybe because they didn't like his brother either. I had no idea what the story there was, but nothing bonded people as much as mutual dislike for someone else. Okay, except maybe mutual love. In this case, it was definitely dislike.

"At least Parker and I have a brain cell between us," Hunter retorted. He grinned and offered his twin a fist bump.

Tiger rolled his eyes. "You guys are dickheads. I guess this is all the help Reuben is sending."

"We're all the help you need." Parker looked as

smug as any of the guys ever did. "If we and the whole Dusk Bay Demons ice hockey team can't deal with one little Fiorelli, then we suck. And I know we don't suck."

"There's more to this, isn't there?" I asked. "More than one little Fiorelli."

"Ding ding ding, give the girl a prize," Parker said. "I bet you'd love a pack of Kink or Drink cards." His smile faded slightly. "There's always more to it. Geneva Mancini had a greater reach than we suspected. Reuben tried to step in and claim her assets and connections once she was dead."

"Nicholas got to them first," I guessed.

"First, or they maintained their loyalty to the Fiorellis," Hunter replied. "Nicholas has a lot more resources than we thought he did. In fact, the muffin and shooting this place are small acts compared to what he's potentially capable of."

"He's trying to distract us," Tiger said. "Make us think he's desperate."

"You think he's planning something big." A feeling of dread started in my stomach and quickly grew. "Like the attack on the arena."

"Asshole better not do that again," Hunter said. "Parker and I were cranky as fuck when we heard about it. We *almost* got Caleb to give us the team before that, but then Reuben said he needed Aidan to take care of the Fiorellis and he wanted Caleb to keep that connection."

"Those of us who could have died that night weren't too happy about it either," Bray said.

"No, we weren't," Tiger agreed. "The team wouldn't have been much good if either of us were dead."

Parker leaned over to pat Bray's knee. "Lucky for all of us that didn't happen."

Bray shifted his knee away. "Sounds to me like Nicholas is a lot bigger than an ant. Is he big enough to rival Reuben?"

"Maybe we should step out of the way and let Reuben deal with him," I suggested.

"I like that idea," Lex said. "All of this is starting to seem like a Reuben problem."

"He's not that big," Hunter said. "Reuben wants him dealt with before he is. That means all players on the ice."

"Why aren't you having this conversation with Aidan?" Tiger asked. "He's the one who reports to Reuben, not us."

"Just following orders," Hunter said. "Reuben wanted us to assess the damage to the building. Also, we're friends. We want you to know what you might be up against. You already know not to let your guard down. This should drive it home, if you didn't. We'll talk to Aidan after this and tell him what he needs to know. Between us, we'll make a plan. Something that will end this once and for all. Parker and I have spent too much time cleaning up after shit caused by the Fiorellis."

"What happens after that?" I asked carefully. "Are Reuben and Samuel Bell going to fight over what the Fiorellis left behind?" Since they were dating Samuel's daughter, they'd be caught right in the middle.

Hunter and Parker exchanged glances. "Hopefully not, but that's a bridge we'll cross when we get to it. We have bigger fish to fry in the meantime."

They were clearly not going to elaborate on that, so none of us asked.

"So we're supposed to sit tight and wait for someone to tell us what to do?" Tiger asked.

"No, you're supposed to get on with your daily lives," Hunter said. "Play hockey. Make goals. Focus on winning the cup, but just stay alert for threats. We'll keep working on which direction they'll come from."

That didn't sound like much of a plan to me, but they were right. The guys couldn't stop playing until all of this blew over. For all we knew nothing may happen again for months.

# CHAPTER 27

## WREN

"Isn't this fun?" Parker gestured around the dressing area and grinned.

With Elenna working tonight, Sinclair and I opted to stay behind the scenes with her and the team. We were happy to help wheel hampers of towels and jerseys back and forth from the laundry, while she and Finley dealt with broken skates, sticks and padding.

The atmosphere was different to the one in the stands. As electric, but more tense.

Like before every game, it was also a lot quieter back here. The guys were all lost in their own thoughts. Each focused on pre-game mental warm-ups and rituals.

Tiger put on his skates right foot, then left, before lacing them up.

Bray chugged a full bottle of water to make sure he was hydrated.

The rest of the team had their own rituals.

As far as I knew, none of the guys dipped their hockey stick in the toilet, but that was a thing at least one player used to do. Once they did a thing and then won, it was difficult to let that superstition go. Even something as gross as that.

"Why do you want to own the team?" I asked. "Seems like a lot of hassle to me."

"I think it'd be fun," Parker said. "It's super handy for smuggling shit." He leaned in and lowered his voice. "Don't tell anyone this, but part of it is because we think the Demons deserved better than someone like Caleb, who doesn't give a shit."

"You'd give a shit about the team?" I asked. Neither he nor Hunter seemed like the kind of guy who'd bother with a sporting team.

"I'd like to think we would," Parker replied. "We're not as evil as we let on. Owning the team is a business opportunity, and a way to give back to the community. You know, encourage kids to play and all that stuff." He winced. "Now I sounded like a do-gooder."

I snorted. I didn't think anyone would mistake them for honest, decent citizens. Not for long anyway.

"There's nothing wrong with being a do-gooder. Not everyone in the world has to be an asshole."

"I keep telling Hunter that, but he just laughs." Parker shrugged and smiled.

I doubted he'd ever said anything like that to his

twin in his life. I wouldn't trust either of them as far as I could throw them, but it was difficult not to like them. Parker in particular. He seemed to roll with the punches, so to speak.

"It would be nice to have someone in charge who actually cares if the team wins or not," I said. "I get the impression Caleb doesn't, one way or another. As long as the team does what he needs it to do." Smuggling and laundering money, for example.

"Exactly," Parker agreed. "Hunter and I have been to more of the Demons games than he has. And more Wolf Venom concerts."

"Right." I'd forgotten one of their older brothers was the lead singer in the same band as Tiger's brother played keyboard. The drummer, Asher, was the cousin of Phoenix, the Demons' goalie. If I thought about all of that for too long, my brain would hurt.

"Could you convince Wolf Venom to play at a charity concert here?" Sinclair walked up to us and playfully bumped her hip against mine.

I grinned and bumped her back.

"I can't claim to have much influence with Zeke or the others," Parker admitted. He looked pained to have to say that. "Try asking Abbie. She'll probably like you. But don't mention me or Hunter, or she'll hang up on you before you even ask. She has a grudge against us for some reason." He shrugged.

"Okay, I will," Sinclair said.

Abbie Hart, the singer, was dating all of the members of the band, and their manager. The idea of seven boyfriends also hurt my brain.

"You work in PR, right?" Parker asked Sinclair. "When we convince Caleb to give us the team, we'll have to sit down and have a chat."

Sinclair looked nervous. "Okay," she said slowly. "Why?"

Parker chuckled at the expression on her face. "Because we don't want the team to look bad. Whatever Hunter and I need to do to make them look like the poster boys for Australian ice hockey, we'll happily do."

"Because it's much easier to get away with illegal shit when your image is squeaky clean?" Sinclair suggested.

Parker grinned. "Exactly. You can make more money with a good reputation than a bad one. More than one person has fucked themselves by screwing someone else over. So Lila says anyway. She's studying business, so I guess she'd know."

"She sounds smart," Sinclair said.

His expression softened. "She's crazy smart. And a complete badass. There's no one else in the world like her." He was clearly a man head over heels for his woman.

"You better not be trying anything with my girlfriend." Tiger stomped over on his skates.

Coast Riggs wasn't far behind, a similar expression

on his face. He snaked an arm around Sinclair's waist and pulled him to her like she was his possession and how dare Parker even be this close to her?

Parker held up his hands. "I was just talking to these two lovely women about business. They were both very interested, right?" He looked from me to Sinclair, and back to Coast. Of course his words were carefully chosen to be just provocative enough.

"Literally business," Sinclair said. She put a hand on Coast's chest to stop him from lunging at Parker.

I grabbed Tiger's hand to do the same thing. "If he and his brother own the team someday, we're all going to see a lot more of them."

"Whatever, but if he touches you, I'll rip his fucking arm off." Tiger kept his gaze on Parker.

"He won't," I assured him. Parker was more interested in stirring up trouble than he was in me or my friend. He was definitely more into Lila than he was into anything else.

Parker held up a hand. "I really won't. Scout's honour."

"As if you were ever a fucking scout," Coast said.

Parker chuckled. "Fine. Mobster's honour then. Is that better?"

"More accurate," Tiger said.

"Get out there," Aidan called out. "Warm up." He'd been off to the side, talking to Hunter. Whatever he thought about the conversation, I couldn't tell. He usually looked angry about something, so his expression was no different from normal. As far as I knew, he only ever smiled around Elenna, even when the team won.

Tiger kissed my mouth, then reluctantly slipped his hand out of mine and stepped out to the ice.

I didn't tell him good luck. One of his superstitions was that if someone said that to him, the team would lose. So I said nothing.

I stepped back and kissed Bray as he too passed me. "Have a good game."

He didn't have the same superstition as Tiger, but I didn't like to say 'good luck' to him either. If it was bad for one, it might be bad for all of them.

It wasn't just players who had their superstitions.

I felt a hand on my shoulder and looked over to see Lex standing beside me. He watched the guys walking onto the ice, his expression intense and focused.

Of course, part of his job was making sure they warmed up properly and weren't going out on the ice with an injury they'd tried to hide.

Ideally, the coaching team wanted to prevent injuries before they happened. Lex helped them to do that by running them through exercises to build their strength in a variety of muscles. That way, a player wouldn't put too much strain on one in particular.

"The vibe in here is good tonight," I said softly. I didn't want to break his concentration unnecessarily.

He didn't take his eyes off the team. "It is. They're going to smash the opposition."

"I'm in the wrong line of work," Parker said. "I should have done something that let me beat the shit out of people and get paid for it."

"Isn't that what you do?" I asked.

He looked surprised for a moment, then grinned. "Oh, yeah. I guess it is. We don't get to do it as often as they do though, and we don't have an arena full of people to cheer us on."

"You missed your calling," Lex told him. "You should have been a Roman gladiator."

Parker laughed. "I'll remember to discuss that with Reuben. He might be interested in bringing back a blood sport like that. Just for shits and giggles."

If that was Reuben's idea of fun, he was fucked up in the head.

"Just out of curiosity," I said slowly, "you're interested in business ventures to invest in?"

"You might say that," Parker agreed. "Why?"

I told him about Danglies. "I could ask the guys to invest, but I think they're biased. I'd prefer to have someone who really thinks the business can get off the ground. But I only want a silent partner and a short-term loan. Five years at most."

"Sounds interesting," Parker said thoughtfully. "You'll have to show me your pussy sometime." His eyes shone with mischief.

Lex pushed his chest forward, towards Parker. "You want to reword that?"

"I should have said pussies," Parker said unapologetically. "And cocks. If we're investing in anything, we need to see what we're investing in first." He patted Lex on the chest.

"What are we investing in?" Hunter asked.

"Cocks and pussies," Parker told him.

"Two of my favourite things," Hunter said. He grinned as Parker elaborated. "Even better. I'll take three cocks. Lila will get a kick out of having little gold representations of me, Parker and Slade." He added, "Slade is Lila's other boyfriend. He teaches at Brutham Academy."

"If you make one bigger than the other two, that's mine," Parker said.

"What is it about men and dick size?" I asked Sinclair.

She laughed. "It does seem like an obsession with dicks, doesn't it?"

"I might have a thing for them too," I said. I wouldn't make cock-shaped pendants if I didn't like the way they looked and felt.

"Who has a thing for what?" Elenna asked. She approached us, Finley behind her, pulling him along by his hand.

"They were just expressing their appreciation for penises," Hunter said.

"Seems we arrived at just the right time," Finley said with a grin. "I'd hate to miss that conversation."

"Speaking about missing things, we're going to miss

the game if we stay here and talk about dicks," I pointed out.

"We don't want that," Hunter said. "Parker and I are going to watch from the owner's box. Practice for when we actually own the team." He rubbed his hands together in anticipation.

I still wasn't sure I fully understood their interest in owning the team, but it seemed to be something they wanted very much. Guys like them tended to find a way to obtain the things they wanted, when they wanted them that much.

"We'll talk to you later about your pussy," Parker said, casting a teasing eye in Lex's direction. "*Pussies.* I meant *pussies.*" He stood just out of reach of Lex's fist. "See you all later." His eyes on Lex until the last moment, he turned and followed his twin away.

Lex grunted and watched them carefully as they walked away. "That's exactly why they call them the evil twins."

"Because they flirt with girls like us?" I asked. As pastimes went, it seemed harmless enough to me, except that sooner or later someone may have a fist planted in their face.

"Flirting with danger might be more accurate," Finley said. "Judging by the expression on Lex's face right now, they might be lucky if he doesn't arrange for them to be run over by the Zamboni."

Lex snapped his fingers. "There's an idea."

I slapped him lightly on the centre of his chest with

the back of my hand. "They're on our side, don't forget. Save the violence and testosterone for Nicholas Fiorelli."

"I'd consider it a practice run," Lex said easily. "Don't worry, I won't really do anything to them. We might need them yet."

# CHAPTER 28

## WREN

"The more nothing happens, the more I feel like something is going to happen." Bray sat back on the narrow hotel couch and propped his feet on the table in front of him.

If we were at home, doing that would have earned him a glare from Tiger. Bray would have ignored him and done it anyway. Here, no one bothered to call him out.

"I think that's the plan," Lex said into his beer. "They want to drive us insane with speculation. They are evil assholes, after all."

"Joke's on them, we're already crazy." I drank the last of my vodka and orange, and placed the empty glass down on the table. I sat back with a weary sigh.

I was starting to understand why the guys were always so tired when they got home from being on the road. To me, it felt like an endless blur of airplanes, hotel rooms and arenas. In between that, they had training and games, and games and training. Tonight was a rare night off, where we could sit down and regroup for a while.

I needed it almost as much as they did. I'd taken to helping Elenna and Finley, so it didn't look like I was along for the ride. I was more than happy to work to earn my keep.

As an added bonus, I got to spend more time with my friend, and learn the ins and outs of the team.

Aidan gave me a funny look the first time I turned up at the airport with the guys, but they all stared him down. Lex had already arranged for me to sit in the players' section of the aircraft, and I stayed with the guys, so there was no need for an extra hotel room.

There were more than enough seats on the bus to and from the airport, and if there weren't, I'd sit on one of the guys' laps. Even if that meant wrinkling their suit pants.

In the end, Aidan shrugged, turned away and dealt with something more important than a stowaway.

"Speak for yourself," Bray said. "I'm not crazy."

"I knew there was something wrong with you," I teased.

"Right back at you." He was struggling not to smile. "In fact, I made a list. Want to see?" He reached for his phone.

"You do *not* have a list of what's wrong with me," I said, pretending to be outraged. "If you do, it's super short. Shorter than Aidan's temper."

Bray frowned. "Are you feeling okay?"

My smile faded. "I think so, why?" I felt all right. Unless I was hallucinating this whole conversation. Was that what was happening? Had I eaten anything I shouldn't have? I was sure I'd only had one drink. Hadn't I?

"Because you had the perfect opportunity to say I have a really short cock, and you didn't take it," Bray said. He grinned like he scored a goal without an assist.

Tiger snorted loudly. Lex chuckled.

Asshole. I was on the verge of freaking the fuck out. "I thought I'd be nice. If you want to admit it's really short, that's up to you. It shouldn't always be me pointing out these things." I stuck my tongue out at him.

He chuckled. "You're such a brat. I should put you over my knee and spank you for that." His eyes turned darker. His definitely-not-short cock tented the front of his track pants.

"Why don't you?" I lifted my chin in challenge.

His eyebrows rose. "You might like it too much."

"You say that like it's a bad thing." I placed a hand on my hip and popped it out to the side. "Would it hurt you to live a little?"

"Me? No. It might hurt you, but it seems like you'd

welcome that." He glanced at Lex and Tiger. "What do you guys think? She could use a little smacking?"

"She can use a little whatever she wants," Lex replied. Judging by the front of his track pants, he was hoping I'd agree.

"Where's the fun in that?" Bray asked teasingly. He grabbed my hand and pulled me until I was lying across his lap. He tugged down the top of my leggings and my panties and swiped his hand over my ass cheek.

I wriggled with delight at the slight sting. "Is that the best you got?" I grinned at him over my shoulder.

"Not at all." He brought his hand down harder, hard enough to make me jump. "Is that better?"

"I can hardly feel it." I could, but I wanted more, harder still.

That was exactly what he gave me, spanking a couple of more times until my ass cheeks were red.

"I should have done this a long time ago," he said. "If I spanked you every time you got a smart mouth, you might have been better behaved." He didn't sound like he believed it either.

I snorted a laugh. "No chance. I would have done something like put live snakes in your bed."

"Or peanut butter in his sandwich," Lex offered.

Bray winced. "Whose side are you on?"

"Wren's," Lex said, grinning. "Sorry, bro. For what it's worth, I wouldn't do that. I don't want you dead."

"Yet," Tiger said ominously. His eyebrows twitched and his mouth curved up slightly.

Bray shook his head at them and pushed my leggings and panties down further. I kicked them off, letting them fall to the floor.

He parted my legs and ran his hands over my ass and down between my thighs. He dipped his finger into my damp pussy, coating it in my arousal before moving it up and pressing the tip into my rear hole.

"I want to fuck you here." He pushed his finger in deeper.

I quivered. "Yes please," I said softly. Just having his finger in there felt incredible, but I wanted more.

The guys exchanged glances and helped me up off the couch and over to the bed.

They stripped off their T-shirts and track pants and Lex lay down on his back, pulling me on top of him. His hands on my hips, he guided me down onto his erection.

I closed my eyes and savoured the feeling of my pussy sliding down his cock all the way to his balls.

"Fuck, Wren, you always feel incredible," he said.

"So do you," I said, breathlessly. Every centimetre was seated so wonderfully deep inside me. Was that the vein in his cock throbbing or my clit? Maybe a combination of both.

"Lean forward." Bray pulled a tube of lube out of his bag and squeezed a large dollop onto his hands.

I glanced at his fingers. My heart did a tap dance in

my chest. I swallowed down a flutter of nerves and did what he said.

He smeared the lube around and into my rear hole, making me smooth and slippery. Careful but firm, he pressed two fingers into me, then three, stretching me and making me ready.

Finally, he straddled Lex's legs and positioned his cock with the tip pressing into my ass.

"Ready or not, here I come," he said with a slight laugh.

I choked back a laugh of my own. "You're so silly."

"That's one word for me," he agreed. He gripped my hips and pushed himself in deeper.

"Holy crap," I breathed. I'd done anal a time or two before, but I'd never felt anything like this. Two guys with their cocks deep inside me at the same time. I never imagined this would feel so good. So absolutely full and arousing as hell. I could have come then and there, without even moving.

"You okay?" Lex asked.

"Better than okay," I replied. "I glanced sideways at Tiger, whose fist was wrapped around his own erection.

He bent over to kiss me, softly at first, then deeper. I moaned against his mouth, revelling at the way his stubble lightly scraped the skin of my cheeks.

Lex cupped my breasts with both hands and palmed my nipples until they were as hard as stone.

Holy shit, these men.

Tiger broke off our kiss, leaned over and pressed his mouth to Lex's.

Lex looked surprised, but then he was kissing him back, with his lips and his tongue.

When they finally broke apart, Lex said, "If you want to…" His tongue darted over his lower lip.

That was all the invitation Tiger needed. He lowered himself down beside Lex and pressed his cock between the coach's lips.

"Holy fuck," I whispered.

That was the cue for Bray to start moving inside me, thrusting slowly into my ass. In turn, he pushed me onto Lex's cock, setting the rhythm for all four of us.

"Your ass is perfect," Bray breathed. "Fuck… I can feel Lex when I'm deep inside you."

Lex's eyebrows twitched in acknowledgement that he could also feel Bray's cock with each thrust, but his mouth was busy licking and sucking and enjoying the taste of Tiger.

"Like what you see?" Tiger asked me.

"Very much," I agreed. "I love what I see and what I feel."

One thing was for sure, I could never go back to only having one lover. Especially not now. I'd told myself so many times in the last couple of months, but I could have done this for the rest of eternity and had no regrets. Just when I thought things couldn't get more incredible, they did.

"You like how his mouth feels?" I asked with no jealousy. Not even a hint. I loved sucking cock, but watching it was just as hot.

"Yeah," Tiger said on an exhale. "He's as talented at this as you are."

Lex smiled around his mouthful and thrust up into me faster, harder. My clit rubbed against him each time, pushing me quickly to and over the edge.

I threw back my head and cried out as I came, my whole body shaking with the overwhelming flood of bliss that shattered me right to my core, over and over like a king tide.

"Fuck, Wren," Bray grunted and came a moment later, falling still and letting his balls explode his release in my ass.

Tiger slid his cock out of Lex's mouth long enough for Lex to breathe while he too came hard. He thrust into me desperately, eyes half closed, his own release filling me, held in for now by the thickness of his cock.

The moment he could breathe again, Tiger slid his cock back between Lex's lips, in time for his own orgasm.

I watched Lex's eyes as Tiger filled his mouth with his cum. The coach seemed to like what he tasted. He looked from me to Tiger and back again, holding it in his mouth. Lex waited for Bray to slide out of me before rolling us over and pressing his mouth to mine. He pushed my lips open with his tongue and squirted Tiger's release onto my tongue.

I swished it around in my mouthful a moment or two before swallowing. "Delicious."

"Yes it was," Lex said. He placed his hand on the back of Tiger's hand and pulled him down for his own kiss. "You both are."

Fuck yeah, we definitely needed to do this again.

My phone vibrated in my back pocket. I shifted the pile of padding to my opposite arm and pulled it out to glance at the screen. It lit up with a message from Elenna.

> We're missing jerseys from Javey and Orion. Can you check laundry plz?

I managed to type a quick response, and shoved the phone back in my pocket before I dropped everything.

I turned around and headed back down the corridor towards the laundry.

Strange, I wasn't the one who grabbed the last load out of the dryer. I was surprised Elenna or Finley wouldn't have missed anything. They were usually careful.

"No one's perfect," I said to myself.

I turned around, pushed the laundry door open

with my back and dropped the padding onto a folding table. Really, it was a trestle that predated my grandparents. The surface was scratched and dented, but the table itself was stable enough. Mostly.

I peered into one dryer. It was empty. The other was still drying a load. I put it on pause and opened the door.

If nothing else, I could tell Elenna where the missing jerseys were. After a quick search, I decided they weren't in there. I restarted the dryer and looked into the industrial washing machines. Both of those were empty. Not even a missing sock stuck to the side.

I pulled out my phone to text Elenna that they weren't here.

The device was snatched out of my hand.

"What the—" I whirled around.

My heart stopped dead.

I recognised the two men who stood in the laundry doorway. Roach and Otis. Formerly minions of Sawyer Mancini. Two of the men who kidnapped Sinclair and me last year.

"How did you get in here?" I asked.

Security in the arena was supposed to be crazy tight. No one should have been allowed to walk through the front doors unless they were staff. Or... held tickets.

Still, they shouldn't have been able to get into this part of the arena. Granted, we were in Melbourne. Their security might not be as tight as in Dusk Bay.

Fuck. Of course they'd waited until we were some-where like this to make a move.

"If you did anything to Elenna—" How had they sent a message that looked like it came from her phone? The technology existed, it was used by telephone scam-mers all the time, but to hijack her phone? It felt to me like a violation. Better her phone than her, but Aidan would kill them both for this. If he got to them before Tiger did.

"Your friend is fine." Roach leaned against the door like we were having a casual conversation. "She's the brunette, right?"

I wasn't going to dignify his question with an answer. Instead, I ran through the items I'd seen in the laundry, trying to figure out if I could use anything as a weapon and if it was close enough to grab.

Back in Dusk Bay, Finley kept hockey sticks here and there for times like this. That would be helpful if I was bigger and only facing one asshole. With two of them… I ruled out everything I could think of. One by one.

The only plan I had left was to play nice and hope like hell I walked away from this in one piece.

"It's been great to catch up with you guys, but if you'll excuse me, I have work to do." I swivelled my upper body and reached for the pile of padding.

"I wouldn't do that if I were you." Otis had a gun in his grip, aimed at my hands.

Since I was very much attached to my hands, I stepped back and raised them. "What do you want?"

If I was lucky, they'd cut to the chase and get the hell out of here. Then I could do the same. Right now, all I wanted was to be with my three guys, their arms around me, holding me until I stopped shaking. I hadn't realised I'd started, but I realised it now. My whole body was trembling.

"We don't want to hurt you," Roach said.

That was good to know. Or it would be if I believed it. I was one hundred percent sure if their boss told them to maim or kill me, they'd do it without a second thought or lingering regret.

I stayed silent, waiting for them to continue.

"We're going to need you to come with us," Otis said. "Do as you're told and you'll walk away when this is over."

"Why don't you let me walk away right now?" I said.

Fuck, I shouldn't provoke them, but the words were out before I could stop them. I mean, it was a reasonable request. Right?

Bray always told me my big mouth would get me in trouble some day. Just before he told me my big mouth was perfect for his big cock. He couldn't help himself.

"You know the answer to that as well as we do," Roach said. "We have a job to do, nothing more. If we turn up without you, we're dead."

Honestly, them being dead worked for me. Was that mean or wrong? No, the motherfuckers were holding a gun on me. Again. They could go to hell and burn there for all eternity as far as I was concerned. The sooner the better.

"You could tell them I ran away from you," I suggested. "If we put our heads together, we can come up with a plausible scenario. Maybe you couldn't get into the arena in the first place. I'm sure Nicholas would buy that."

I snapped my fingers. "I know, he can come and see for himself. In fact, this is my invitation to him to do just that." As if he'd be that stupid. Shame, we could set up a nice little trap just for him.

"Maybe you can shut the fuck up and move," Otis snapped. He was always the cranky one of the pair. He dropped my phone on the ground and stomped on the screen with the heel of his heavy boot.

The last time, when he and Roach abducted Sinclair and me, they used our phones to reply to texts from the guys, pretending we were fine.

Apparently that wasn't happening this time. They weren't pretending. They wanted the guys to know they had me.

"How about I deliver a message?" I suggested. "That's the point, isn't it? Drugging me with that muffin —that was you, wasn't it?"

"I've always wanted to be a baker," Roach said. "The muffin tasted good, didn't it?" He actually looked hopeful. Even proud. Dickhead.

"It was amazing," I gushed. "If it wasn't laced with hallucinogen, it would have been incredible. I think you should give up being a goon and go back to school to learn to be a baker." Right now would be perfect.

"You think so?" Roach straightened up.

Otis shot him a dark look. "Not the time, idiot. We have a job to do, remember?"

Roach slumped back against the door. "Right."

I sighed to myself. At least the seeds of dissent were planted in his brain. Maybe that would lead to something, like him deciding to be on my side. Yeah, okay, it was a long shot, but a girl could hope.

I rallied myself again. "The shooting thing, that was a warning too, right? I eyed the gun in Otis' hand. "Was that you? That was some impressive shooting."

He twitched. Looked slightly disappointed. "Not me."

His cranky mask snapped back into place. "Shut up and start walking." He stepped back out of the doorway and gestured with the gun, indicating for me to move in front of them.

I stayed in place. I reminded myself I should not be poking the hornets' nest, but I knew if they took me out of here, my chances of surviving were considerably reduced. There was nothing to stop them from getting annoyed and killing me, regardless of what they were ordered to do.

"Nicholas didn't give you the chance to try?" I asked. "That's a shame. You look like a guy who could shoot through bulletproof glass."

"Otis wanted the job, but Nicholas gave it to—"

Otis elbowed Roach in the ribs. "Shut the fuck up. If you keep blabbing like that, I'll shoot you myself."

Roach raised his hands. "Chill out, bro. I'm on your side, okay? I just thought it wasn't fair. Fargo hasn't worked for the boss for as long as we—" He caught Otis' glare and closed his mouth with a snap of his teeth.

"I don't think either of you want to be here doing this," I said. "I tell you what, put the gun away, turn around and leave and I won't say anything about this to anyone."

Not least until I reached my guys. Then I'd tell them *everything*. They'd hug me, then chase after these two and tear them apart. That was firmly in the 'not my problem' basket.

Roach actually looked like he was considering the offer.

Otis, on the other hand, raised the gun and pointed it at my chest. "Enough talk. If I have to tell the boss your death was an accident, that's what I'll do. It's easier for everyone if you do as you're fucking told."

He might be right, but desperation and panic were warring with each other for the right to uncoil in my stomach and spread throughout my entire body.

I shook my head. "I'm not going with you. You'll have to kill me instead."

I never thought much about how I'd die, but it hadn't crossed my mind it would be in a laundry room, in a hockey arena in Melbourne.

To be fair, I couldn't have guessed that, up until recently. It's not exactly a bucket list item. I put it firmly on my fuck it list instead. I didn't want to die here.

In retrospect, I should have told Aidan I was coming along for my safety and stayed as close to the guys as possible. But no, I had to go and try to be useful. If it was any consolation, Javey and Orion probably had their jerseys with them.

All of that flashed through my mind before I grabbed up the backup goalie's padding I'd placed on the table and raised it up in front of me, a barrier between me and them.

The first bullet slammed into the centre of one of the knee pads. It passed through that and into the one behind it and the one behind that.

It stopped short of exiting and striking the centre of my chest.

The second shot did almost the same thing. This time, instead of stopping, it struck just below my collarbone. Searing pain lanced through me.

Without the padding it would have gone a lot deeper, but it still hurt like a motherfucker.

I braced myself, but the third and fourth shot didn't hit the padding at all.

I heard the gunshots, but felt no strike. Nothing.

My mind couldn't put the two things together. Unless I was dead. That was why I didn't feel an impact. That wouldn't explain the pain though. My mind was a fog of agony and confusion.

"Wren!"

That was Bray's voice. He sounded frantic. More worried than I'd ever heard him.

I didn't *think* this was a hallucination, but his tone made me wonder. Since when did Bray talk to me like that?

Tentatively, I lowered the padding, just enough to peer over the top.

Tiger stood with a gun in his hand, pointed toward the two bodies that lay on the floor between him and Bray.

Lex was right behind them.

Blood was already pooling around Roach and Otis's heads, spreading across the worn linoleum.

"I'm okay," I said in a small voice. "Just a little... Shot."

Fuck, I was *shot*. The pain was incredible. Blood was starting to soak into my shirt and hoodie. I could feel it, damp, the smell tangy.

Suddenly faint, I dropped the padding to the floor and let the guys grab me before I landed in a heap beside it.

# CHAPTER 30

## BRAY

"How did you know where to find me?" Wren still looked pale and shaken, but according to the team doctor, she'd be fine. The bullet had grazed her skin. If it wasn't for that padding...

"Elenna," Tiger said. "She said you'd been gone for longer than it should have taken to grab what Finley sent you down for. She was worried you got lost."

He sat on the chair beside Wren's hospital bed, looking furious. He'd had that exact expression on his face for the last hour. If I looked in the mirror, I'd probably see the same one.

I was still trying to get my head around the fact those two assholes dared to walk into the arena and try to abduct my woman. Again.

"It is a rabbit warren," I said. "If it wasn't for that first gunshot, we might not have found you in time. We were searching in that area, but hadn't thought to check the laundry yet. We would have, soon enough," I added quickly when she looked like she might take the opportunity to give me shit.

"Says you," she said weakly. "At least you got there."

"Exactly," I said, trying to look smug. I probably didn't pull it off. Yeah, judging by her smirk, I definitely didn't. Whatever, I was happy to see her alive and more or less well.

"I'm sorry we didn't get there sooner." Lex sighed heavily. "It would have been better if you didn't go down there by yourself in the first place. Aidan is still looking into how the hell they got in. As you can imagine, he's out there tearing the arena management a new one. As far as anyone knows, they entered, intending to steal valuable equipment. That's the official story."

"Sounds accurate to me," I said. "Wren *is* valuable equipment. Especially her pussy." I grinned and waggled my eyebrows at her.

She rolled her eyes at me, which was totally fair. "My equipment is a lot more valuable than yours."

"Definitely," Tiger said with a grunt.

I turned to him with a mock scowl. "Whose side are you on?" First Lex and now him. They'd both joined in on Wren ribbing me. I loved it. They made me feel like I belonged.

"Me and my cock," Tiger replied unapologetically.

I sat back in my own chair and pretended to sulk. I succeeded in lightening the mood at least. In my experience, humour always helped make a situation easier to handle.

Lex cleared his throat. "Anyway, the arena lockdown just lifted. The cops and arena management insisted we postpone the game, so we're done for the night."

"Good," I said. "Personally, I had no intention of leaving Wren and going back to the arena. She's more important than hockey."

Wren pressed the back of her hand to her forehead. "Now I *am* hallucinating. Did I just hear you say something in life is more important than hockey? Not just something, but…" She paused dramatically. "Me?"

"Don't let it go to your head," I teased. The smile I gave her was anything but teasing or sarcastic.

I had no idea exactly when I fell in love with Wren, but I had and I fell hard. If I had to give up hockey for her, I'd do it right this minute. Yesterday. Last fucking week. Nothing else mattered.

"Too late, it went straight to my head." She smiled and sank back against her pillows. "I don't have to stay here, do I? I hate hospitals and I hate hospital food."

"You and everyone else on the face of the planet," Lex said. "But no. I've organised a car for us. You just need to sign the release forms and we can get out of here." He rubbed his chin. "My preference is for going straight to the airport and back to Dusk Bay. Or we could drive."

"You have a game in Adelaide in two nights," Wren pointed out. "You can't go home yet."

"Didn't I just mention something about things being more important than hockey," I said with a slight hint of a teasing sneer. "Maybe the doctor should have cleaned your ears out while she was there."

Wren flipped me off, which was also totally fair. "You can make statements like that, but then you have a contract to do something you love."

I wanted to tell her I didn't need a contract to do some*one* I loved, but the words wouldn't come. Yeah, I might be the worst kind of coward. She could have died and I couldn't tell her how I felt. I would. I made a promise to myself and to her, I'd tell her soon.

"If they try anything again—" Tiger started.

"You'll be right there to deal with them," she said. "If I have to take you all down to the laundry with me to get the jerseys, then that's what I'll do." She shrugged and winced. Her shoulder was going to be stiff for a while, until the stitches came out.

"Maybe I'll get to kill one next time," I remarked.

"Sorry if Wren's safety was more important than stopping and handing you the gun so you could deal with one of them," Tiger said sarcastically. "I'll bear that in mind next time. And still not do it. The fuckers got what they deserved, and they got it quickly."

"I almost feel sorry for Roach," Wren said slowly. "I have a feeling he wanted a better life than that. He was the one who made the muffin."

"Only you would feel sorry for someone who drugged you." I rolled my eyes toward the ceiling. She had a bigger heart than anyone else I knew. Too big sometimes, but maybe mine was too small.

"It's not that," she said with a small voice and a frown. "It was a really good muffin. If he had the chance to do what he wanted to do, he wouldn't have been trying to abduct people, and hold them at gunpoint. He would have been happily making cakes. He was good enough to go on one of those cooking shows. That muffin at least…"

"Excuse me if I don't lose too much sleep over him," I said.

If I thought about it too much, I might also feel a twinge of regret. Some people made the choice to embrace this lifestyle and become a goon, or someone like Reuben who lorded it over the rest of us. Others fell into the job, or had no choice because everyone has to eat.

If I wasn't any good at hockey, that could have been me. Braylon Ellis, hired goon. It had a ring to it, but not as much as Bray Ellis, Dusk Bay Demons' winger.

"I know," Wren said. "There's no point dwelling on the past anyway. They're both dead and presumably all over the news already."

"Aidan made sure of that," Lex said. "He wanted Nicholas to know he didn't succeed here. In case not hearing from his goons wasn't obvious enough. With any luck, this will make him angry enough to make a mistake. When he does, we'll be right there, waiting to kick his ass."

"I'll shoot his ass," Tiger said. "Right before I put a bullet in his head."

"Priorities," I said approvingly. "Make him suffer before putting him out of his misery. And ours."

"That sounds good," Wren said. "Personally, I'm getting tired of him coming at me. At least now I know it's personal. I mean, it's me he's targeting."

"Because of me," Tiger growled.

"And me," Lex said. "And Aidan, Coast, Orion, Finley, Phoenix, Javey and probably Bray." He looked like he was going to add something, but changed his mind.

I suspected he was going to point a finger at Elenna and Sinclair. Elenna had killed Nicholas' younger brother Oscar in retribution for murdering her brother Ike.

Sinclair had worked with Aidan and the rest of us to try to ferret out who was feeding information from the Demons to the Fiorelli slash Mancini family.

They were both in it as deep as anyone. But they were also Wren's best friends and bringing them into the conversation right now was probably not a good idea. Wren needed to rest and recover.

"Definitely me," I said to distract from Lex's expression. "From now on, we're making sure one of us is with you at all times. Two or three would be better, but at least one."

I slid Wren a sly grin. "You know the situation is

serious when I'd voluntarily spend time with my stepsister."

She groaned playfully. The sound went straight to my groin.

"Crap, does that mean I have to spend time with you too?" She wrinkled her nose. "I'm starting to think I should have let them abduct me."

"I could try to contact Nicholas and offer you up?" I said. As if I'd ever do something like that.

"Not if you like your balls intact," Tiger said.

"What he said." Lex nodded to Tiger. "I don't think you'd like how it would feel to have us put a clamp on each of your balls and pull them in different directions."

My balls tried to retreat up into my body.

I winced. "No thank you. Wren will have to learn to put up with me, because she's going to be seeing me every time she turns around."

She sighed, but the expression on her face suggested she was actually looking forward to it.

So was I, but I hated the reasoning for it. If Nicholas had balls of his own, he'd go after one of us, not her. Clearly, he was trying to piss us off. It was working. At the same time, he was making himself look like a coward.

"I don't know about you, but I think we should get out of here." I pressed my hands to the chair on either side of me and pushed myself half the way up.

"Wait a minute," Wren said. She turned to Lex. "Did Aidan say anything about someone in the arena working with them? There's a possibility someone let them in, right?"

I lowered myself back down with a bump. "Fuck."

I was so busy worrying about her, I hadn't given any thought to the way things went down. Judging by the look on the other guys' faces, neither had they. No regrets, Wren came first, but it was something we needed to consider now.

Lex rubbed his forehead with the tip of a couple of fingers. "Yeah, it's certainly possible. They might have been paid to let them in. In which case, we might find a money trail. That'll take time though."

Tiger asked. "We can deal with those assholes after we deal with Nicholas. Those dickheads are small fish."

He pointed a finger at Lex and me before we could reply, both surprised he wasn't ready to jump up and rip off heads right now.

"If they're working with that asshole, that's one thing. Chances are, they're just some stadium staff member who needed some cash. They got exploited by their own desperation. If we find out it's more than that, I'll be right there planting bullets in brains."

"Tiger is right," I said. "People like Nicholas look for vulnerable people to use in situations like this. It would be a lot less expensive and a lot less hassle than planting someone here and waiting for us."

"Tiger is usually right," Tiger said. He crossed his arms and waited for one of us to contradict him.

I raised one eyebrow at him, but wisely said nothing. I saw the way he effectively and efficiently shot both of those goons. Getting on his bad side would be a bad idea. Not to mention it might cause friction with Wren and if I was going to annoy her, it wasn't going to be like that. No, I preferred more creative ways to get under her skin.

"Okay, let's get out of here," Lex said. He helped Wren get up off the hospital bed and walk with us to the door.

# CHAPTER 31

## WREN

"You're on babysitting duty?" I smiled teasingly at Lex.

The flight from Melbourne to Adelaide was uneventful, apart from the usual hectic movement of a whole hockey team and all their equipment. The plane wasn't hijacked. No one died. No one even aimed a gun at me.

Bonus.

"I don't mind." He draped an arm over my shoulders.

Neither of us cared we were sitting right beside the rink while the guys practised. Let people look, we had nothing to be ashamed of. I'd already ignored several funny looks when I kissed all three of my guys. You know what they say about jealousy being a curse. If they saw the bandage under my hoodie, they might be less envious.

"I get to be with you and watch them at the same time. Win-win." He glanced over at me and smiled.

"They're looking good this season." I leaned against him. "The team, I mean." Although, Bray and Tiger specifically. Of course. "I feel like they've come together so much better than they did last season. So to speak." The memory of being double stuffed by Lex and Bray made my clit take notice. Added to that remembering Lex sucking Tiger off, and the temperature in the arena seemed to go up by about two dozen degrees.

"Nothing unites people like going through the shit we've gone through in the last year," Lex agreed.

He turned his attention back to the ice. The first line was practising against the second. Neither was going easy on the other. Nor should they. All of the second line players were ambitious to take a spot on the first. Eager to prove themselves. The first line players had to work hard to keep their contracts. Put those together and you had some good, healthy competition.

Coast skated around a couple of the opposition, ducking and weaving before he flicked the puck off his stick and into the goal from several metres away. The goalie hardly saw it coming. He had no time to react or stop it before it was flying past him and into the net.

"That was incredible." I applauded along with everyone else watching.

In typical Coast Riggs style, he looked cool and calm, like he made shots like that every day. He skated away, back into the centre of the rink, already focused on where the puck might go next.

"He wouldn't have pulled off a shot like that last year," Lex said. "Sinclair has been good for him. Phoenix too. He's always had the talent, but now he has the confidence."

"I wouldn't have thought Coast lacked confidence," I said dryly.

Lex glanced over and grinned. "There's a difference between confidence on and off the ice. Not to mention faking it until you make it. He likes to put on a show that he's a big, bad, cocky hockey player, but he's a regular guy underneath. Just like the rest of them."

"Even Bray and Tiger?" I asked. "Never mind, I know the answer to that. Underneath the swagger, Bray is as regular as they come. And Tiger is really a big teddy bear."

"A big teddy bear that holds a grudge," Lex agreed. "If I was Nicholas or anyone else who pissed him off, I'd be shaking in my shoes."

"Like Gus," I said. I hadn't seen any sign of the third guy who abducted me, but I assumed he was still out there, taking orders from Nicholas and fucking up other people's lives.

Lex squeezed my shoulders. "We'll find him and deal with him. If he has any brains, he's lying low right now, but sooner or later he'll resurface. We'll be ready."

"I know," I said. "Thank you."

"For what?" Lex asked.

"Keeping me sane." After a moment I added, "Mostly sane."

"You're the sanest person I know." He leaned over to kiss my mouth.

I kissed him back, then laughed. "I believe you. I'm familiar with the people you know."

He laughed. "That wasn't what I meant and you know it." His smile faded and he lightly touched the bandage under my collarbone. "I wish this hadn't happened."

"Me too," I said. "But it's feeling a lot better now. Just a little stiff and sore."

His smile was back. "Can relate."

I glanced down at his lap. "Is that right?" It certainly *looked* right. And getting more and more right by the moment.

"Around you, always." He kissed my temple and nuzzled his face into my hair. "I don't think anyone will notice if we disappear for a little while."

"They'll definitely notice," I said, my voice getting husky. "But I don't care if they do."

I stood and offered him my hand. I glanced back over my shoulder to see Bray and Tiger watch us disappear. They wore similar wry smiles on their faces, slightly envious of Lex, but knowing he'd keep me safe wherever we went.

"Focus!" Aidan snapped at them. "Otherwise I'll—"

We slipped out the door before I heard the rest of what he said. Probably something along the lines of banning me from watching practice. Good luck with that, considering Elenna did the same thing frequently.

Lex and I made it the handful of steps to the empty visitors' dressing area before he pressed me back against the wall, the full length of his body against mine. He slid his hands up the front of my shirt and over my belly.

His cock prodded into me, hungry and insistent. He pinched my nipples through the lacy fabric of my bra, making them hard and as needy as my pussy.

"How do you always know the right way to touch me?" I asked.

"I pay attention to the way you respond," he said. "I see what you like and give it to you. I love feeling you wriggle and groan because of what I'm doing to you."

"I like it too," I said. "I like making you feel good." One of my favourite things was having my guys come inside my body. Whether it was my pussy, my ass or my mouth. Together, we created the friction that drove us wild. Giving and receiving pleasure with our bodies. Every time, I felt closer and closer to them in every possible way.

We were both aware someone could walk in at any moment, but I didn't resist him pushing my shirt up and over my head. He leaned down to pull one of my nipples into his mouth, sucking it through the fabric of my bra.

I moaned softly. Aroused by his touch, and the sound of the play out on the ice. Close enough to hear, but out of sight. If I could hear them, then they might be able to hear me.

Now I was very, very wet.

"Just like that," Lex said. "Moan for me, baby." He switched to the other nipple, before pulling down my cup and palming the first. "I want them to hear you. Let them know what I'm doing to you."

I moaned louder. I could barely hear myself over the rush of blood in my ears.

"That's my girl," Lex soothed. He reached around to unhook my bra and tug it down my arms and onto the floor. "You're so beautiful."

He leaned back to admire me, the colour in my cheeks and the roughness of my breathing. "So fucking beautiful. So fucking mine."

Out on the ice, someone else scored a goal. That was followed by cheering and shouting.

I imagined they were egging me on instead. Encouraging Lex to touch me and fuck me so close to where they skated.

I shoved up the front of Lex's shirt and ran my hands over his flat belly and tight abs. He was as rock hard as any of the players, firm and warm under my fingers.

"And this is so fucking mine," I whispered.

Feeling bold, I pushed down my leggings and panties in one go and stepped out of them.

How did I go from someone who was shy about taking photos of herself to a woman who was naked in the locker room where anyone could come in at any time?

Maybe I preferred to be seen, than to capture those moments myself.

"You're incredible." Lex slipped out of his pants and boxers and kicked them aside. He grabbed my ass and picked me up until I wrapped my legs around his waist.

With no hesitation or care that we might be caught, he pressed his cock into me, sliding all the way in to his balls. My back pressed against the rough, painted brick wall, he started to thrust into me, quick and hard.

My breasts bounced with each stroke, keeping the rhythm, along with the rocking of my hips, encouraging him to thrust in deeper still.

I dropped my head back and groaned. "That feels amazing. Keep doing that, right there." The cold air and my arousal made my nipples pebble and ache.

Between thrusts, he leaned in and suckled on first one, then the other. His lips and tongue were warm on my sensitive skin, sensual as hell.

"You taste delicious," he said, kissing my breast just above one nipple.

"You feel amazing," I said breathlessly.

In the corner of my eye, I caught movement in the doorway.

Aidan stepped into the locker room, took one look at us and turned and walked back out to the ice. Under his breath, he muttered something that sounded like, "Get a fucking room next time."

Lex chuckled, but didn't slow his thrusts. If anything, they became faster, more desperate.

My face heated, but I was equally undeterred. If anything, I was more turned on then ever. Excited at having been caught, but not embarrassed.

With his body, Lex would have blocked off the view of all but my legs and feet, and maybe the top of my head. If he wasn't concerned about Aidan seeing his back and ass, neither was I.

It wasn't like nudity in a locker room was anything new. Fucking maybe, but not naked butts.

I kept a tight grip on Lex, my arms around his neck. He was hitting my clit just right. I didn't want to let him go. Not now. Maybe not ever.

"I'm so close," I said between ragged breaths. "Don't stop. Please don't stop."

"I have no intention of stopping," he said. "Come for me. Come for me, little bird. Come on my cock."

I dug my nails into the skin of his back as I came, my pussy tightening around his cock and stealing an orgasm from him at the same time.

We matched each other breath for breath, groan for groan, thrust for thrust.

Hearing him coming made my orgasm last and last. We weren't in a locker room anymore. We were floating in a universe that existed of him and I and nothing else. Just our bodies giving each other bliss. Giving and taking in equal measure. The moment strung out for seventeen eternities until we both slumped against the wall, panting heavily and trying to catch our breath.

"Wow, that was something else." Lex said softly.

Out on the ice, someone scored another goal and the arena echoed with cheers.

"Apparently they agree," I said with a breathy little laugh. "I think we both scored."

He laughed softly beside my ear. "At the end of the first period, I call it 1-1."

"Only the first period?" I asked.

"Definitely. Time for an intermission and then we can commence the second period."

*Hell yeah.*

# CHAPTER 32

## WREN

"Stop that." I swatted away Bray's hand after he pinched my ass.

He pressed the front of his body against my back and leaned down to say, "Hurry up then."

I glanced at him over my shoulder. "In case you haven't noticed, we're on a plane full of people and everyone is trying to get off."

Tiger and Lex were right in front of me, half the team still in front of them. All dressed in suits, in case the press appeared to take photos or ask questions about what happened in Melbourne. Couldn't have them looking their usual, scruffy selves when they were representing the team.

"I can't argue with that." He pressed his groin into my hip.

I pushed back, making his cock respond. "Not that kind of getting off, dickhead. Everyone is trying to *disembark*."

"That's a big word, stepsister dear," he teased. "Do you know how to spell it?"

I half turned around and grinned. "I…T."

He snorted a laugh. "Always the smartass."

"Better than being a dumbass." I reached the steps and followed Tiger and Lex down to the tarmac.

Both of them stopped until I was clear of the plane, then all three guys herded me to the waiting bus. The same one, with the same driver, who picked up Sinclair and I from the side of the road after our abductors let us go. I suppressed a shiver while I stepped on board and gave the driver a warm smile. I had to give him some credit for helping to find me as fast as they had.

"Hey, Fred," I said cheerfully.

He nodded politely. "Wren." As far as I could tell, Fred was a man of few words at the best of times.

I hurried down the bus aisle and flopped into a seat covered in faded, slightly worn blue and red fabric. It looked a little tired, indented from years of ass cheeks, but it was comfortable.

Bray slipped in beside me. Tiger and Lex right behind us.

"It'll be nice to be home," Lex said.

"Been too long," Tiger said with a grunt. He leaned forward and placed a hand on my shoulder. "Got a surprise for you when we get there."

"She's already seen your cock," Bray said.

Tiger smirked at him. "My cock is worth seeing again and again. That's not the surprise."

"She's seen your balls too." Bray grinned.

"You want me to tell the driver to drop you off halfway there?" Tiger narrowed his eyes at Bray.

"You wouldn't do that." Bray placed his hands in his lap, one over the other.

"He might not, but I would," Lex said. "Just for a laugh."

"No one is telling the driver to drop anyone off," I said. "You three behave yourselves or I'll have to spank all of you."

"I think you just said, 'Please keep giving each other shit so you have an excuse to spank us,'" Bray said. He gave me a knowing look.

"Don't pretend you wouldn't enjoy it," I told him.

He cocked his head and one side of his mouth drew up. "Bring it on," he drawled.

"Count on it." I leaned against him as the driver pulled the bus away from the plane and towards the exit. We passed through a boom gate beside a security booth and out onto the highway that led into Dusk Bay.

"If you're not careful you're going to—"

My words were interrupted by the squeal of brakes.

The bus skidded sideways down the road. The vehicle listed heavily to the right before straightening up with a thump and going on sliding.

I grabbed onto the seat in front of me, while Bray held on to me.

"Duck your head," he said. He placed a hand on the back of my neck and pushed my face down towards my knees. At the same time, he doubled over, pulling me close.

I screwed my eyes shut while the bus continued to skid.

It seemed to slide on for days. A million thoughts passed through my mind.

They began with— What the hell? It was too early in the winter for ice on the road, wasn't it? If not that, then what?

That was followed by— Had I told my father and Jenny I loved them? Had I told my guys? If I had, had I told them enough?

"I love you," I managed to grind out before the bus slammed into something hard.

Metal shrieked and groaned. People screamed.

After a moment, I realised one of those people was me. The sound was wrenched painfully out of my mouth, leaving my throat raw.

After an eternity, the bus finally came to a complete stop.

I slumped further forward as the silence hung heavier than a thundercloud.

"Wren?" Bray broke the silence. "Fucking hell. Are you okay?" He sounded pained.

I managed to force my eyes open. I moved my shoulders, wriggled my fingers and toes. "Yeah, I'm okay. You?"

"I seem to be more or less intact."

His tone made me turn my face and look at him. Blood trickled from a gash on his forehead.

"You're bleeding." I straightened up a little more. "Are you—"

Bray pressed his palm to his forehead for a few moments. He lowered his hand and glanced down at the smear of red on his fingers. "It's just a scratch. Nothing is broken. You'll be relieved to hear my cock and balls are still intact."

"Yeah, you're fine all right," I said dryly. "Priorities still in place."

The brief smile that flashed across his face looked forced. He was trying to lighten the mood. Neither of us was fooled.

I grabbed hold of the seat in front of me and levered myself to my feet. On wobbly legs, I turned around.

"Tiger? Lex?" I tentatively peered behind my seat.

Like Bray and me, Tiger and Lex were just straightening up, their arms around each other, heads down.

Tiger shook his head and grimaced. "I'm fine. Takes more than a bus crash to slow me down."

Lex was a little slower to respond. "I think my wrist is broken."

He held up his arm, his wrist bent at an angle wrists don't usually go. "Otherwise, I'm just fine." His face was paler than usual, expression drawn, brows furrowed. He was clearly in pain.

"We need to get off this bus," Tiger said.

All around us, people were stirring.

"Stay in your seats!" Aidan called out.

I glanced back to see him and Finley head towards the rear of the bus, where a locker sat in place of a row of seats.

Tiger looked like he was about to argue, but Lex curled his good hand around his shoulder. "This isn't an accident."

I knew that. We all did. Until now, I hadn't let myself acknowledge that fact.

I sat back down in a hurry, looking out the window into the darkness.

I could have imagined it, but I was sure I saw a shadow pass by the side of the bus.

My trembling hadn't stopped, but now it increased twofold. Someone was out there. Most likely several someones.

People who wanted us dead.

Aidan and Finley moved through the bus, tossing guns to anyone able to use one.

I caught a glimpse of Elenna and Sinclair each with a gun in her hand. Both appeared unhurt.

A couple of players had broken bones, or gashes to their heads. I didn't know what the bus struck, but where it struck… There was no way the guys sitting there survived.

I thought back, trying to remember who it was. Fuck. A few second line players, a rookie or two and one of the coaching staff.

Someone would have to tell their families, but that was something we'd have to worry about later. Right now, we had to focus on the rest of us not joining them.

I looked through the gap between my seat and Bray's as Tiger pulled off his suit jacket and shirt. He ripped it at the seams and made a sling for Lex's wrist.

"Try to keep it still." His tone was a mixture of worry, fury and determination. If he had to, he'd kill everyone who did this to us, all by himself. Even if he was killed in the process.

"Thanks." Lex leaned over to kiss Tiger's mouth. "I love you."

Tiger looked gruff. "Love you too. Let's deal with these assholes."

"Everyone move to the centre aisle," Aidan called out. "Keep down low. Those who can, make your way to the front of the bus. Those who can't, stay where you are. Elenna—"

"I'm coming with you," she said firmly.

"Me too," Sinclair called out.

"Me three," I added.

There was no way I was being left behind.

Aidan sighed. "Fine." He moved through the bus, his expression grim. "We have some idea what we're up against. Nothing we can't handle."

A bullet slammed into the window a couple of metres from him. He turned and regarded it with what almost looked like amusement.

Bray snorted. "As if the Demons wouldn't travel in a bulletproof bus."

The windows were tinted so the shooter wouldn't even know what or who they were aiming at. If it wasn't for the sound of voices and movement, they might have assumed we were all dead.

As it was, they had no idea how many of us were left alive. A factor Aidan no doubt kept in mind.

"Coast, Orion, Finley, Tiger, Phoenix and I are going out first," he said. "Lex will decide when the rest of you will step off." He and Lex exchanged glances before all five men were moving towards the front of the bus. Aidan nodded to Fred, who seemed shaken but not injured.

Fred leaned over to press a button and the doors opened slowly and with protest.

The guys stayed back, bodies tense, waiting.

My eyes were on Tiger.

He was illuminated by a sliver of moonlight. Bare chest shining silver against the darkness. Muscles coiled like a spring, waiting for the moment of release.

I wanted to shout out that I loved him, but distracting him right now could be fatal.

I held my breath and waited with them.

No one stormed onto the bus, guns blazing or whatever happens in action movies.

There was no sound from outside. Just an eerie silence that did nothing to steady my nerves.

Aidan gestured for them to move forward, stepping off the bus quickly and quietly.

On a signal from Lex, the rest of us rose. Those of us who could.

"Is there any way I can convince you to stay here?" he asked me.

"Save your breath," Bray advised. "She's got that look on her face." He'd seen it too many times before to bother to argue with me, at least, not for very long. He knew once I dug my heels in, they were dug in deep. Whether it was the right thing to do or not.

"Yeah, she does," Lex said, appraising me, more or less resigned. "There's times when being stubborn isn't the best way to go. Bray and I could tie you down to your seat."

His eyebrow twitched as though he was considering exactly the right way to go about that. We didn't have a length of rope or handcuffs handy, that I could tell.

Although this was the Demons' bus, it wouldn't surprise me if both were stashed somewhere.

"I'm also armed," I pointed out sweetly. I held up my gun and waved it around slightly. "And I don't have a broken wrist. Maybe you should be the one to stay here."

The idea of him going out there, basically one-handed, facing fuck knows what, scared the shit out of me. He wasn't defenceless, but he was at a disadvantage. No doubt he hated that fact as much as I did.

"If I thought you'd stay with me, I would," he said.

The sound of gunshots from outside the bus, forced us all to immediate silence.

Footsteps crunched on the road outside, trotting or running. A shout sounded from a handful of metres away.

Shivers slid up and down my spine. Part of me was terrified, but part of me was itching to come face-to-face with Gus and Nicholas Fiorelli.

I could already picture them with a neat bullet hole in the centre of each of their foreheads. Courtesy of me or someone else, I didn't care.

By the end of this either they'd be dead or we would.

"Okay," Lex said. "Let's go and help them finish off these assholes."

We surged towards the front of the bus and stepped off into the night.

# CHAPTER 33

## WREN

I half expected to find us surrounded, the whole ordeal over.

Maybe the bad guys standing quietly with their arms raised above their heads, guns tossed to the ground.

Instead, we were met with darkness, broken by the occasional light in the distance.

The only sounds? The crunch of our shoes on the road and the pounding of blood in my ears.

The bus' engine popped softly a couple of times as it started to cool. From this side, it looked intact, undamaged. The other side rested against the trunk of a tree. Several branches hung at an angle over the back of the vehicle, threatening to fall and cave the roof in. Another good reason not to stay on board.

"Where are they?" I whispered.

I squinted into the shadows. They couldn't be too far

away. Hiding a full-sized hockey player was difficult, much less several of them.

"Be careful," Lex said, his voice low. "Stay close."

I caught a flash of his expression in the moonlight.

He looked like he might order us to get back on board, branches or no branches.

I suspected the only thing stopping him was the fact we'd be sitting ducks inside a tin can.

The windows were bullet-proof, but we'd fucked if they got in through the door. The bus was too mangled to drive, or we would have left on it already.

No, the only way out of here was on foot.

I froze at the sound of a scuffle. Listened, trying to identify the direction and distance.

A gunshot sounded, followed by a grunt and a thud. The sound carried through the night, eerie as hell.

My heart hammered faster. Sweat sprung up on my palms and under my arms. My mouth was drier than the Simpson Desert in the middle of summer. My stomach churned with anxiety.

With everything in me, I wished like hell that wasn't Tiger or one of the guys from the team that hit the ground. If it was...

My heart broke a little at the idea of it. I blinked away tears that had no business pooling in the corners of my eyes.

I dashed them away.

*Fuck nope*, I told myself. It would take a lot more than that to bring down a guy like Tiger. Or any of the others, for that matter. Whoever now lay on the ground in the cold of the night, it wasn't Tiger. It couldn't be.

Besides, if he or one of the guys just died, the others would immediately end whoever did it. The thud was followed by a lengthy silence.

I'd like to say I was reassured, but a sliver of fear was starting to expand into something much bigger. I didn't mind admitting I was scared. Hell, I'd surrender my badass card right now if it meant we all walked away in one piece.

"This way," Lex whispered. He gestured us forward with his good arm. Even his breathing sounded pained, but he was doing his best not to let on. If I handed in my badass card, I'd give it to him. He deserved two of them. Two at least. And a dozen blow jobs. And a bunch of other things I couldn't think of right now.

I found myself almost surrounded, with Elenna on my left, Sinclair on my right and Bray right behind me.

"Come on, Socks," Bray whispered. "We've got some goonholes to deal with."

I held back a snort. Goonholes? That was a new one. I liked it.

*"You* come on, Bray-Bray," I whispered back. "Don't get yourself killed."

"You too, little birdie," he said. "And try not to kill me."

Now I snorted, but softly. "I make no promises." Honestly, I didn't know how we could joke at a time like this. Apparently dark humour was a good coping mechanism, but it was a strange one, for sure. For us, it was basically par for the course. If it helped to keep us sane, then that was a bonus.

Realistically though, if anything I did resulted in his death, I'd never forgive myself. For a guy who used to be the biggest pain in my ass, he meant a lot to me now.

If I was honest with myself, I'd admit he'd meant a lot to me for a long time. The expected reactions from other people stood in our way for too long. Not to mention our own stubbornness. One thing we'd excelled at, was getting in our own way.

I was grateful we weren't doing that anymore, I just hoped he didn't stop giving me shit and taking it back. I'd miss our banter and mock arguments.

Or real arguments, but for those we had make up sex. I might keep calling it hate sex, to get under his skin.

"I could shoot you in the ass right now and leave you here," he offered.

I glanced back and smirked. "You wouldn't do that."

"Only because Elenna and Sinclair would choose a cheek each and shoot me in retribution," he replied.

"Yes, we would," Sinclair said.

"Then a ball each," Elenna added.

"Sinclair isn't looking at another man's balls," Javey snapped.

"Not for long," Sinclair agreed. "It would be for a good cause, not because I want to *touch* them."

"My balls are starting to feel uncomfortable about this conversation," Bray said.

"Sorry, not sorry," Sinclair said. "If you're lucky, Wren might kiss them better later." Her smile was a brief flash of white in the darkness.

My pale skin was probably visible from a kilometre away. I should smear some dirt over my face if I got the chance. Getting shot because I was a pale-skinned redhead would suck. The fact my death would be avenged quickly wasn't as much consolation as you might think.

Bray grunted but fell silent. No doubt imagining me kissing his balls. Hopefully not enough to distract himself by forcing all of his blood out of the head on his shoulders and down into the one in his groin.

I smiled to myself. Sometimes it was too easy to get to him. On the other hand, we were all jumpy and on short fuses. It wouldn't take much to get to any of us.

If someone leaped out of the shadows and shouted, 'boo,' I'd probably scream. I couldn't afford to react like that. If I was on edge too much, I might make a mistake. None of us could afford that.

"You okay?" Sinclair whispered.

"As okay as I can be," I replied. "You?"

"I'm fine, but I wasn't the one who was drugged, shot at, and then almost abducted again by those two pricks. And then *actually* shot. It's okay if you're not okay." She took my hand and squeezed it.

She was right, I wasn't completely fine. If this wasn't

over soon, I was going to come apart at the seams. If not for my guys and my friends, I already would have. They were the stitches keeping me together, bound tighter than the ones in my shoulder. It would take more than a pair of scissors to break us apart.

I squeezed her hand back. "I'll be better when this is dealt with. Then we can get on with our lives and things can go back to normal. Whatever normal is."

"Normal is coffee and cake at our favourite café," she said. "And celebrating after games at Hazards. Not having to look over our shoulders wherever we go or whatever we do."

"Or being nervous to eat chocolate chip muffins," Elenna said.

"Especially that," Sinclair agreed. "No one should be scared of chocolate chip anything."

"If you keep talking about that, you're going to make me hungry," I joked weakly.

"If you keep talking at all, they'll know we're coming," Javey pointed out, his tone blunt.

We abruptly stopped whispering at both his words, and at the sound of another scuffle, closer this time. The shuffling of feet, grunts, the snap of twigs and the crunch of leaves underfoot.

"I know this place," Bray whispered. "There's a track leading off to a stream. On the other side of the stream is a cliff. If I was going to lead someone somewhere to deal with them, that's where I'd lead them."

I didn't ask how he knew; that didn't matter right

now. Chances were, he saw the track and got curious one day. Took a walk down there and found the stream. He wouldn't be the first or last to do something like that.

"They might be heading into an ambush," I said.

"Aidan won't let them—" Elenna started.

Several gunshots rang out in the night, unexpectedly close.

For half a second, I expected to be hit, or for one of the people around me to fall to the ground.

We all dropped to a crouch. Ducking down on instinct, hours of training in our younger days, kicking in.

Yeah, this is shit kids in Dusk Bay learn, like they learn to read and write. The kids whose parents worked for mobsters anyway.

"Down there!" I recognised Aidan's voice.

"There's at least a dozen." That was Coast.

"Not for long."

I smiled at the sound of Tiger's voice. The smile was short-lived.

The men weren't making any effort to hide their presence. The enemy knew exactly where they were.

I blinked against the sudden glare as a pair of headlights came on, a high beam illuminating the bush ahead of us.

"Get back," Lex hissed. He waved us into the shadows under the trees by the side of the road.

My heart raced harder than ever. Had they seen us, or were they focused on Tiger and the others?

We stayed down low and waited. A minute passed. Two. Three. No one converged on our location.

Shadows danced on the very edge of the glare from the headlights. Barely visible as they passed between the trunks of massive gum trees.

People. All of them moving slowly, guns in hand.

"Gus," Sinclair hissed.

I glanced over at her quickly. "Are you sure?" All I could make out was a silhouette, flowing through the trees.

"Yes. I'd know that shape and movement anywhere," she replied. "It's definitely him."

She must have spent more time studying him while we were held in that motel room, then I had. That kind of attention to detail was her thing. It shouldn't surprise me she noticed. Or maybe she was more traumatised than she let on and she was projecting.

Fuck knows if that was him or someone else entirely. As much as I wanted to believe her, caution seemed wise. In the meantime, she had my complete support, like I'd have hers if the tables were turned.

"Then we need to deal with him," I said.

I glanced at Lex. Would he argue with me? Would he say we should stay here, out of sight? He looked like he was thinking it. I could barely make out his expression in the corner of the glow from the headlights, but it was enough.

He nodded. "If they herded our people to the stream, we can put the goonholes—" he smiled briefly at Bray for the term "— between us and them…"

"Let's do it." Bray was already on his feet. Javey too, a moment later.

Lex nodded and rose. "Let's get this done."

# CHAPTER 34

## WREN

"Quiet as we can." Lex whispered. He led the way, Bray behind me, my friends to either side. Javey walked close behind Sinclair.

The headlights illuminated the track, making it easier to see. Several other vehicles were parked beside the first, all dark, their lights off.

How much planning went into all of this?

"I'm tempted to slash their tyres, but we may need them to get out of here," Bray said.

I was thinking the exact same thing. Stopping the bad guys from getting away from us might be to our benefit. Trapping ourselves definitely wouldn't be.

I suspected this would come down to either us surviving, or them.

Whoever walked away from this, the cars were all theirs. Slashed tyres wouldn't help us if we were dead.

Imagining them triumphant and coming back here

to find they couldn't leave, gave me a slight spike of petty amusement. Only a small one. I didn't want to picture us dead all that much.

"That would be a waste of time," Javey said.

"Quiet," Lex said. "Spread out a bit."

He gestured to the other players and coaching staff who survived the crash. They quickly complied, putting a metre between each other. That should make getting past us unseen, more difficult.

At a shout, and more gunshots from up ahead, we all broke into a brisk trot.

If we had the element of surprise, we wouldn't have it for long. They'd expect us to get off the bus and do something at some point. Or maybe they'd expect us to stay and wait for them to come and take us out.

Either way, they knew we existed and would have to be dealt with sooner or later. Speed was more urgent than stealth right now.

We skidded to a stop at the top of a rise. I was puffing lightly. Running around in forests wasn't something I did regularly. Or anywhere else, for that matter. I wasn't as fit as the guys. That was something I'd have to rectify when this was over. Powell Tower had a state-of-the-art gym Tiger and Bray made use of. I could do the same. I was sure Lex could give me a few pointers.

The glare of the headlights wasn't as bright below the rise, but it was enough to make out the stream Bray mentioned. The cliff right behind.

Elenna let out a squeak.

The guys stood in a loose semicircle, facing at least ten armed men. Including Gus.

Before I could even think, Sinclair raised her gun and aimed at him.

I couldn't see where the bullet went, but it must have missed him. His brains weren't spread in every direction. He didn't fall to the ground with a satisfying thud.

Instead, he turned and fired back.

The shot caught one of the coaching staff in the stomach. He went down with a cry of pain I'd probably hear until after I was dead.

The wound wasn't immediately fatal. He'd suffer for a long time before he died, unless we could get him to a hospital in time. We had to. Too many of us had died already. We couldn't lose anyone else. He'd survive, but we had to do this quickly.

I sent thoughts of gratitude to past me. The Wren of a handful of minutes ago, agreeing that slashing the tyres was a bad idea. We might need those vehicles sooner than we thought.

We all dropped down and melted into the trees, goonholes, players, coaches and badass women alike.

A shadow loomed in front of me, gun aimed at my head. Without thinking, I fired before he could. He let out a grunt of pain and ducked back away. Unless I was mistaken, I got his shoulder, not his heart where I was actually aiming. Bummer.

With any luck, it would be enough to put him out of

commission for a while. I knew there was a reason I focused on shoulder shots when I was learning to shoot. Who knew my animosity towards Bray might actually come in useful someday?

*That's for* my *shoulder*, I thought. It was aching like a bitch right now, but I had to ignore it and focus on the job at hand.

A moment later, a different goonhole rose from the bushes and aimed at Lex.

*No you fucking don't*. My hand trembled from the recoil of the last shot, but I acted on instinct. I swung around and squeezed the trigger. The bullet flew out of my gun and hit my target exactly where I intended it to. Right in the back of his head. It blasted his skull apart, killing him before he even knew I was there.

Fuck yeah, I still had it.

I glanced away from the spray of blood and chunks of brain and swallowed to keep down my last meal. I had a strong stomach and I'd seen death before, *killed* before, but it was never something I relished. I'd be no good torturing people or as a serial killer. I'd stick to making jewellery.

Lex turned back to look over his shoulder. "Good job." He flashed me a brief grin. "Thank you."

I shrugged as though I was unmoved. "You're welcome. Nothing any of you wouldn't have done for me."

"Of course, but it's the first time anyone has killed for me," he said.

A smile crept onto my lips.

I had to cut short my celebration to duck back down as a barrage of bullets struck the trees all around me.

"No one shoots my girlfriend." Bray rose and took out two of them with two perfect shots. One to the head and another to the chest.

"No one but you?" I asked as he sank back down beside me.

He grinned. "Exactly. And vice versa."

I couldn't imagine a scenario in which we'd have to shoot each other, but I laughed softly anyway and squinted through the trees.

"In case I don't get a chance to tell you later, I love you," Bray said.

I glanced back over him and resisted the urge to make a comment about his timing. "I love you too." That seemed more important right now than ribbing him.

"Good." Apparently he felt the same way. "Don't get dead."

"You either."

Where the fuck was Gus? Was Nicholas here at all, or had he left all of this to his goonholes? That would be the kind of cowardly thing he'd do. Let them deal with us, and potentially die. As long as he was safe and well. Asshole.

Not unlike Reuben and Caleb, now I thought about it. I didn't see Hunter and Parker along with us either.

Of *course*, when push came to shove, they were nowhere to be seen.

"Let's make our way forward," Lex said. "Stay low and move carefully."

"I thought we could run out there like crazy people and wave for their attention," Bray said sarcastically.

Lex glanced back at him and rolled his eyes, but grinned. "Go ahead. If you want to explain to Aidan later why you're full of bullet holes."

"Doesn't sound like I'd be in much shape to explain," Bray said.

Evidently he didn't like that idea much, he stayed low and moved quietly, staying close to me.

I startled at the sound of gunshots behind us.

The goonholes must have gone around, trying to pin us between them and the cliff, with the rest of the team.

Cries of pain and thud after thud made everything inside me recoil. They were killing our people.

I turned and waited. Watched the converging shadows approaching our position. They eventually drew close enough for me to make them out individually.

*A little closer*, I thought. I didn't want to waste bullets by missing.

*Almost. Almost.*

*Now.*

I aimed, taking out one goonhole before she could fire at Bray.

"No one shoots my boyfriend," I said. "Except me."

"Nice shot, Socks." Bray took out another of the enemy with a clean shot to the chest, and narrowly missed being shot in the head. The bullet embedded in the tree right beside him.

Hot fury coursing through me, I shot the man who aimed that bullet. "What did I just say?" I asked rhetorically.

He couldn't answer with half his face missing.

Slightly nauseous, I crouched back down, my hand on the tree trunk next to me. I'd rather kill than be killed, but this was getting to me more and more. Especially when all this death was so unnecessary.

We had no particular gripe with these people, just the ones they worked for.

Correction, we'd had no particular gripe, until they picked up guns and aimed them at us.

Let's face it, all bets were off at that point.

"There can't be many left," Lex said.

I wasn't sure if he was referring to the enemy or us. Possibly both.

The bush was a scene of carnage. I'd hate to see it when the sun rose. There would be blood and brains everywhere, bodies attracting flies and rotting in the filtered light under the trees.

"Gus," Sinclair hissed.

I looked in the direction she pointed. He and several goonholes were heading for Tiger and the other guys. He must have assumed we were dealt with. There really must not be many of us left.

"I think we can agree no one shoots our boyfriend," Lex said.

"Absofuckinglutely not," I agreed.

The six of us rose and stalked the goonholes, moving as silently as we could. Like before, we needed to get close enough for clear shots. Otherwise, they'd turn and end us before we could end them.

As the goonholes drew closer, Aidan gestured for the others to wait. The enemy was too far for them to get a good shot either.

The distance was closing quickly. Gus and his companions were making no effort to hide their presence or be slow and careful. They were so sure they were about to end this, they were getting cocky and, with that, they got sloppy. They should have known being sloppy gets you dead.

As if to punctuate my thoughts with a dash of irony, I almost tripped over a stick in my haste to keep up. I caught myself at the last moment and hoped like hell Gus didn't hear.

Evidently he didn't. The crunching of sticks and leaves under his boots were loud enough to cover mine.

"When I say the word, run," Lex whispered. "We can't let them get too close."

We all nodded our understanding.

I kept an eye on him and the other on the ground in front of me.

Gus stepped to the open track, back into the glare of the headlights. Trying to intimidate us by illuminating him and his people. They looked like a scene out of an action movie. The kind where the bad guys roll into town, just about to end the good guys.

I snorted to myself. *Good luck with that, asshole.* None of us were that easily intimidated.

I hoped.

"Run," Lex hissed.

As one, we bolted towards the road until we were close enough. Before Gus could turn, we aimed and shot half of his people in the back.

He whirled around and aimed back at us.

"Not today, Satan," Sinclair declared. She pointed a gun at him and shot him in his left temple.

"Fuck yeah, that's my girl!" Coast shouted.

Aidan ordered them all forward. They ran, taking out the last two goonholes who were closest to them.

Realising I hadn't stopped shaking since the bus crashed, I lowered my gun and sucked in a long, slow breath. "Is that all of them?"

"All of them except for Nicholas," Aidan said. He had his arms around Elenna, him, Orion and Finley giving her a hug.

I found Bray, Tiger and Lex's arms around me and nestled into them all.

"We still need to deal with Nicholas," Tiger said. "I saw him about half an hour ago. There were other people with him." He shot Aidan a glance, no apology for contradicting him.

I sighed into the side of Bray's chest. "It's not over then."

"It will be soon," Bray said. "Let's find this asshole and deal with him."

"Agreed," Aidan said. "No one goes home tonight until Nicholas Fiorelli is dead." He didn't add 'or we are.' Enough of us had died here tonight. We weren't going to let any more be killed.

# CHAPTER 35

## WREN

"We need to split up." Aidan scrubbed his face with his hand. He looked tired. As tired as I felt. As tired as we all were.

None of us would walk away until this was done. "Lex, you go that way with them." He gestured toward a couple of players who had appeared out of the trees shortly after Gus' death. They'd become separated from the rest of us and missed out on the fun.

If you could call it fun.

"Finley, take Javey, Phoenix, Tiger, Bray and Wren and go that way." Aidan pointed.

"Sinclair goes where I go," Javey said. His mouth was set in a firm line. If Aidan tried to send her off in a different direction, he'd follow.

Evidently, Aidan was in no mood to argue. "Fine, take her too. Coast, Orion, Elenna and me, will go this way. Nicholas knows we're here, but not that we're alive. Let him assume we're Gus. He'd have no reason to sneak around. Don't do anything wild, but stay in touch and keep your eyes peeled." Sure we'd do what he said, he turned and led his group into the trees.

"Come on," Finley said. He started off in the direction Aidan had indicated. "Let's find this dickhead before he finds us. Preferably before the other groups find them."

"This isn't a competition," Sinclair said.

Javey, Phoenix, Tiger and Bray all looked at her with raised eyebrows.

She held up her hands in surrender. "Sorry, it *is* a competition. I should have remembered who I was talking to. You guys are competitive for a living."

Phoenix snaked an arm around her and tucked her in close to his side while they walked. "Don't say you don't want to find them first too."

"As long as *someone* finds them," she said.

Phoenix let out a sigh like she just didn't get it.

"Don't fight it," I told her. "They're guys, and professional hockey players. Whatever they do, they have to win."

"She gets it," Finley said. "I've always said redheads were especially smart." He offered me a fist bump without breaking his stride.

I grinned and bumped my fist against his. "I know right? I've been saying that for years, but no one seems to believe me."

"She's not joking," Bray said. "I don't know how many times she said it when we were growing up. Although, I seem to recall it had something to do with having a pussy."

"That too," I agreed. "Women are amazing."

"Some more than others." Javey shot Sinclair at half-lidded glance.

"Are you trying to make me blush?" she asked with a laugh.

"He's trying to remind you of the truth, because you don't seem to remember it for yourself," Phoenix said. He gave her a similar look. They were adorable together. The three of them and Coast.

"That is not a problem Wren has," Bray said. "She has a very healthy ego. Ouch." He rubbed his ribs where I elbowed him. "Hey, it's not a bad thing."

"It is when you say it like that," I told him. "I am not conceited."

"Definitely not," Tiger agreed.

Bray stifled a laugh when I threatened to elbow him in the ribs again. "Fine, I'll be nice. As long as you don't suggest we need some kind of dorky group name. Like the Searching Kangaroos."

I pulled a face at him. "You're such a drongo." The affectionate Australian slang for 'idiot' was perfect for him. "Anyway, I was going to suggest the Redhead Brigade."

"You were not." Sinclair laughed.

"No, I wasn't," I agreed. "Because I'm not as big a dork as my stepbrother."

"Yes you are," Bray said. "We're at least on equal footing in the dork department."

I flipped him off and started to say something, but I was interrupted by a scream of sheer agony.

"Lex!" All thoughts of finding Nicholas were immediately driven out of my mind. I turned toward the sound and started off at a run, staggering through the trees and tripping every few steps.

I barely registered that Sinclair and the guys were right behind me.

I barely registered anything. All I could think about was getting to Lex, and what happened to make him scream like that.

Lex screamed again. He was definitely close at this time, the pain in his scream doubled.

I sprinted across a narrow track and back into the trees. A handful of metres later, I skidded to a stop on the edge of a clearing.

Lex lay on the ground, his broken wrist held close to his chest. His expression was a mask of pure agony. The players who went with him lay dead on the ground, the backs of their heads all but gone.

Nicholas Fiorelli was standing over Lex, a handful of goonholes arrayed behind him.

"Fucking prick," Tiger snarled. He raised his gun and aimed it at Nicholas.

Rather than flinch, Nicholas kicked Lex in his broken wrist.

Lex screamed out for a third time.

Tears poured down my cheeks. The sound ripped my heart straight out of my chest.

"You're outnumbered," Nicholas said.

Several more goonholes moved out of the trees behind us. Each held a gun to our heads.

"What do you want?" Finley called out. For once, he wasn't smiling. The cheerful Irishman was gone, replaced by cold, ruthless fury. He sounded a lot like Aidan right now.

"I want you all dead," Nicholas said. "Every one of you is responsible for the deaths of my family."

"You're responsible for Sawyer's death, dickhead," Phoenix said. "And Celine."

"Geneva is responsible for her own," Tiger added. "She could have stayed in her lane and lived a long and prosperous life. But she had to go and attack the arena."

"It was one of you who killed her," Nicholas said. "And my brother Jamison. Once you're all dead, we'll be even."

"That doesn't work for us," Bray said. "We'd prefer it if you were dead." He was shoved forward a step by the goon whose gun was now pressed hard to the back of his head.

"Kill him," Nicholas said as though he was bored by this conversation.

"No!" The word was ripped from my lips so

violently I barely knew it was coming. It tore out of me, leaving my throat raw.

Without thinking, I turned and fired a shot at the goonhole. The bullet struck his cheekbone, shattering it and the rest of his face before slamming into his brain and ending his life.

All hell broke loose.

Sinclair and the other guys turned and shot at the goons behind us.

At the same time, I was vaguely aware of shots behind Lex and Nicholas. I aimed and squeezed the trigger while waiting for a bullet to end me. If I was going to die here, I was going to take as many of them with me as I could.

No bullet came.

Aidan and Elenna came running out of the trees and helped us to dispatch the last of those goonholes.

When the final one went down, I whirled around to see Coast and Orion standing over dead goons, guns aimed at Nicholas. The bullets I thought would kill me must have come from them.

I sagged down in relief. It only lasted a moment, until I pulled myself together and trotted over to drop to my knees beside Lex.

He managed to sit up, but he was pale and cradling his wrist. "Assholes snuck up on us," he groaned. "I've decided he's not very nice."

I responded with a husky laugh and gently kissed his lips. "I agree. We need to get you to a hospital."

"I'm having déjà vu," he said. "Didn't we say that to you only a couple of days ago? Because of the same asshole." He looked up at Nicholas sharply.

"He won't be doing that to anyone else ever again," Tiger said. He knelt down beside Lex and fixed the sling, which was still hanging around Lex's neck. "Told you to keep it still."

Lex grunted softly. "I tried." He looked over to Aidan, who stood near Elenna, eyes on Nicholas.

Aidan raised his chin. "You know there's no way you're walking away from this alive?"

Nicholas raised his own chin, still defiant. "I don't know why I'm not dead already."

"Neither do I," Tiger said.

"Is this where we draw sticks to decide who's going to kill him?" Finley asked.

"No thank you," Elenna said quickly. "I've done my share of killing."

"Me too," I agreed.

"Me three," Sinclair said. "I'm not going to fight anyone here for it."

Tiger, Bray and Lex exchanged glances. Something passed between them.

With Bray and Tiger's help, Lex got to his feet. I handed him my gun and stepped back.

"On the count of three?" Bray asked. He nodded to Coast and Orion as well. They both looked down at Nicholas, their expressions grim but ready.

"One," Lex said.

"Two." Tiger's hand was firm on the trigger.

"Three." They all fired simultaneously.

---

We left Nicholas lying where he was.

Aidan said something about organising a cleanup in the morning, preferably before the police discovered the scene. Following the glare of the headlights, we trudged back up the track to the vehicles.

A couple of the guys carried the coach who was shot in the stomach, but was somehow still alive if barely conscious.

We were a silent group as we approached the vehicles. Each lost in our own thoughts, until we saw another two vehicles parked with the others.

My heart sank. Fuck, this wasn't over after all.

I was ready to rally any energy I had left, until the doors of each of the dark vehicles opened.

Hunter and Parker Brantley climbed out of one, and Caleb Brantley out of the other.

"We saw the crashed bus and came to find you," Hunter said. "It seems like you didn't need us after all."

Most of the second line and a handful of coaches were dead. We'd needed them, but it was too late for that now. We'd done exactly what they asked us to do, but we paid a fucking heavy price for it.

"Figures you'd turn up now." Tiger looked at them sideways, scowling in undisguised annoyance.

"Better late than never," Parker said lightly. He glanced over at Caleb.

Caleb regarded all of us, his eyes sliding from one to another, to another. "Nicholas Fiorelli?" He directed the question to Aidan.

"Dead," Aidan said. "He's the last of them." He held onto Elenna's hand like she was the only thing keeping him upright.

Caleb nodded. "Reuben will expect a report in the morning." He looked over to his younger brothers. "You can have the team." Without another word, or gesture, he climbed back into his car and shut the door behind him with a thunk. The driver reversed the car up the track and disappeared down the highway.

Hunter and Parker were both grinning like they won some kind of prize.

"The first order of business will be replacing some players," Hunter said. "And convincing the public the ones who didn't make it died in a terrible bus crash."

That figured. No one but us would ever know what went on here.

I supposed it was better this way. Some of those players' families didn't know what they got up to with the Demons. They wouldn't want to know.

Mourning their lost loved ones would be difficult enough. I didn't envy anyone the task of having to make all those phone calls.

I wiped tears off my cheeks. It felt like too many

deaths in the family all at once. At some point, it might sink in that it was over.

Aidan nodded. "We can deal with that in the morning. Everyone get out of here."

No one needed to be told twice.

# CHAPTER 36

## WREN

"So then he said, you can have the team," Parker said into his phone.

I rolled my eyes and turned my attention back to where the nurse was plastering Lex's wrist. He'd had it x-rayed and left for a while to reduce the swelling.

"Can I sign it first?" I asked. "Before the guys on the team draw cocks and balls all over it."

Lex managed a tired laugh. "Sure. You can make it look pretty before they deface it."

"You could let Wren draw all over it," Bray suggested. "Like a mural. People usually can't bring themselves to graffiti over those."

I glanced over at him. "Did you just say I'm talented?"

He scratched the side of his nose with the tip of his finger. "I guess I did. Don't let it go to your head." He couldn't offer more than a half-hearted smirk.

"Too late." I hooked an arm around his neck and pulled him over for a quick kiss. "It's already there. But I don't mind sharing Lex's cast with a bunch of cocks and balls. I'd be a spoilsport if I didn't let them draw all over it. He is their coach, after all."

The nurse gave us all a funny look before slipping out of the room. The cast would have to dry for a while before we could take Lex home.

"You make us sound like a bunch of schoolboys," Bray observed.

"If the helmet fits," Tiger said.

Bray leaned back in his chair and placed his hands behind his head. "She's including you in that, Pennington."

"No shit, Ellis," Tiger retorted. His eyes were on the twins just outside the door, in the hospital corridor.

"What are you thinking?" I asked.

"I'm thinking the team might get more money now. An upgrade to facilities. Better... Everything." He was cautiously optimistic. Not making assumptions just because the twins were friends of his.

"If there's anything the Demons have proved in the last year, it's that we can kick ass even with what we had," Lex said. "Once we came together as a team, we started killing it. Now we won't have the distractions of people coming after us and trying to kill us. But upgrading everything would rock too. Aidan's probably putting a list together as we speak."

"What is Aidan putting together a list of?" Hunter asked as he and Parker stepped into the room.

"Equipment the Demons need if we're going to continue to dominate the AIHL," Lex said evenly.

Hunter rubbed his hands together and grinned. He didn't seem affected by all the dead players and coaches. Of course he wasn't. He'd seen death probably more times than he could count. This was just another night in Dusk Bay.

"I'm thinking we could add a bondage dungeon," Hunter said. "Maybe a nightclub."

"How about a Zamboni that doesn't break down every second day?" Lex said.

"New sticks," Tiger said.

"Those new, state-of-the-art skates that let you go faster, smoother," Bray said.

"New boards around the rink," Lex added.

"New helmets," Tiger said.

"A new goalie coach until the one who was shot in the stomach makes a full recovery," Bray said. "Not to mention the ones who died." He glanced down at the worn, linoleum floor.

Hunter's enthusiasm wasn't even slightly dented. He actually listened and nodded. "We can start with all of those things. Whatever it takes to make you the most winningest team in the AIHL. Then maybe we could expand into other sports. What do you think, Park?"

"I've always wanted to own a gridiron team," Parker

said. "Rugby, baseball, soccer... We could be the kings of owning sports teams."

No one could say they weren't ambitious.

"Can I suggest you do one at a time?" I said. "If you're going to be hands on, it'll be a lot of work for you."

"Good point," Hunter said. "Lila would be pissed off if we spent all our time at the arena and not with her. Once she's finished school, she can come with us. Slade too."

"That'll be fun," Parker said. "I guess we'll wait for Aidan's list. I have a feeling it might be longer than the one we just got."

I mimed opening a scroll and letting the length of paper roll and roll and roll across the floor. "That might be underestimating it."

"Once again, I find myself admitting Wren is right," Bray said. "Caleb not caring about the team has meant a lot of things need fixing or replacing. It had an effect on morale for the last few years. If it wasn't for Aidan kicking our asses into gear, we'd still be right at the bottom of the ladder."

"You weren't thinking of replacing him?" Lex asked quietly.

Hunter cocked his head. "Aidan? Fuck no. Or you, if that's what you're really worried about. The Fiorellis were a pain in our asses for so long. If it wouldn't bring attention to you that none of you'd want or appreciate, I'd get medals for all of you."

"None of us need medals," Tiger said.

"I'd settle for chocolate chip muffins that aren't drugged," I said.

Hunter pointed a finger gun at me. "That, I can arrange. All the chocolate chip muffins you can eat. No drugs."

"And coffee," I added.

"And coffee," he agreed. "I'm not a Neanderthal."

"That's debatable," Tiger said mildly. There was no hint of malice in his brilliant blue eyes. Exhaustion and relief, but no aggression. It was a good look for him. Maybe at some point, he'd learn to relax.

"That's what I keep saying to him." Parker ducked from Hunter's half-hearted swing at his head.

"If I'm a Neanderthal, so are you," his identical twin told him.

"Keep telling yourself that." Parker gave him a shove.

"Anyway, it's late." Hunter regained his footing and glanced at his phone. "We'll get going. The team should take a couple of days off. Parker and I will deal with funeral arrangements. First thing Monday morning, we can all jump back in. I might even learn how to skate."

"You, learn how to skate?" Parker teased Hunter as they headed out the door. Their voices and banter faded away gradually, before they were finally out of earshot.

"They're a pair of pricks, but they're okay at times." Tiger rubbed a hand over the back of his neck. "Don't tell either of them I said that. Their egos are healthy enough."

"They won't hear it from me." Lex poked his cast with the pad of his thumb. "It feels dry."

The nurse stepped back into the treatment room and checked the cast out for herself. "Okay, you should be good to go. Remember not to stick anything down there to scratch it. Wouldn't want it to get infected under the plaster." She looked at him sternly. She must have said the same thing to patients hundreds of times. Some of them probably listened.

"I'll try to behave," Lex said. "Thank you."

She gave him another look before waving us all out the door.

"They should hire her to work at the arena," Bray said, loud enough for her to hear even though we were out in the corridor. "She'd give Aidan a run for his money. The injured players might even do what she tells them to."

Athletes were notorious for pretending they weren't injured so they could keep on playing. Hockey players were no exception to this. If anyone could get them to sit still when they were supposed to, they'd be worth their weight in pucks.

"No thank you," she called out behind us. "I get enough hell from patients without getting any from boys like you."

I laughed at the expression on Bray's face. "Boy, you got owned."

He stopped to tangle his fingers around my hair and pulled me closer to him. "After we get some sleep, I'm going to show you who's the one who is owned." He kissed me roughly.

I kissed him back, before pulling away. "Promises, promises, Bray-Bray."

"It's definitely a promise and I keep my promises," he said. "Now, let's get the hell out of this place. I don't know about you guys, but I've had enough of hospitals for a while."

I couldn't agree with that more. Me with my bullet wound, Lex with his broken wrist and Bray with a swollen lump on his forehead. We were like the walking wounded. It was a miracle Tiger was relatively unharmed. He'd earned himself some scratches and scrapes, but that was about it.

The mental scars— Those would take longer to heal.

# CHAPTER 37

## WREN

"I was actually getting used to the bullets in the glass," I remarked.

Tiger grunted. "We can have them put the old panes back if you like." He took a step towards the glazier before I grabbed his arm and pulled him back.

"Let's not," I said quickly. "They look much better without them."

It was a difficult process to bring the large panes up to the twelfth floor and remove the old ones before putting in the new. We all stayed well back, out of their way, especially when the windows had no glass in them at all. None of us felt like falling to our deaths. Honestly, the glaziers were brave to do the job they did, even if they wore safety harnesses the entire time.

"Good, I think so too." He looked relieved.

"You would have actually told them to put them back if I asked you to, wouldn't you?" I asked him.

"There's nothing I wouldn't do for you." He drew me into his arms and grazed his lips over mine. "Even put up with bulletproof glass full of bullets. If you wanted the panes tinted pink, I'd even do that. You don't want that, right?"

I laughed softly. "No, I don't think so. Although, it would make the outside look like a beautiful sunset all day."

I rubbed my chin and pretended to seriously consider it. Finally, I smiled. "Okay, no pink tint. Not even a purple polkadot tint. Not even cocks and pussies in place of the polkadots."

"That would look interesting," Lex said. "Like stained glass in the shape of genitals." He put one arm around me and rested his cast-covered wrist on Tiger's shoulder.

"We could start a new trend." I leaned into both of them and smiled.

"Let's don't and pretend we did," Tiger said dryly. "I don't want to look at those kinds of dicks and pussies all day."

"Who's looking at dicks and pussies?" Bray asked as he stepped into the apartment. In his hand he held a large paper bag with the top rolled down.

"I don't want to know," Dad said. He followed close behind Bray, Jenny behind him. They both held similar paper bags.

I stepped away from the guys to give Dad and Jenny a hug. "It's good to see you both."

"It's good to see you all alive," Dad said. "I gather things got a bit hair-raising." He hugged me back and handed me the bag.

I opened the top and peeked inside. "Chocolate chip muffins!"

"Without drugs," Bray said. He placed his bag on the island beside Jenny's. "Apparently if you want yours made with weed, you have to order in advance."

"Good to know." I pulled out a muffin and bit into it. If anyone else delivered them, I'd hesitate. The last thing I needed was to hallucinate and walk straight out the window. I'd bear weed in mind for another day.

"What's good to know?" Sinclair stepped in through the open doorway, carrying a tray of takeaway coffee cups. Her three guys followed behind her.

Elenna and hers were on her heels. Some carrying coffee, others with more bags of muffins. All still looking tired and battered, but relieved to be alive.

"Looks like the whole team is here." Tiger took two cups from Sinclair's tray and handed me one before taking a sip from his.

"The ones still alive," Aidan said. "Brandon will make a full recovery. It'll take time." He already had an arm around Elenna, coffee in his other hand.

"Become a hockey player, they said." Coast smirked. "It'll be fun, they said. The pamphlet never mentioned any of this."

"Yes it did," Tiger said. "You just didn't read the fine print."

"I never read the fine print." Coast grinned.

"Obviously," Sinclair said teasingly. "It seems like most of us didn't. We wouldn't have signed up to be abducted, drugged, in a bus crash, hunted, shot at..." She frowned. "Am I forgetting anything? Oh, right." She snapped her fingers. "Held at gunpoint, kicked, had bones broken, threatened..."

"Being forced to sit directly on the ice." Phoenix shivered.

"Losing half the team," Finley said. That made the mood more sombre.

Coast broke it by saying, "Having to put up with Pennington."

Tiger flipped him off. "Having to tolerate Riggs."

"I know you secretly adore me." Coast made a kissy face at Tiger.

"We all do," Lex said. "You brought coffee." He toasted Coast with his cup.

Coast grinned, completely undeterred by the teasing. "I live to please." He draped an arm around Sinclair's shoulders.

"I don't want to get sentimental," Aidan said, his voice low, "but I'm glad to be here with all of you. We're all still standing at the end of the day because we all stood together. If we hadn't had each other's backs, we would have been fucked a long time ago."

"Not in the good way," Coast added.

Aidan nodded in his direction to acknowledge the centre's words. "Definitely not in the good way. In all likelihood, we'd be dead right now. Most if not all of us. This is why I keep trying to impress upon you assholes that you need to be united. On the ice as well as off."

He wouldn't be Aidan without a dig at the guys, but this time it was said with affection, not animosity. The guys weren't just a team, they were family. When their careers were over and they were no longer playing hockey, they'd still be friends. Brothers.

Finley closed his eyes tight. "Why do I feel like there's a but in there?"

Aidan sighed. "Because we'll know better than to get complacent. When one door closes, sometimes a window opens." He nodded to where the glaziers were sealing the last section of window. "The Fiorellis are gone, but we don't know what and who might take their place. Whatever it is could be a hundred times worse." He glanced down at the hardwood floor, then back up again.

"If there's something Reuben Brantley is good at, it's making enemies and his enemies are our enemies. Sooner or later, someone or something is going to come for us. We have to be ready."

"We will be," Elenna said. "No one messes with a Dusk Bay Demon without dealing with the rest of us."

"Amen," Orion said softly.

We all lifted our coffee cups in toast. With any luck, we'd have a year or two to rest before life went to hell again.

# CHAPTER 38

## WREN

"My shoulder feels so much better with the stitches out." I raised my arm a couple of times, testing the way it felt.

"The scar is next level." Bray peeled back the fabric of my shirt to take a look. "You know what they say, dudes dig scars." He lightly kissed the healing skin.

"I thought the expression was that chicks dig scars," I said.

"It is, but that can go both ways." He grabbed a fistful of my shirt and pulled me to him for a kiss.

"That or you got hit on the head harder than I thought you did," I teased. The swelling on his forehead had long since gone down, leaving him more or less back to normal. Normal for him anyway.

"That's possible too." He swiped the tip of his tongue across my lower lip. "I mean, I still want to kiss you and be with you. Clearly something in there is damaged."

I snorted a laugh. "Finally, we agree on something. Just remember, you said it, not me."

He laughed and swiped his tongue back the other way. "I don't care. As long as I get the girl."

"We all get the girl," Tiger reminded him. He stepped away from where he'd been inspecting the new glass, and slipped his arms around me from behind. He pressed his quickly growing erection against my hip.

"Yes we do." Lex's wrist was still in a cast, but he went without the support of a sling now. It didn't seem to be giving him any pain, but he was clearly looking forward to having the plaster removed in a few weeks.

He was the kind of guy who didn't want to slow down for anything, especially something like that. Although, if it was Tiger or Bray, they'd be a hundred times worse than he was. He could still coach with a broken wrist, they couldn't play. That would drive them both up the wall in about thirty seconds flat.

"Should we show her?" Bray asked.

"What if I don't want you to?" I asked teasingly.

They exchanged a glance.

Tiger stepped away, into the kitchen. He opened the drawer and pulled out a long tea towel. Standing behind me, he placed it over my eyes before knotting it behind my head.

Without another word, he turned me around, picked me up and threw me over his shoulder.

"Bray can drive. I'll tell you where." He wrapped his arm around my legs, keeping me in place so all I could do was dangle there while they took me down in the elevator.

I guessed where we were going. The smell of oil confirmed my suspicion. The beep of a car unlocking was followed by the sound of a door opening.

I was tossed into the back seat of the car, where I bounced before coming to lie across the smooth leather.

"Well this is—" I started to say. Exciting. Intriguing. Arousing.

"Quiet," Tiger snapped. He climbed in beside me and reached to pull the seat belt over me. "Do as you're fucking told. And remember the safe word, highland cow." He added in a gentler tone.

And there went another pair of panties. "If you want me to be quiet, you're going to have to make me."

I don't know where he got the roll of duct tape from, but he tore off a piece and pressed it over my mouth.

"There, that will shut you up."

I responded with a sniff and a hum. I could still say the safe word if I needed to, but I was effectively gagged.

"I don't think that's enough," Bray said.

Footsteps went around to the back of the car, followed by the sound of the hatch opening and closing. The door opened beside me and I was hauled around until my face was in Tiger's lap, my arms behind me. What felt like rope was wrapped around my wrists and tied firmly.

"Much better." Bray sounded satisfied and smug as

ever. "I've always wanted to tie her up and gag her." He slapped my ass hard.

I kicked out and connected with some part of him. Since he responded with a laugh, not a cry of pain, I guessed I missed his balls. Bummer.

He shoved my feet away and closed the door.

He and Lex climbed into the front seats and the engine started.

The only thing I could do for the next while was lie still with my cheek pressed against Tiger's half erect cock, and wait.

I had no idea how long we drove or which direction we went. Eventually, the surface under the SUV's tires sounded like gravel or dirt instead of a sealed road. The going was bumpy here, bouncing me around. Tiger became harder and harder each time my face landed on his groin.

We'd just come to a stop when I heard the zipper on his pants slide down. He gripped the side of the duct tape and tore it away.

I barely had time to wince when he was gripping a handful of my hair and shoving my mouth down and around his cock. He pushed me down until I gagged, then went on pushing and pulling me up and down his length. At the same time, his hips shoved him up into me fast and rough.

I tried to catch a breath, but he was relentless in fucking my mouth. I gagged over and over.

"That's the best way to shut her up," Bray remarked.

As far as I could tell, he was still in the driver's seat, watching.

Tiger grunted and pulled me off his cock. "Let's get her inside."

The door beside me opened. Strong hands grabbed me and pulled me out. I guessed it was Bray by the way Tiger scrambled out of the car behind me. Lex's wrist wouldn't have allowed him to yank me around like this. Not yet.

I found myself draped over Bray's shoulder and carried into a place with what sounded like wooden floors. I imagined some abandoned cabin deep in the forest. The kind of place devious people took victims to do unspeakable things to them. Somewhere they could do whatever they wanted to me without being over-heard or seen. Use me however they wanted.

That thought sent shivers through me. With no tape over my mouth, I could say the safe word easily and clearly if I needed to. What could they possibly do that would force me into saying it? I didn't know, but I was looking forward to finding out.

I was tossed down onto a surface that felt like a thin mattress on the floor.

They rolled onto my side. My leggings and panties were tugged down and off. My legs were shoved apart and fingers rammed straight into my pussy.

"She's wet." Bray's voice was rough and deep.

"Of course she is." The tea towel was shoved up off my face. Tiger was looking down at me. His eyes were dark with need. He grabbed my wrists and undid the rope.

"She knows who owns her. We do. We're going to show her that now. We're going to take her body. We're going to use every part of her until she forgets everything but the fact she belongs to us."

"Sounds perfect." Bray shoved his fingers in and out of me, fucking me with his hand with no restraint. "I've been meaning to teach her that for a while now. I've owned her for a long time, but she doesn't seem to have realised it."

I gave him a look of defiance.

Lex sat down beside me and grabbed a fistful of hair in his good hand. He yanked my head back until I was looking at him. "I've owned her since the night we first talked in Hazards. The night I ate her out on the pool table. That night, her pussy became mine."

He kissed me equally roughly. Still holding my hair, he turned to Tiger and kissed him too.

"When will you admit you own each other too?" I asked.

Tiger and Lex exchanged a long look. Lex let my hair go and wound his hand behind Tiger's head and kissed him, his tongue pushing into the player's mouth.

Bray pushed me onto my back, pressed my legs apart and pulled my pussy straight onto his mouth.

I couldn't suppress a gasp at the sudden touch of his lips and tongue on my clit and folds. Instinctively, my back arched, pushing myself harder against him.

Tiger and Lex broke off the kiss and Tiger went to work on Lex's pants. Hungrily, he pulled them down, freed Lex's erection and lowered his mouth onto him so far his head must have touched the back of Tiger's throat.

"Fuck," Lex groaned.

Yeah, I was thinking about the same thing.

Bray lifted his face from my pussy and hauled me over to Tiger's groin. He shoved my mouth down onto his cock. Almost in the same motion, he lay behind me, parted my legs again and rammed his cock into my pussy so hard I gave a muffled scream.

"That's it, scream." He reached around to pinch one of my nipples so hard it hurt. "Scream to show you know I own you."

He slammed in harder than before, making me scream again. "Just like that." He rammed in over and over while I choked on Tiger's cock. While Tiger choked on Lex's.

Lex had his head back, eyes closed, looking completely blissed out. He moved in perfect rhythm with Tiger's sucks and licks.

Unable to stop myself, I came, muscles clenching around Bray's cock, slowing his relentless slamming as he too came, spilling himself inside me.

I lifted my mouth from Tiger so I could breathe while I was swallowed in a vortex of orgasmic perfection. Punctuated by the slap of skin on skin and the smack of Tiger's mouth, the orgasm went on and on until I finally drifted back down. At the same time, Bray slumped forward, panting.

He eventually slid out of me and lay beside me, chest rising and falling as he caught his breath.

Lex touched the side of Tiger's head, encouraging him to open his mouth and let him slide his cock free. "Lie back."

Looking slightly confused, Tiger did as he was told.

Lex leaned over to a bag I hadn't noticed before, and pulled out a tube of lube. He motioned for me to spread my legs wider and smeared a handful around and inside my pussy. He did the same to his cock and then Tiger's. Tossing the lube aside, he gripped my hips and encouraged me to straddle Tiger and lower my pussy onto his cock.

"Lean as far forward as you can," Lex said.

I glanced back over my shoulder, but did what he said. My eyes widened as Lex straddled Tiger behind me and pushed his cock into my pussy, so both of them were inside me at the same time.

Two cocks both inside my pussy, so full and tight.

"Holy fuck," Tiger breathed. "You both feels so fucking good."

"You two, too." Lex eased in deeper, moving slowly to give me time to stretch and fit him in there too.

Just when I thought I couldn't be filled any more, I was.

Gradually, they were both all the way inside me, their cocks pressing against each other. Slowly at first, they started to move, thrusting into me and sliding against each other. There was nothing frantic about this fucking. It was careful, deliberate and restrained. And fucking amazing.

"I'm going to come again," I whispered.

"Come for us," Lex said from behind me.

"What he said," Tiger grunted.

"Come with me," I told them. "All of us." I couldn't have held myself back if I tried, I pitched over the edge, but I took both of them with me. All three of us came in near perfect unison. Grunting, grinding and gasping. They both spilled themselves into me at the same time, coating my insides and their cocks with each other's cum.

My orgasm this time was stronger and more intense than any I'd ever had before in my life.

I tilted my head back and screamed at the top of my lungs. Screamed because I felt good. Screamed because I loved these three men. Screamed because they owned me and I owned them, and they owned each other.

Because there was nothing else in the world that mattered more than us.

# EPILOGUE

## WREN

"I can't take this anymore." Sinclair gripped my hand so tight it hurt. "I can't watch." She didn't take her eyes off the ice.

Neither did I. Nor did I take my hand from hers. It would hurt later, but I barely felt it now. All of my attention was on the players who skated down below the team box, eyes on that little black puck.

"This is so intense," Elenna whispered. She sat on the other side of Sinclair, brown eyes wide, her hands still in her lap. I hadn't seen her wring them once since Nicholas' death. Him dying seemed to have unlocked something in her. She was finally able to relax and get on with her life.

This was the only unfinished business the team had. The Demons and the Koalas both had an equal amount of wins in the division. The Demons had hoped to take out the Goodall cup last week, but the Koalas won in overtime.

Tonight's game was do or die. Not literally, thank fuck. We'd all had enough of that to last a lifetime.

Elenna squealed with excitement as Tiger slammed the puck to Orion, who put it into the goal, evening the score. "A goal on Tiger's assist." She did a little dance in her seat, which I joined in on after a moment.

"It's going to go into overtime," Sinclair said. "I really can't watch." She put her hands over her eyes but peeked between her fingers.

The guys had a couple more minutes and two more shift changes before the horn sounded for the end of the third period. Sinclair was right, they would go into overtime.

"We can't say it's not exciting," I said.

"Are you saying you haven't had enough excitement for one lifetime?" Sinclair looked over to me and lowered her hands.

"Outside the arena, I have," I agreed. "Inside, there's always room for more."

The guys headed off the ice for a break before overtime. They wouldn't get any shifts when they went back on. They'd go on playing until one of the teams scored.

"To think, they've gone from being the worst team in the AIHL, to being this close to winning again," Elenna said.

"Because of Aidan," Sinclair said reluctantly. "And Lex."

"And because of their unity," I added. "Next year will be interesting." The AIHL was expanding, adding more teams from all over Australia. Some minor teams, some major. I'd bet they'd all be hungry to prove themselves.

"It will," Sinclair agreed. "We can all focus on hockey and living our lives."

"The guys are going back on," I said.

We all held our breaths while the players got back into their positions, each of them with concentration etched on their features.

The puck dropped and Coast was quick to take possession.

Like I was watching a tennis match, my eyes went back and forth as the puck went in and out of our defensive zone.

After a few minutes, the players were all becoming visibly tired, but none willing to concede a millimetre.

As if to prove the point, Javey snuck the puck past the opposition and over to Bray.

"Come on, come on," I said under my breath. If he got this in, scoring the winning goal of the finals, his head would be enormous, but I wanted this for him. I wanted it for the team.

As if he was merely skating around at practice, Bray tapped the puck in front of him. He fainted to the left before splitting to the right and smashing the puck right into the basket. It flew into the back of the net before coming to rest on the ice.

The entire arena erupted in cheers and shouts and singing.

I found myself in the middle of a hug with my two best friends, all of us crying and laughing at the same time.

"They fucking did it," Sinclair said. "They won!"

"Yeah, they did," I agreed. They actually did it.

The Dusk Bay Demons won the cup. The celebrations were going to go for weeks.

I couldn't wait. I wiped away tears of pride before we all headed down to the ice to congratulate our guys.

Wren here—thank you for reading! If you'd love a sweet bonus scene, you can find that here. If you need more hockey, check out the up and coming Opal Springs Ghouls in Pucking Hearts Collide.

# ABOUT THE AUTHOR

Maggie Alabaster writes reverse harem romance.

She lives in NSW, Australia with one spouse, two daughters, one dog, and countless birds.

Jo Bradley writes contemporary romance.

Sign up for Maggie's newsletter! Sign Up!

Join Maggie's reader group! Join here!

Follow Maggie on Bookbub! Click here to follow me!

Check out Maggie's website- www. maggiealabaster.com

Sign up for Jo's newsletter

## ALSO BY MAGGIE ALABASTER

Dusk Bay Demons

Puck Drop

Breakaway

Power Play


Brutal Academy

Book 1 Heartless

Book 2 Cruel

Book 3 Vengeful


Court of Blood and Binding

Book 1 Song of Scent and Magic

Book 2 Crown of Mist and Heat

Book 3 Sword of Balm and Shadow

Book 4 Whisper of Frost and Flame


Dark Masque

Book 1 Bait

Book 2 Prey

Book 3 Trap


Saving Abbie

Book 1 Pitch

Book 2 Pound

Book 3 Session

Book 4 Muse

Book 5 Rhythm

Book 6 Encore

Novella Venomous

Saving Abbie books 1-4

Saving Abbie books 4-6 + Venomous


Ruthless Claws

Book 1 Ivory

Book 2 Crimson

Book 3 Elodie


Harmony's Magic

Book 1 Summoned by Fire

Book 2 Summoned by Fate

Book 3 Summoned by Desire


Shifter's Vault

Book 1 Discarded

Book 2 Deceived

Book 3 Disgraced


My Alien Mates

## ALSO BY JO BRADLEY

**Dusk Bay Sharks**

Prequel Novella Sidelined

Spike

Punt

Intercept

Snap